# FORBIDDEN FRUIT

LaShawn Hewlett-Wilson

Bittersweet Publications, LLC

Published by Bittersweet Publications, LLC
Forbidden Fruit
Copyright © 2011 by LaShawn C. Hewlett-Wilson

*This book is a work of fiction. The characters, incidents, and dialogues are products of the author's imagination and are not to be construed as real. Any resemblance to actual events or persons, living or dead, is entirely coincidental.*

ISBN: 13: 978-0615610504
ISBN-10: 0615610501

Book Cover Designed by Dzine Detail, Duane Brannon
2900 W. Clay Street
Richmond, Virginia

Cover Model: Crystal Rose Anthony

Edited by E. Claudette Freeman
www.eclaudetteliterary.com
LaTonya Hewlett

Printed in the United States of America

**This book is dedicated to the loving memories of:**

*Alexander Hewlett*
*Mildred Mcrant*
*Howard Evans*
*Leon Hewlett*
*David LaShawn Wilson*

# ACKNOWLEDGMENTS

Through all the trials and tribulations, it has not been easy for me to get to where I am today, and I am truly grateful I made it. With that being said, I would like to first and foremost give all the glory and praise to God, for giving me the gift of writing and use that talent to write this book, and inspire others to go after their dreams and goals.

To my loving husband Michael Wilson, who I truly adore. Thank you for all your love, support, and being there for me when I needed you the most. You understand this journey took sacrifice, determination, hard work, perseverance, and you stood patiently by my side. You're the greatest and I love you with all my heart and soul.

To my precious little angels, Tavon, Michael Jr., and DeAyrra, thank you for the patience and understanding in knowing my attitude was never personal when I was having my fits because nothing was going right with my book, or I didn't have the time to do something you wanted me to do. Always remember I love you guys no matter what. Continue to make me proud and always strive to be the best in life, do the right thing, and know you all are destined for success.

My parents, Carol and Beverly Jerome Hewlett, Sr., without you guys there will be no me. I love you both very much. To my brothers, Jerome, Jason (Wiggy), and Christopher, remember who is the oldest and know I love you all dearly.

A very special thanks to my editors E. Claudette Freeman and LaTonya Hewlett. I would have not been able to keep my head above water without my cheering squad. Ms. Freeman, you were a blessing sent to me, and I will always be grateful to you. You have really taught me a lot about story development and challenged my writing ability to the fullest. It was exhausting, but without you, I could have not brought this story to life. I look forward to working with you again.

LaTonya Hewlett, your contribution will not go unnoticed. If it wasn't for you, this book would be all over the place. You have graduated from editor to literary advisor. I think we made a pretty good team. It's time to start writing your own book. There is a story brewing inside you. Follow your heart and dreams; I know you can do it.

My cover model, Crystal R. Anthony, you are the best. You did the damn thing on the front cover. I wish you much success in your modeling.

Duane Brannon, you are truly talented and gifted. You brought my vision to life with the most beautiful book cover. I appreciate your help in seeing this project through.

Thank you to my sister-n-laws, Kischa, Regina, Tanika a.k.a. (Nicky), and Cheri, for listening to me whine, complain, and go on and on about this book. You girls are the best! Kischa, you brainstormed the idea for the book cover, and I must say the cover is the bomb (tick, tick) BOOM!!!.

To my best friend in the whole wide world, Melissa Bodrick, we've been through it all: the good, the bad, and the ugly. I always admired your go-getter attitude you possess. I love you dearly with your mean self (lol).

Last but not least, sincere appreciation to Sabrina Daniels, Jessica Bolling, Verlene Reynolds, and Forondo "Pee-Wee" Holmes. Thanks for showing me so much love. Don't let me forget Zakia Mckensy for the flawless job done on my makeup, and Tonya Brown for hooking up my hair so that I could look good for my cover shoot.

To all my other host of family, friends, and fans, thank you all for your support, words of encouragement, but more than that, believing in me. If I have forgotten anyone, charge it to my head and not my heart. Peace. Love

# Back in the Day

# 1

It was July, the summer of 2000, and Rayne's sixteenth birthday party was going to be off the chain, without a doubt. Her parents were throwing her a huge pool party, the biggest her neighborhood had ever seen; everybody and their mamas were sure to be there. Except for the one person she despised: Rachel Poindexter. Drama was the last thing Rayne needed, and there was no way in hell that loose-booty tramp was coming anywhere near her party.

Rayne turned around and struck a pose to show off her purple two-piece bikini. The two-piece displayed her washboard stomach and toned legs.

"How do I look?" she asked Kenya.

Kenya gave her two thumbs up, smiled and responded, "Girl, you look good. You're going to knock Rashard off his feet."

"That's if he even comes to my party." A sad look instantly washed over Rayne's face.

"I'm sure he'll come. Rashard is a smart guy and I don't think he believes that lie Rachel spread about you. Are you sure Rachel is not going to show up starting any drama? That is all you need, her crashing your party. You know she's dying for revenge after that fight ya'll had a week ago."

Rayne's lips pursed, the mention of Rachel's name evoked a mental picture of their fight. She was finally making progress at winning Rashard over. They were talking on the phone every day and hanging around each

1

other a lot more. It started to feel like they were a couple, but not officially.

Rayne was anxiously waiting by Rashard's locker because they were going to have lunch together. The mean expression on his face as he approached her gave an indication that something was wrong.

"Hey, Rashard. Is everything ok? You look mad about something."

Rashard didn't speak. He simply ignored her as he opened up his locker.

"Rashard, I asked you a question. What is the matter with you?"

Rashard slammed the locker door, and stared at Rayne for a brief moment before finally speaking.

"Man, I thought you were different. You just like all the rest of these trifling girls in this school."

"Who shit in your cornflakes? I don't know what you're even talking about." Rayne barked at Rashard's rudeness.

"Don't play dumb, Rayne. I heard all about you and Jason. I heard you got with my boy the other night and ya'll made out."

"Are you serious?!" Rayne shouted. Her outburst stopped students in their tracks. All eyes were now on them, but Rayne didn't care. She gave Rashard a piece of her mind.

"How dare you believe a disgusting rumor like that! I never been with Jason, and whoever told you that is going to get their ass kicked. You are a jerk for believing such a nasty rumor. Go to hell, Rashard Armstrong!"

"Ooohhh, you just got your feelings hurt." Troy said laughing, walking up behind Rashard and slapping him on his shoulder.

Rayne rolled her eyes at Troy's cynical remark, and stormed off to find Kenya and Zoey. She had to get to the bottom of who spread the rumor about her. Her gut instincts told her there was only one person that would try to ruin her reputation: Rachel.

Rayne confronted Rachel when she learned that it was indeed her that created the rumor. Anger started to manifest as she stared into Rachel's eyes. Rivalry against rivalry, Rayne's fists were clenched tight ready to annihilate her enemy. A crowd of student's gathered around them hoping it would be a fight. Rayne was not intimidated by Rachel's two-hundred plus size frame. As soon as Rachel started talking shit, Rayne hit her across the face and shoved her to the ground. Rachel managed to grab a lock of Rayne's hair. Rayne struggled to get her hair free from Rachel's vice-like grip, and with all the strength she could muster, she dug her nails in the side of Rachel's face. Both girls continued to tussle across the hallway floor. In the background you could hear the student's chanting, "Fight, fight, fight, fight, fight." The girls fought to their death until the principal finally broke them apart, and several teachers immediately cleared the hallways of all the commotion. That day was definitely hell day for Rayne. Not only was she suspended for five days, her parents threatened to cancel her party. Luckily for her after pleading her case, they had a change of heart.

Thinking about that moment was making Rayne mad all over again. She pushed it out of her mind. There was still a party to get ready for. She walked over to her vanity, picked up her brush and started brushing her long hair.

"I'm not worried about that girl. Trust me, I already warned her she better not step foot on my property or she'll get more than her ass beat this time. You know Kenya, I wanted to seriously hurt that girl." Rayne slammed the brush down on the vanity and turned to face Kenya, "I think the whore is mental!" Rayne hissed.

Kenya chuckled at Rayne's feisty demeanor, "I did not mean to work you all up and get you mad."

Rayne walked towards her closet. "I am not mad. I just hope Rashard show up because I'm excited and determined to win him over today without Rachel's interference. Anyway, Zoey should be here soon so let's finish getting cute and head out to the party."

Rayne was walking on cloud nine when she walked out to her family's backyard. Her mother and father spared no expense making her day special. The yard was decorated perfectly: purple and crème balloons floated overhead, the area was surrounded by lawn chairs amidst beautiful palm trees and lighting that hung delicately. There was a table filled with party favors for girls and boys, float beds, volley ball nets and beach balls nestled in the pool, purple and crème beach towels accented tables with umbrellas in the center, and a bar filled with fruit and mocktails. Happy birthday signs and streamers were posted all around the house and tables. The grill was filled with a little of everything: hotdogs, hamburgers, chicken, steak, sausages, and corn on the cob. As guests arrived, they were given flip flops to wear and keep as mementos. The DJ was off to the side mixing. The sounds of Aaliyah mixed with R. Kelly were blaring through 15 inch speakers and two 18 inch subwoofers.

An hour had passed since the party started and there was still no sign of Rashard. Since the fight with Rachel, she hadn't talked to him for two weeks. He wouldn't answer her calls, and he evaded her every chance he got at school. Rayne, Kenya, and Zoey were talking to Crystal, captain of the cheerleading squad, when Rashard walked through the backyard with his cousin Troy. Rayne was stoked but totally surprised he showed up. *I wonder what gave him a change of heart*, Rayne thought to herself.

Rashard was one of the finest brothers who had moved into her neighborhood. Every girl in her high school wanted him. He stood six feet two inches tall, with a caramel complexion, head full of curly hair, deep dimples, soulful eyes, and luscious lips. A whole year of chasing after Rashard was not easy. You see, Rayne set her plan in motion by pretending she was failing the math class they shared. It was her tactic to snag him early in the semester. *I'm gonna pretend to fail this class*, she thought. *What better way to get close to my future boyfriend?* She was nowhere near dumb, and she had an A average in the class. She made Rashard think she was having a hard time understanding the work just so he could tutor her. She would show up at his house with the cutest short skirts and fitted tops. She always wore her hair hanging down because she learned that he loved girls with long hair. She asked him what was his favorite woman's perfume and he told her Obsession by Calvin Klein. She ran out and purchased a bottle. Rayne's coochie would ooze every time Rashard told her how good she smelled. Needless to say, her plan flew off without a hitch.

The pool party was jumping and everybody was having a

good time. Mystikal's song, "Shake It Fast" had the girls putting in extra hip thrusts as they moved to the lyrics. Some girls were playing volleyball against the boys in the pool. The smell of juicy hotdogs and hamburgers filled the air as they sizzled on the grill. Rayne's and Kenya's mothers were passing out mocktails to all the teenagers. With all the excitement around Rayne, everything started to fade as she gazed in Rashard's direction. He was looking fine as hell in his white wife beater, red swim trunks, and white Nike flip-flops. She wanted to rip off his shirt and run her hands up and down his well-defined biceps and chest. Rayne was in a trance when Rashard started walking towards her. She was drawn to him like a magnet. His voice broke her gaze.

"Hey, Rayne. Happy Birthday."

"Hey, Rashard," Rayne said, blushing as her heart began to flutter uncontrollably.

"I brought this for you," Rashard said, while handing her a medium-sized box wrapped in her favorite color purple.

Rayne reached for the box, catching the grimaced look on Troy's face. Troy was very attractive, but his bad disposition made him hard to get along with at times. Rayne couldn't help but notice he favored Rashard with the slight frown on his face and wrinkled lines on his forehead when he got mad. She could definitely tell they were cousins.

"I hope you like your gift." Rashard said.

"Thank you. I'm sure I will. It's very sweet of you to remember my favorite color is purple." Rayne was feenin' for Rashard even more and wanted to kiss him on his cheek, but decided not to in case her father was looking.

Rashard had the widest smile as he stood there admiring Rayne's beautiful features. She had a five feet five inch frame, long jet black hair, hazel eyes, caramel complexion, and a beauty mark right above the right side of her lip. Her apple bottom behind was perfect, and her legs were well defined from running track.

Troy couldn't take it anymore watching Rayne warm up to Rashard. It was making him nauseous so he brushed pass Rashard and shoved his gift at Rayne's chest.

"Here," said Troy, as he stormed off. Rayne didn't have a chance to catch the falling box or say thank you. She didn't care because with his bad attitude, she didn't want anything to do with him. The gift hit the ground and that's exactly where she was going to leave it.

"You're not going to pick that up?" Rashard asked.

Rayne retorted, "Why should I? Your cousin was the one that threw it at me."

Rashard bent down to pick up the gift and handed it to her. "Here you go."

"You should have left it there." Rayne said coolly, folding her arms tightly across her chest.

"No need. Troy is just going through something right now. Plus he's upset because he likes you, and you won't give him the time of the day."

"I don't care. That doesn't mean he can come to my party and act rude. If he feels that way he can leave."

Rashard started to smile. Her feisty attitude always gave him a hard on.

"Why are you smiling?"

"You're cute when you're mad. I mean, um, you, um, beautiful," Rashard said.

"Thank you." Rayne's smile was a mile wide. "So what made you show up at my party? I thought you were mad with me."

"I can't stay mad at you. I felt pretty stupid thinking you would do something like that with my friend. I avoided you because I felt bad that I may have hurt you. I hope you forgive me and we can start over."

Jackpot! Rayne had Rashard right where she wanted him. Finally, her persistence and determination was paying off. She was starting to see some progress. *This is going to be the best birthday yet,* Rayne thought to herself.

Zoey and Kenya interrupted Rayne's moment with Rashard and grabbed her by her arms.

"Come on girl, our song is on!" Kenya yelled over the music blaring from the speakers.

The girls made their way to the center of the yard with the other kids and started shaking their asses to Sisqo's, "Thong Song." Rayne poked out her apple bottom and started swaying from side to side. The music coursed through her body, excited her senses, took her to a state of euphoria. Her hips rotated in a circular motion. She began to imitate some of the dance moves she saw in the video for the song. Rashard's presence inspired her to act out of character, her sultry moves were bold. She moved with sexy confidence, intoxicated by her own sexual energy. Rayne was filled with desires that were forbidden at a young age.

The party was a hit. As everyone was leaving, they told Rayne and her parents how much fun they had, how delicious the food was, and how beautiful the yard was decorated. Some of her friends were huddled up still jamming as the DJ played the last few tunes.

"Hey, guys the party is over." Rayne told them.

They replied, "Ah, man." Rayne knew for sure her party would be the talk of the school for the next two weeks. Hell, for the next month.

Twenty minutes later, Rayne was engaged in a deep conversation with Kenya and Zoey, telling them about her scheme to hook up with Rashard that night. Zoey was about to say something when Tyreke came up from behind and interrupted.

"You know pop is going to whip your fast, hot ass," said Tyreke.

"Shut up!"

"You shut up before I go tell pop you out here scheming with your girls."

"You are such an asshole, Tyreke. You don't know what we talking about, let alone what's going on, so mind your business."

"I saw you dancing all nasty because you knew Rashard was watching you."

Rayne smacked her gums and rolled her neck like a snake. "You don't know what you're talking about."

"Whateva, don't play dumb. I'm older than you and a lot wiser. Game recognize game, girl. Anywayz, I'm out 'cus you young'uns are cramping my style."

"Good-bye, square head!" Rayne shouted out after her brother.

Kenya and Zoey laughed at Rayne's remark.

"Girl, your brother is a piece of work," said Kenya.

"I know right. He's always in my biz."

As soon as Tyreke walked into the house, Kenya turned her attention back towards Rayne. "Ok, so what makes you think this plan of yours is going to work?"

7

"Well, since we are staying over Zoey's house tonight, Rashard and I figured this was a perfect opportunity for us to hook up."

"What about his parents?" Kenya asked.

"Rashard said they visiting his dad's aunt in Emporia, and they plan to be back home by noon tomorrow."

"I sure hope you know what you're doing?" Kenya asked, feeling uneasy about the whole situation.

"I got this under control. Zoey, just make sure you leave the window unlocked so I can get in. I'll be back at your house by nine at the latest."

Rayne spotted her mother at the back door and pulled her friends off to the side so she wouldn't hear their conversation. She was certain her mother had radar ears.

Kenya raised an eyebrow and looked at Zoey. "Are you sure your mom won't wake up?" she asked.

"Trust me, she won't. She'll be too drunk to even hear or notice anything wrong," said Zoey, with a look of disappointment in her eyes.

"You hear that Kenya, we good. Rashard and I already worked it out, and if you two play your roles, we shouldn't get caught."

"What about Troy? You know he is all salty about you and Rashard." Kenya said, with uncertainty in her voice.

"He supposed to be staying over Smoot's house tonight. So you see we got this situation under control. Relax, you two more nervous than I am."

"We should be. Your daddy will have a cow if he found out you stayed over Rashard's house over night when you should have been at mine. As a matter of fact, he will kill you. Kill you both," Zoey said.

Rayne's eyes kept darting at the back door, making sure neither her mother nor brother was in sight. The last thing she needed was to get busted before she got the chance to hook up with Rashard.

"Look, if we stick together nothing should go wrong. Let's finish cleaning up and then go. When we get in the house, please act normal. I don't need my mom thinking we're up to something and getting all suspicious." Rayne turned around and faced her friends. She held her hand out, "Three Musketeers?"

8

Zoey and Kenya put their hands on top of Rayne's hand and they all said in unison, "Three Musketeers."

\*\*\*

The moment felt so surreal, and Rayne couldn't believe she was finally at Rashard's house cuddled up alone with the boy she desired. Ms. Winters was passed out drunk like Zoey expected and Troy was gone.

They were sitting on the sofa watching a re-run episode of the TV show *What's Happening*. Being in the company of Rayne started to arouse Rashard's senses; he cautiously started running his hand up and down Rayne's arm, sending chills along her spine.

"Am I making you nervous?"

"No, not really." Rayne said.

Rashard began to giggle. "I can't tell I'm not making you nervous. As soon as I touched you, you started bouncing your left leg non-stop. I know this is our first time being alone without my parents being home so I know you got to be shitting bricks. I just want you to be comfortable, so if you not up to this I can walk you back to Zoey's house."

"I'm good Rashard. Trust me, I really am." Rayne said, with a smile.

"Ok. What else you want to watch on TV?"

"I don't know. Whatever is good."

"Well, I can tell you nothing on is good. Cable sucks. Would you like something to drink?"

"No thanks."

Rayne palms started to sweat. With her heart racing, she asked, "So are you sure Troy is not coming back tonight?"

"Yeah, I'm positive."

Rashard turned the volume down on the TV. He pulled Rayne closer to him and placed his soft lips onto hers. He slid his tongue into her mouth and it was the most intense French kiss she had ever experienced. At one point, she thought he was going to suck her face off. On a scale from one to ten, he got a nine. He was a decent kisser. At last they came up for air.

"Can I ask you a question without you getting upset?"

"Sure."

Rayne could sense he was nervous by the way he was fidgeting with his hands.

"Are you a virgin for real?"

A puzzled look crossed Rayne's face, she was curious as to why he would ask her again when she already told him she was a virgin.

"Why would I lie about something like that?"

Rashard shrugged his shoulders. "I don't know. I mean, don't girls lie about stuff like that?"

"I guess it depends on the person. I don't have any need to lie about something like that. I'm proud of my virginity."

"Have you had someone lie to you before about not being a virgin?"

"I don't think so. I couldn't tell. I thought you weren't going to like me anymore when I told you I wasn't a virgin."

"Why would I not like you? You know how I feel, and I'm not going to judge you."

Rayne's genuineness made him blush.

"I think you're special for being a virgin."

"Thank you," Rayne smiled.

"Were you serious about wanting me to be your first?" Rashard asked.

Rayne's heart started to beat wildly. She was certain but hesitantly said, "Yes."

They started to kiss again for what seemed like hours. Rashard really wanted Rayne and grabbed her, leading her towards his bedroom. Once inside he laid her on his full size bed.

*Oh my God. Is this really about to go down? Am I really going to let Rashard hit?*

Rashard started to kiss her again, his hand slowly trailed up her skirt to her inner thigh making his way to her panties. He pulled her panties to the side and began to finger fuck the hell out of her coochie. He knew how to get a girl in the mood because his older cousin, Ronnie, told him girls like it when guys finger them. He was praying like hell it would work on Rayne. It must have because the deeper his fingers went, the wider Rayne spread her legs apart. He pulled out her right breast and started to lick, suck, and roll his tongue over her erect nipple. The double pleasure made Rayne tremble like an earthquake. Rashard whispered, "Take off your panties."

At that moment, Rayne knew she was at a point of no return.

Rashard stood up in front of the bed and took off his wife beater. Rayne marveled at his fine body. For a young man who was just seventeen, Rashard's body was tight and fit. Damn, milk does a body good. He pulled down his boxers and indeed, he was hung like a horse. It was the most beautiful thing Rayne had ever laid her eyes on. Rayne tried to control her eagerness. The anticipation was growing inside her like a rapid wild fire. She had never been that close to a dick before. The sight of it put her under a spell. Her wish was about to come true, she was about to let Rashard explore her insides and make her feel like a woman.

Rayne was breathing heavily as she watched Rashard slide the condom over his erect penis. When he was done, he laid her back onto the bed and lowered himself on top of her. He could feel her tense up as he eased inside of her.

"Are you ok? Am I hurting you?"

Rayne took a deep breath and said, "No."

Rashard knew this was Rayne's first time, so he wanted to make her experience special. He didn't want to rush and move too fast, so he deliberately took it slow. After a deliciously, long hour of making love, twice to be exact, Rayne loved it and she was beat. From the many positions and the name screaming, not only was she sore, but she knew she would be hoarse the next day. Rayne didn't care; just being with Rashard was well worth it.

The next morning, Rayne hurried to put on her clothes. It was five minutes to nine and she told Zoey and Kenya she'd be back by nine o'clock. Although Zoey lived around the block, she still didn't want to risk being caught. Rayne was in the middle of getting dressed, but froze like a popsicle when she heard Troy stomping up the steps reciting the lyrics to Jay-Z's rap song "I Just Wanna Love U." Rayne's fear began to manifest.

"Oh my God, Troy's home!" Rayne exclaimed.

"Don't worry," Rashard assured. "While he's in his room, we can quickly go out the back door before he comes out."

Rayne shook her head in agreement, hurried up and

slipped on her skirt, then rushed to the bedroom door.

"Wait!" Rashard said above a whisper. "I can't let you leave without telling you this." Rashard placed a soft kiss on Rayne's lips. "You are officially my girl now."

Rayne couldn't resist the way the spark from Rashard's soulful eyes and his smile made her heart melt like ice cream. She was speechless but at the same time in bliss.

"I like the sound of that." Rayne wanted to do jumping jacks, but her fear instantly kicked back in when she realized she had to leave to avoid running into Troy. She and Rashard ran out of the bedroom, sprinted down the steps and Rayne bolted out the back door.

On the way to Zoey's house all Rayne could think about was her magical night spent with Rashard. She was no longer a virgin and she was elated that her first time was with the boy she desired and he desired her. Now she would be the one telling a story like Kenya and Zoey who were always bragging about their sexcapades with their boyfriends. She finally had something to tell.

Climbing through the window was a piece of cake. She couldn't wait to get inside and tell her girls all about her sexual experience. Unfortunately, that conversation would have to wait. Standing in the middle of Zoey's bedroom floor was her father with a thick leather belt, and Kenya and Zoey sitting on the bed with horror smothered across their faces. Rayne was busted! Now ain't that a bitch.

# BETRAYAL

# 2

***The present...***

Rashard and Rayne were curled up on the floor naked. Tender moans had faded away in the distance and the smell of sweet sex lingered in the air. They were basking in the afterglow of their love-making activities. Rayne was panting as if she had just run a 100 yard dash. Rashard was nibbling on her ear lobes, making trails of kisses on her neck, and repeatedly whispering how much he loved her.

Rayne sat up from Rashard's embrace and looked around the living room that was filled with moving boxes. The sun was streaming through the blinds, giving the dim room lighting. The canyon brown paint on the walls had a somber tone from being bare. Her life was picture perfect. Rashard was a civil engineer and was taking over his father's engineering company. His father took an extended leave of absence to take care of his ailing wife. Rayne successfully opened up her own real estate company. To put the icing on the cake, she and Rashard were moving into their first home. What more could a woman ask for? Rayne was on cloud nine.

Rayne loved her husband more than life itself. In her eyes, he was the perfect package. Besides being so damn fine, he took good care of her financially and sexually. They started dating in high school and off and on throughout college. Rayne started to remember how they were destined to be together from the moment they went on their first date.

Her parents promised that when she turned sixteen she could start dating. They didn't have their first date until their junior year in high school when Rashard got his driver's license. She would never forget how Rashard was so nervous when he asked her out to the movies.

"Would you like to go see that new Eddie Murphy film, *Nutty Professor II* this weekend?"

Rayne was tickled watching Rashard fidget with his hands while she slowly contemplated her answer. She couldn't believe he had the jitters asking her out on a date.

"I don't know...I have to check my calendar...it depends on if my mom don't need me around the house. I'll get back with you later."

"Ok then," Rashard said sounding so pitiful.

Rayne fell out laughing, and finally decided to put him out of his misery and responded, "I would love to go out with you this weekend. I was just kidding."

He rolled his eyes but gave her a cheerful smile. "You love giving me a hard time."

"I do because I know you like it." Rayne said, batting her eyelashes. She could tell by the way he blushed and stared at her with his soulful eyes.

Saturday had finally arrived and Rayne was rummaging through her closet trying to find the hottest, cutest outfit for her first date. She decided on her mini denim skirt, tight pink printed tee, and wedge heel sandals. Her hair was pinned in an up-do, face immaculately done, accessories on point, and her nails and toes were polished in hot pink. She pulled out her strawberry lip gloss from her purse and applied it to her lips. She looked herself over in the mirror, marveling at her stunning look that was sure to make Rashard drool.

Rayne's mother walked into the room, breaking her concentration from the mirror. She stood up and spun around so her mother could see her outfit.

"You look beautiful, baby." Her angelic smile made Rayne feel good. She walked closer to Rayne and gently touched the side of her face. "Too bad your father is not here to share this experience with you. He would be so proud of how his little girl has grown up to be respectful, intelligent, and beautiful."

Six months had passed since the death of her father. His death had briefly put a strain on her relationship with Rashard, not to mention it was hard for her, her mother, and brother to cope with their loss. Tyreke was staying on campus. It was his freshman year at Old Dominion University. It was just Rayne and her mother, but they got to see Tyreke every other weekend, during breaks, and when the campus was closed for holidays.

Rayne hugged her mother tightly. "Thank you momma, I love you."

Thirty minutes later, Rashard arrived at her house. He looked too damn fine in his blue jeans, white tee with the word Converse written across the front, and a fresh pair of all white Chuck Taylor sneakers.

They arrived at the movies where they ran into all their friends. Rayne saw Kenya and Zoey who were hugged up with their boyfriends. They managed to get in five minutes to gloat over their boos and complement each other on how good they looked in their outfits before returning to their dates.

The first hour of the movie, Rayne and Rashard watched the movie sharing popcorn and Goobers, laughing hysterically at Eddie Murphy, but the remainder of the movie they were engaged in heavy kissing and necking. The date ended with them going to Byrd Park. A lot of teenagers frequented there because they saw it as a romantic spot to make out in the back seat of their cars. They climbed in the back seat of Rashard's Nissan Sentra where heavier kissing, necking, and Rashard fingering Rayne took place. The park was closing at nine and although they had thirty minutes, they spent the rest of their time making love. When they finished, Rayne looked deep into Rashard's eyes and said, "I love you." Not only did Rashard tell her he loved her back, but he gave her a beautiful customized initial gold necklace. He put the necklace around Rayne's neck, and tears trickled down her cheeks making her realize he was the one she wanted to spend the rest of her life with.

In their packed up apartment, he was still the one. Rashard ran his fingers through Rayne's hair, breaking her moment of reflection. He kissed her on the forehead before getting up to head towards the kitchen to get a glass of water; he felt like he was dying of thirst. He returned to the living room with two glasses of water in his hands. Rayne licked her lips and fell into a hypnotic trance as she watched Rashard's balls swing back and forth in a pendulum motion against his thighs. Rashard handed her the glass of water, breaking her trance. Her returned smile let him know she was grateful for his thoughtfulness. She anxiously took the cold liquid to her mouth, appreciating the relief it brought as it soothed her throat. She felt hoarse from all the screaming and hollering Rashard had her doing. She handed her glass to Rashard, and he set the two glasses off to the side. He pulled Rayne into his arms and moved his fingertips up and down Rayne's arms, along down her side, and then stopped at her waist. He started to blush then said, "Did I tell you how much I love you?"

"For the hundredth time," she confirmed.

"Then why such the gloomy look?" he asked.

"I was just thinking about how much I'm going to miss this apartment. We are leaving behind a lot of memories and good times." She started to pout.

"I know we did have some great times in this place." Rashard shook his head and started smiling. "Besides...we moving up like the Jeffersons. Don't look so down, Weezie."

Rayne startled to giggle. "You make me so happy," she said, leaning over and kissing him gently.

"Don't worry, I'm going to always protect and take good care of you."

Rayne couldn't help but to laugh at his sincerity. "Please, I don't need you protecting me. I can handle myself," she said and playfully nudged him in his arm.

"You are so right about that. You have always been feisty, fearless, and never took any shit from nobody. I've always loved that about you." Rashard knew the moment he laid eyes on Rayne, she was the one. In his eyes, no other woman could emulate her beauty, sensitivity, and devotion that he found quite desirable.

Rashard slid his tongue inside her mouth and their tongues intertwined as they felt the warmth of each other's breath. Rayne loved his kisses. She could feel his passion every time his lips would touch hers. Rashard laid Rayne onto her back and buried his head in between her thighs, licking and sucking the outside of her universe. She let out a satisfying moan. He nursed her swollen clitoris with his tongue, and then gently inserted his index finger inside her wetness. When he finished licking and sucking all the juices out of her, she let out a loud orgasm that left her breathless. She finally gathered her composure and wasted no time taking his manhood into her mouth and returning the favor. Damn, I love me some Rashard Armstrong was all she could think about as she was putting in work on his penis.

Rashard let out a series of loud moans that echoed through the vacant apartment. Rayne's warm mouth around his penis gave an intense sensation that made his toes curl. A wonderful feeling of pleasure made its way through his body like electricity. He could feel himself reaching his climax, and as much as he wanted to fight it, he screamed out, "I'm coming. I'm coming!" His knees gave in and he collapsed to the floor.

When they finished, Rayne was grinning from ear to ear. "You never cease to amaze me. Round one was off the chain, but round two was explosive," she said with happiness in her voice.

"I'm glad you like it, because I aim to please." Rashard was not cocky, but he knew his sex game was on point.

As much as Rayne wanted to remain in his arms and not get up, she couldn't because they had to finish packing. The movers were scheduled to arrive at their house 8 o'clock the next morning. She walked across the room to grab her tank top and a pair of shorts thrown across the floor. Rashard sat mesmerized at her beauty. There wasn't much that changed about her looks since high school except she was slightly taller, her breasts were bigger, and her hair had bronze highlights to complement her skin complexion. Rashard had the widest smile knowing he was the luckiest man alive to be blessed with a beautiful human being. He got up to put on his sweatpants and before he could pull them up, there was a knock at the door. They both looked at each other puzzled because neither one of them was expecting any company.

"I wonder who that could be."

17

Rashard shrugged his shoulders. "I don't know, but while you get the door, I'm going to take a leak."

Rayne slipped on her tank top and shorts, then took her hand to smooth back her hair that was disarrayed. She didn't want to answer the door looking like she just been in a brawl: even though she did look like that after two hours of non-stop, intense love making. There were three more knocks before Rayne reached the door. She had a perplexed look on her face when she opened the door and saw a tall, slinky white man with short blondish hair. He was wearing khaki brown pants with a red polo shirt. He had a clipboard in his hand and the first thing that came to Rayne's mind was a salesman. He smiled at her and said, "Hello, are you Mrs. Armstrong."

This made Rayne more curious because he addressed her by her last name. "Yes I am. How can I help you?"

"I have a package for you. Can you please sign here?"

Rayne reached for the clipboard as she stared attentively at the yellow envelope. Wondering what was inside, she quickly signed her name and handed the gentleman back his clipboard.

"Thank you," he said pleasantly and turned around to walk away.

There was no return address which made Rayne nervous than curious. She slowly opened up the envelope and pulled out several pictures. Seized with horror, her mouth flew open as she gazed through each picture.

"Honey, who was at the door?"

She slowly turned around to face Rashard when she heard him walk up behind her.

The frown on Rayne's face made him question, "What's wrong with you?"

Rayne was so choked up that she couldn't speak for a moment. When she could, she said in a sarcastic tone, "I don't know Rashard, you tell me."

He was baffled by her attitude and glanced down at her hand, warily eyeing the contents she was holding. "What's that in your hand?"

With her free hand, Rayne repeatedly jabbed at his chest with her index finger. "I loved you more than anything in this world. Damn it, Rashard, I loved you more than I loved myself. How could you do this to me?"

"Do what Rayne? I don't know what you're talking about?"

"Don't play me for a fucking fool! You have been lying to me!"

The look in Rayne's eyes made Rashard scared. "What's wrong with you? I can't give you a straight answer if you don't tell me what's the matter!" He beseeched her.

"You bastard! How could you?" Rayne slung the pictures at Rashard, and started to throw punches like a mad woman. Rashard was stunned and tried to disengage himself from her tirade.

He finally grabbed her by the arms and held her steady. "Will you please calm down?!" he demanded.

"Get the hell off of me!" Rayne growled through clenched teeth.

When Rashard didn't let go, she yelled, "Now! You son of a bitch!"

Rashard slowly let her arms go and backed away. He touched the side of his face that was bleeding from her scratches. He was puzzled as to why Rayne went off into a frenzy. He looked down at the floor where the scattered pictures laid and bent down to pick them up.

The room started to spin. Then suddenly an overwhelming wave of anxiety hit Rayne like a ton of bricks. "I hate you! I hate you!" She screamed and stormed off.

Rashard thoughts were a jumbled mess. He was in a state of shock as he looked through the pictures one by one. The images shook him to the core, his heart thumped fiercely from panic. It was beating like a drum. When he discovered what set Rayne off, there was no justifying the pain that he caused. He tightly clenched the photos, anger began to manifest, his heart wounded by the ricochet of his own betrayal.

Rayne was curled up in a ball on the floor crying uncontrollably. It felt like her heart was being ripped out of her chest. She cried harder. She couldn't force those images from her mind. She was grief-stricken by the indecent images of Rashard with Rachel. The image of Rachel sucking Rashard's penis dangled in her head, his betrayal dismantled her heart, pain refusing to dissolve. Her heart fluttered as she started to slowly faint listening to Rashard's impassioned pleas for forgiveness. His cries began to fade into thin air, and before she knew it everything went black.

# Sabotage

## 3

A Touch of Style Hair Salon was packed. The Maury Povich Show boomed through the television, mixed with the sound of clients' heels clicking against the hardwood floors as they were being escorted to the shampoo bowl, gave a rhythmic counterbalance to the lively chatter that filled the room. The sunlight beamed through the ceiling-high windows reflecting off the earth tone walls which were beautifully decorated with fine art. Different conversations sparked throughout the room amongst the customers and hairstylists. Rayne sat in the swivel barber chair feeling out of her depth while Tyreke curled her long mane in big pink rollers. She was flipping through an Essence magazine, not really reading the articles because her mind was distracted and diffused.

Bell Biv DeVoe couldn't have said it any better, "that girl is poison." Rachel Poindexter was a snake. It shouldn't have been a surprise that Rachel went after Rashard because that is what snakes do. Like the saying goes, "better cut the grass so you can see the snakes." Rayne's worse fear had come true. But never in a million years would she have thought Rashard would betray her with that skank. Rayne and Rachel, along with many other girls in her high school, would bid for Rashard's affection. But ultimately it was Rayne who stole his heart. She tried to suppress a smile that was about to form on her face when she thought about the shenanigan she pulled on Rachel during their tenth grade year before she and Rashard became boyfriend and girlfriend. She remembered it like it was yesterday's news.

Rayne, Kenya, and Zoey were at Regina's house playing double dutch. Rayne stopped jumping rope when she looked over at Rashard's house and spotted Rachel tugging on Rashard's t-shirt, and the sight of her rubbing her body up against his was making her blood boil.

Rachel had an awful reputation with guys and girls; can you say stank ho? That's what Rayne and her two best friends, Kenya and Zoey called her. All the guys including Rashard wanted to dig her out because she was known to give the best blow jobs. Standing at five feet four inches tall and treading over two hundred pounds, Rachel had an ass on her. She definitely gave meaning to the phrase 'junk in the trunk.' Guys foamed at the mouth when they saw her coming because her ass shook like a bowl of jello. She had a funky walk, and you would always see her sucking on a lollipop. Rayne figured that was her signature display to let everybody know she could suck a good dick. Rachel sucked and licked a lollipop very sensually, arousing every boy she knew that was watching. Her face was ok, typical light skin chick with a good grain of hair, but she was no dime piece. She had very small breasts. The girls would tease her saying she belonged in the itty bitty titty committee. But that still did not matter to all the boys, because what she lacked up top, she made up for it in the ass area.

Rayne threw her hands on her hips. "I hate that loose booty tramp!" she shouted.

"What's wrong now?" Kenya demanded to know.

"Don't ask me any stupid questions?" she retorted with a sneerful look on her face. "Duh, don't you see that whore all up on my man?"

Rayne was fuming with anger. "Come on ya'll. I'll teach her not to mess with me."

Kenya and Zoey took off running with Rayne around the block to her house. They raced towards the kitchen, and Rayne flung open the refrigerator door and grabbed a Mountain Dew soda bottle. She twisted off the metal cap and gulped down the beverage leaving only half of its contents.

Kenya and Zoey just stood with confused expressions on

22

their faces. "What are you doing?" Kenya asked.

"You'll see," Rayne assured her.

To their disbelief they watched as she pulled up her skirt, pulled her panties down to her ankles, and peed in the bottle.

"Are you out of your mind?!" Kenya yelled out.

With a devious smile, Rayne covered the top of the bottle with her hand and shook the contents, making sure the urine was mixed well with the soda. She grabbed three more sodas and handed one to each of her friends and kept the other one for herself.

"There, now let's go offer Miss Thang something to drink. I'm sure she's thirsty after trying so hard to come on to Rashard."

With uncertainty in her voice, Zoey said, "I don't know about this. We could get in big trouble."

Rayne abruptly stopped walking. Kenya and Zoey were right on her heels and her sudden stop caused them to bump into her. She spun around to face them, threw her hand on her hip, and waved her finger in their faces.

"Look here you two get wit' the program. Rashard is my man and I'm not going to let that big booty, stanky heifer keep throwing herself at him. Now let's go!"

As they headed back towards Rashard's house, he was sitting on his porch and Rachel was sitting on his lap. When he saw Rayne coming, he shoved her to the ground.

"Hey, what's your problem?" Rachel started to whine.

"That's my problem," Rashard said and pointed to Rayne as she was approaching his house.

Rachel rolled her eyes. "Boy please, she doesn't scare me. Besides, y'all not together, so what do you care for?"

It took a lot for Rayne not to smack that heifer. She brushed passed her so that she could stand next to Rashard; just being next to him made her all tingly inside. "Hey, Rashard," she said provocatively.

"Hey, Rayne, watcha want?" She could tell by the nervousness in his voice, he was feeling uneasy about her being there.

"We just came to see if Rachel wanted to come play double dutch with us."

Rachel spun her head around so fast because she was

caught off guard with Rayne's sudden case of niceness. "When since you started being so nice?" she snapped.

"Since now, and to show you there are no hard feelings, I brought you a soda."

Rachel stared at Rayne not knowing if she should trust her. She hesitantly took the soda bottle.

Rayne tried her best to suppress the laughter that was building up in the pit of her stomach. She looked at Kenya and Zoey who appeared to be more nervous than a hooker in church. Before they knew it, a screeching howl escaped Rachel's lips.

"Ewww! What the hell you put in this soda!? This doesn't taste like Mountain Dew!"

They all fell to the ground laughing so hard it brought tears to their eyes. Rashard was looking dumbfounded and was curious to know what was going on.

Tyreke waved his hand up and down in front of Rayne's face trying to get her attention. Rayne shifted slightly in her chair, dismissing the memory from her mind.

"Girl, you awfully quiet. I'm just talking to you and you ignoring me. What's wrong with you?" Tyreke asked, as he snapped on the last pink roller. "You feel like talking about it?"

Rayne let out a long sigh. "Not really. If I talk about it it's just going to make the situation even harder to deal with." Rayne shook her head in disgust. She tightened her lips as she tried to hold back the swell of emotion in her chest.

"You still stressing over Rashard, huh? Girl, don't worry about that negro. I know you going through a rough time, but you will get through this. I will see to that because your big brother gon' be there for you."

"Thanks, Tyreke. But nothing or no one can take away the pain that's been pricking at my heart."

"There is something that can help." Tyreke said, raising an eyebrow.

"What's that?"

With a serious look on his face, Tyreke snapped his fingers and rolled his neck like a snake before saying, "Beat that bitch ass!"

"Tyreke, fighting her is not going to bring back my husband or change the fact he betrayed me. It's just going

24

to make me look like a fool and make matters worse. But, I'm not going to lie as much as I want to hurt that girl; I'm going to have to take the high road and swallow my pride."

"Girllll, please! Then I'll beat her ass for you." Tyreke laughed while unsnapping the cape around Rayne's neck, then motioning for her to follow him towards the dryer.

After an hour and a half of sitting under the dryer, Rayne was tired and ready to go home and crawl in her queen size bed, but that was out the question because she promised Zoey she'd hit up the new club Lucien's, downtown on East Main Street. Tyreke had just finish putting the last minute touches to her curls when Troy walked into the salon, and all the thirsty females gravitated like vultures in heat at his presence.

Tyreke smacked his lips and threw his hands on his hips. "Look who the devil done dragged up in here."

Troy was definitely a head turner. He stood at six feet tall, his skin was dark like imported swiss chocolate, his goatee accentuated his face, his physique was well toned, and his smile was an aphrodisiac. Troy always pursued Rayne when they were in high school, but ultimately gave up when Rayne and Rashard hooked up the day of her sixteenth birthday party. Talk about being crushed. That drew a wedge in their friendship, and Troy even stopped talking to her for months. But he eventually got over it. I guess he figured having her as a friend was better than nothing at all. When Rayne and Rashard's marriage fell apart, rest assured, he was there to pick up the pieces. Let's just say old habits die hard.

Troy walked towards Rayne and all the female's eyes were still stuck on him like glue. Rayne flashed a smile as she got up from the chair.

"Hey, beautiful," Troy said.

With a sudden response, Tyreke said, "Hey boo!"

Rayne started to giggle, but Troy didn't find it funny as he shot Tyreke an evil glare. Tyreke flashed a cocky grin, then motioned for his next client to come to his station.

Troy turned his attention back to Rayne. "Anyway, how are you doing today?"

"I'm doing good, and you." Rayne turned around and handed Tyreke three twenty dollar bills.

"I'm good now that I got the chance to run into you."

"Ah, Lord," Tyreke said, rolling his eyes up to the ceiling.

Rayne playfully nudged Tyreke in his arm. "Quit it. I'll see you in two weeks. I love you." Rayne said.

"I love you too sis. I'll call you before you head out tonight. I might just roll up there with y'all."

"Boy, please, you know Craig not letting you out that house."

"Whateva."

Rayne tried to make a dash for the door, sure enough; Troy was following right behind her.

"Hold up baby girl, I'm going to walk you to your car."

*It's really no need*, was what Rayne was thinking and wanted to say out loud, but opted not to because she knew Troy would get all into his feelings and feel rejected.

"Thanks for walking me to my car." *Ok, so I'm lying, but he doesn't have to know that.*

"No problem, baby girl. I feel like you've been avoiding me since the other night. I hope you know I'm truly sorry for crossing the line. You know I can't help the way I feel about you."

Rayne looked into Troy's sexy brown eyes, and as much as she tried to deny it, she found him quite tempting. He certainly would be better than those lonely nights where she curled up in her bed with a bottle of Verdi, listening to a R. Kelly tune, while pleasuring herself with Playboy. Playboy is the name she gave her vibrator. It definitely did the trick on those cold lonely nights. Besides she had needs and a girl has to do what a girl has to do. Although she loved her vibrating friend, she desired a real dick inside her sugary walls.

Troy was starting to make Rayne hot and bothered. "Troy, I have to go."

"Ok. I'll see you tonight and maybe we can continue our little discussion then."

"I'm sure we will see each other. I heard your boy Smoot will be performing tonight."

"Yeah, my boy is doing big things. For what it's worth, Rayne, I really do care about you and hope you reconsider things between us." He leaned in and placed a gentle kiss on her lips.

Rayne was taken completely off guard, but smiled without saying a word. She turned around and got into her Mercedes Benz. She rolled down her window and said to a love-struck Troy who was still standing there waiting for her to pull off, "For what it's worth, I would be lucky to have you, but you know we can't get down like that. It just wouldn't be right."

"That's your opinion, not mine. All you have to do is say the word, and I'm there.

If you just let go and open up your heart to me, I guarantee you I can and I will make you happy."

The manner in which his words rolled off his tongue made Rayne quiver. She gave him a wink and a smile. "I'll see you tonight."

Rayne adored Troy's admiration for her which was flattering, but his persistence was not helping her situation. She weighed the pros and cons, but concluded a relationship with him would only lead to disillusionment and regret. Then there were times she figured messing with him would not be such a bad idea after all, but refused to give into her regressive and untamed desires; even though it would be the sweetest revenge for Rashard's indiscretions. Although there was an undeniable chemistry between her and Troy, she knew that was one forbidden fruit that should be left alone.

# Emotional Rollercoaster

## 4

It was fifteen minutes past eleven. Rashard peeped at the clock. He and his father planned on having lunch at noon. He couldn't concentrate and he certainly wasn't getting any work done. He contemplated leaving the office early and cancelling lunch with his father. Reality was slowly sinking in as he sat at his desk and forlornly gazed at his divorce papers. Frowning at the fact that his marriage was over, he picked up the divorce papers and slung them from his desk. He watched the papers scatter across the floor.

"Damn you Rachel! I hope you burn in hell!" Rashard said aloud to himself. He wanted nothing more than to be married to Rayne.

Brutal pain dwelled in his heart. The day the messenger showed up on his doorstep turned his life into a living hell. To add insult to injury, he learned that he was the father of her child. His indiscretion had finally caught up with him. He could still see the pain in Rayne's eyes as she tried to understand why. He withstood her pained tirade because he knew she had to get it out and he deserved it. Rashard's anger resurfaced every time he relived the day his life was intentionally ruined. Tears began to fall. He tried to fight them back as he let out an exasperated sigh. He remembered what his mother said when he told her, he had finally found true love.

It was the night of their senior prom, and more and more each day Rashard found himself falling madly in love with

28

Rayne. His mother was pinning a purple flower on his tuxedo jacket when she observed the blissful look on his face.

"You look very happy, son." she said, gently touching the side of his face.

"I am mom. Rayne is so special and I'm lucky to have her in my life."

"True love can come around more than once in a lifetime, and I can look in your eyes and tell in your voice that she's the one." An angelic smile lit up her face, and he knew she was happy for him. His mother adored Rayne, and they were always as close as a mother and a daughter could be.

Thinking about Rayne made him want to call her. Her voice resided in his head. He picked up the phone, but quickly hung it back up. He could not handle any more rejection. Every day he apologized profusely, assured her that was the first time, and it never happened again. He asked for her forgiveness or at least time, if she was willing, to let him prove that he wanted the marriage to work.

Rayne sneered and retorted with her reply, "I really loved you Rashard, but you hurt me. There is no way I can get over what you have done and trust you again. Stop trying to make this marriage work because nothing can fix the pain you have caused me."

He wanted to hold her tight and tell her it was just a dream, but the sadness in her eyes didn't give him any hope; it only confirmed that their union was really over. He was the one dreaming if he thought Rayne would consider taking him back. Since his separation, Rashard had several women throw themselves at him. Despite his old player ways, he showed them no interest. None of them could compare to Rayne. He smiled as he ran his fingers through his soft curly hair.

Rashard's ringing cell phone scattered his thoughts. He gathered his composure and cleared his throat.

"Hello."

"Hello, Rashard. This is Rachel, you have time to talk?"

Rashard yanked at his tie and cursed under his breath. Rachel was the last person he wanted to talk to. The sound of her voice stirred up irritation inside him.

"What do you want Rachel?" Rashard snapped.

"What's with the attitude? We didn't get to finish our conversation from the other day. We need to finish our discussion about Moses."

"I told you we'll deal with that situation, but right now, I can't deal with your drama."

"Then when will you be ready? You can't keep avoiding me."

"I'll call you," Rashard said quickly and hung up the phone.

Rachel's call had really put him in a foul mood. He wished he could have reached through the phone and strangled the shit out of her. Rashard knew his father was always prompt and would be walking in his office in any minute. Rashard hastily straightened out his tie, put on his jacket, grabbed the mirror on his desk to check his hair, made sure there were no traces of tear marks from his crying, and picked the divorce papers up from the floor, all in record time. No way in hell was he going to let his father see him in an emotional state, especially over a female. Although his father adored Rayne, any signs of emotional weakness would make him a sissy in his eyes. Just like Rashard expected, his father was walking into his office promptly at noon.

"Hey, pops, how's it going?" Rashard asked, acknowledging his father.

"I'm taking one day at a time, son. Despite your mother's illness, your old man is making it." Alexander extended his hand to shake Rashard's before taking a seat in the leather chair across from his desk. He leaned his cane up against the chair and stretched out his long legs.

"I remember it was me sitting behind that desk, and your mother bringing you up here to see me. You would always tell me that one day you would own this company when I retired. I appreciate you taking over during this trying time. I'm so proud of you son. So what are you up to?"

Despite the tension Rashard was feeling, he managed to force a smile onto his face. "I'm trying to meet this deadline on the Wake Tower proposal. I need to have it in Dan's hands first thing Monday morning, or we'll lose the contract."

Alexander looked at him for a long moment. As much as

30

Rashard tried to hide it, he could look in his face and sense something was wrong. His instincts were telling him it had something to do with Rayne.

Rashard let out a slight chuckle. "What? Why are you staring at me like that?"

"Liar. I know something is wrong with you. You been in here crying over that gal, haven't you?"

Rashard raised an eyebrow, trying to evade the question, he asked, "Would you like a glass of water?" Before his father could respond, he got up from his desk and walked over to the credenza and picked up the pitcher of ice cold water. He poured the water into two glasses, and with his back still turned to his father he asked, "Why do you think I was in here crying over Rayne. I could have been working on my proposal like I said."

"I can look at you and tell you've been moping around like some little sissy. It's written all over your face. I know for a fact you weren't working on no damn proposal. You can't put nothing pass your old man."

"What, you psychic now?" Rashard asked.

He handed his father the glass of water, walked back around to his desk and sat down. He took a quick sip of his water and sat it on the desk, watching his father's eyes trail his every move. He held his stare.

Finally, Mr. Armstrong spoke, "I've been in your shoes and I know how it feels."

"What, crying over some woman?" Rashard asked with an amused look on this face.

"Hell naw, boy! Crying over some woman is for pansies. I know how it feels to lose the woman you love. Before I met your mother, I was with this woman named Claudine for three years. I was madly in love and wanted to marry her. But Claudine broke my heart when she dumped me for her first love. I tell you one thing; your old man never shed one tear. My father always told me, "like many things in life, if you miss one street car catch the next.""

"Well pop, nothing is wrong with expressing how you feel about a woman you truly love. Besides, I was not crying."

"Who the hell you think you're fooling? You can't fool me."

"*Whatever* pops, enough about me." Rashard's tone

changed. He leaned onto his desk and clasped his hands together. "How is mom doing? I'm worried that her condition is taking a turn for the worse."

Alexander fidgeted with his hands before he answered. "You know your mother is a fighter. I strongly believe she can beat this cancer."

"Pop." Rashard hesitated before speaking. "I know you want to believe that, but she has stage four lung cancer. What are the chances—?"

"Stop talking like your mother's going to drop dead today or tomorrow. She's going to beat this dammit!" Alexander jumped up from the chair knocking his cane to the floor.

"I didn't mean to upset you, pop."

Alexander waved him off. "I know you didn't mean any harm. It's just I don't know what I'm going to do if I lose your mother." He eased back down into the chair and began to stroke his gray beard keeping his eyes locked on Rashard. "You know son, I learned that you can close your eyes to things you do not want to see, but you cannot close your heart to things you do not want to feel. As much as we want to be rid of our pain, we can't control the inevitable. If I never told you this, then I want you to know that I always admired your devotion to Rayne. Your love for her reminds me of how I feel about your mother. I know she means a lot to you, and if it's meant to be, you two will find your way back into each other's heart."

Rashard shook his head in doubt, held his breath in then let it go. "I hope you're right, pop. I sho' hope you're right." Rashard was getting restless and was ready to leave the office. "Why don't we go eat before I lose my appetite?"

Rashard and his father headed out to go to lunch, their conversation rested heavily on his mind. What if his dad is right? Can there be hope for him and Rayne to find their way back to each other? After all, he does not believe Moses is his son. However, there was just one problem: DNA tests don't lie. So how was Rashard going to convince Rayne to take him back? Damn.

# Time to let go

## 5

"Talk to you later, baby. Have a nice time at dinner."

Rayne could hear the smile and concern in her mother's voice as she hung up the phone. She couldn't keep her mind on work because thoughts of Rashard kept invading her, bringing back bittersweet memories. Talking with her mother soothed her frantic emotions for a brief moment, but when they hung up; the memories would return and depress her all over again. What do you do when your mind is telling you to do something, but your heart won't allow you to move on? Six months had passed and her divorce was final; yet Rayne was still stuck.

When she laid eyes on him, she knew he was her soul mate. It was love at first sight. Rashard was so attractive, and their connection was immediate and intense. She knew she was in the perfect relationship because her stomach would churn like a slushy machine. Of course like any relationship, they had their ups and downs, but Rayne was devoted and he was devoted to her. She thought he was the perfect partner who would fulfill her in every way, but she got caught up in her own impractical expectations of a relationship, and forgot to separate realism from fantasy. "Damn, I need to get him off my mind and out of my system!" Rayne yelled out. She was beginning to hate herself for giving her ex-husband a second thought. All her time and energy was being wasted on him.

Rayne looked at the mahogany portrait clock Zoey gave

her as a gift for her office. It was 6:30 p.m. and she was waiting for Terrence to finish up his phone call so they could head out to Topeka's for dinner. Her cell phone rang again, and this time it was the ringtone she had assigned to Tyreke, "It's Raining Men." She contemplated whether or not she should answer it, and then hesitantly hit the talk button.

"Hello, Tyreke. What do you want?" Rayne said sounding real annoyed.

"Well damn," Tyreke said with emphasis. "What got your panties all in a bunch?"

"I'm sorry. I just got a lot on my mind. I didn't mean to sound so snappy."

"Well you shouldn't have answered the damn phone then if you didn't want to talk. I forgive your ass this time, but don't let it happen again."

"What do I owe for the pleasure of your call, Tyreke?"

"I have not talked to your ass in two days since I did that nappy head of yours. I wanted to know what was good witcha."

"Nothing exciting or new is going on. The same old stuff, just a different day. I just finished talking to ma on the phone."

"That's nice. What ma talking about?"

"Nothing. She just wanted to talk and see how I was doing."

"Oh, ok. You sound depressed. Let me guess, Rashard must be on your mind."

The sound of his name saddened her all over again. Rayne pondered their breakup for a moment in silence. When Rayne learned of Rashard's infidelity, the pain she felt was like a dagger going straight through her heart. Rashard was her missing rib. Rayne thought she had it all when she married her childhood sweetheart. Like a moth to a flame burned by the fire, she was blinded by his love. She could never love another the way she loved him. His affair was a jolt to her self-worth.

"Hello, earth to Rayne. Are you still there?"

Rayne thoughts snapped back to reality. "My life seems so surreal without Rashard in it. I can't seem to let go and move on. I'm still trying to understand one minute I'm happy with this perfect life, and the next I feel like a woman scorned; like a woman who lost it all. I feel like I'm in a Freddy Krueger nightmare and can't wake up."

"I can't believe it myself. For Rashard to hurt you like this... it's not like him. As much as he adores you, I can't picture him cheating on you with all people that whore, Rachel. The shit just doesn't make sense if you ask me. Sis, if it's meant to be, you two will find a way to work it out."

"What planet are you on? Listen to yourself. My ex-husband cheated on me with a woman I despise. There is no working this out. To be quite honest, he can go straight to hell and take Rachel with him." Rayne started to choke up. "You know what's so fucked about all this? I miss the hell out of him, and the sad part of it all is that I'm not completely over him. I be damn if I let him back into my heart again. He hurt me in the worst way imaginable."

Tyreke responded, "I guess he got caught up."

There was a knock on the door and Terrence poked his head through her office door.

Rayne acknowledged his presence and waved for him to come inside. She let out a long deep sigh, "Well no need to dwell on the past. I'm getting ready to leave the office with Terrence, so we can go to dinner. As a matter of fact, why don't we meet soon for dinner? I'll call Zoey and see if she wants to join us. I'll call you later and we can make plans then."

"That sounds good. I have to go and meet Craig anyway. My boo taking me out on the town tonight."

Rayne shook her head. She didn't know what her brother saw in him. She couldn't stand Craig and thought her brother could do better. She stayed out of it; after all it was his life. Whether or not she approved of his relationship, he was going to continue to see that loser anyway.

"Enjoy your date."

"I'm surprised you don't have anything smart to say?"

"I do not. You are going to do what you want anyway. Good-bye."

"Whatever. Good-bye."

Terrence gave Rayne an indulgent smile. "Let me guess, you were talking to Tyreke."

"Your assumption was right, it was Tyreke."

"Sounds like an intense conversation. I saw the wrinkles on your forehead."

"We were talking about Rashard as usual. You know talking about Rashard can pull me out of my element. But, I'm ready to fix all of that."

Terrence was intrigued. He was anxious to hear what could possibly make Rayne forget all about Rashard. As much as she still loved that man, he figured hell had to freeze over in order to perform that miracle. "I suppose you going to have him killed, because that's the only way I see him no longer suffocating your existence."

"Easy... I plan on letting go of my self-pity and take control of my own feelings and destiny."

"That sounds good, but who are you trying to convince, me or yourself."

"The way I see it Terrence, I need and want a man who can fulfill my sexual desires and leave knowing there could be nothing more between us but an occasional physical encounter with no expectations. I want a jump off and nothing more. Truth of the matter, a relationship would be too damn complicated."

"Good for you darling, but the way I see it, your ass is delusional."

Rayne laughed, "Well it's nice to know I have your support. I'm having a moment here and you not taking me seriously."

"I'll take you seriously when I know you letting some other man taste your chocolate treasure. Until then, Rashard will always be a factor in your life. Now, are you ready to go to dinner? You know Debra have my ass on a curfew."

"Yes, I am ready to go. This day has been exhausting from the sales meetings, closings, house showings, and indecisive ass clients."

Rayne was presumptuous to think she could never lose Rashard. At a time like this, she wished her father was still alive. She missed his fatherly advice. He always knew what to say to make her pain go away. She envisioned sitting in front of him and him saying, "Sometimes, love will hurt, but don't be sad it's over, just be joyful that it was once yours. What don't kill you will only make you stronger." Then he would grab her hand, tell her how much he loves her and seal it with a tender kiss to her forehead. Sad but true, Terrence was right. As much as she wanted to move on, she couldn't let go of the heartbreak. In order to free herself of Rashard Armstrong, she had to let go.

# I want to be that man

## 6

Who said you don't need a knight in shiny armor? Right after Rashard and Rayne's marriage ended, Troy managed to swoop in like a knight in shiny armor to pick up the pieces. He had no intentions of giving up. Unbeknownst to Rayne, Troy had an ulterior motive; and that was to become the new man in her life now that Rashard was out of the picture. You see, Troy had a crush on Rayne who seemed to embody all he ever wanted in a woman. He met her at the age of fourteen when he moved into her neighborhood. He was smitten like a kitten by her beauty. He often fantasized about running his hands freely through her long locks while they sat on his porch and watched the sun go down. Unfortunately for him, it never happened because she was infatuated with Rashard and he didn't stand a chance. He did everything in his power to catch her attention, but Rashard was the only one she saw. He could never understand what she saw in him. In his opinion, Rashard was egotistic, shallow, arrogant, and an asshole.

Troy was fifteen minutes late for his lunch date with Rayne. He was glad she decided to wait. As his car took a beating from the rain, his mind drifted to his freshman year at Virginia State University; Rayne and Rashard were going through one of their frequent stormy days. Rayne had about enough of Rashard's bullshit and broke up with him. While Rashard was seeking comfort in the arms of other females on campus, Troy was happily pursing a vulnerable

Rayne. Troy desperately tried to make Rayne see he was the better man for her while making Rashard out to be the bad guy; chastising his behavior at every opportunity. At first Rayne spurned his advances because he was Rashard's cousin, but it didn't take long to convince her that didn't matter. Although he knew she was vulnerable, he deployed tactics to win over her heart. There was something about Rayne that drew him to her, and although she didn't seem interested, he'd made up his mind that it was her or nobody else.

Everything was going according to plan and Troy found himself spending more time with Rayne than he could imagine. Every day he'd walk her to class, running into Rashard along the way, catching the contorted look on his face as he would reach down and grab Rayne's hand. He would occasionally show up at her apartment and surprise her with a bouquet of roses, take her out to eat or to a movie, in an effort to bridge an emotional connection between them. As much as he cared about Rayne, he had one more scheme up his sleeve. One night he connivingly took her to Red Lobster when he learned Rashard was going to be there with another woman. Rayne was mad as hell, and from the way she acted, she wanted to cut Rashard's heart out and stuff it down his throat. With hindsight, Troy knew his ploy would have a hurtful turning-point. He quietly enjoyed listening to Rayne express her resentment towards Rashard. He wasn't even bothered that he was the sole reason for her being upset. Jealousy smothered Rayne, cut off any common sense that existed, caused her to exact revenge.

"I'm ready to go!" Rayne exclaimed.

"But we haven't even ordered yet."

"Who gives a fuck about ordering any food? I said I'm ready to go now!" Rayne screeched.

She stormed off from the table. Troy was not expecting her next course of action. She stopped at Rashard's table, faced his female companion and with a derisive tone said, "By the way, if you slept with him you better get checked. Word on campus is that he's been giving girl's gonorrhea. I just got my test results back today and they were positive."

With that said, Rayne rolled her eyes and stomped off.

The look on Rashard's face was priceless. Troy knew what he did was manipulative, but like the old saying goes, '*what she doesn't know won't hurt her*'. Besides, he didn't know she would stoop so low in public.

Troy finally arrived at The Boathouse, and once inside the waitress took him straight to his table where Rayne was sitting perusing the menu.

"I'm so sorry I'm late. My meeting ran over." Troy gently kissed her on the cheek, took off his jacket, and placed it on the back of the chair. He smoothed out his shirt before sitting down.

"That's ok. You seem a little flustered. Is everything ok?"

"Sure everything is fine now that I am here with you beautiful."

Rayne tried not to blush, but couldn't because his face took on a loving expression that made her smile. He always had something sweet to say and the look in his eyes made her realize he was sincere.

"I took the liberty to order you a glass of Riesling. The waitress just brought it out, so you are just in time."

"Thanks. I'm so glad you decided to meet me for lunch. I've wanted to see and talk to you. After the other night, I figured you never wanted to see me again."

Rayne said, "We almost crossed the line, and we can't make that kind of mistake again."

There was a pause.

"I know, and I'm so sorry if I made you feel uncomfortable."

Troy waited for her response, but she turned away; stared out the window to avoid eye contact. Rayne's guilt had been eating away at her conscious ever since their shared kiss. A kiss that almost made her commit the unthinkable. For that reason alone, she knew she had to keep her distance to avoid any temptation.

A few days earlier, Troy came to her house to have dinner. What started out to be an innocent meal almost led to a night of passion. After dinner, they cleared the table and washed the dishes. When they were done, she told him she had a long day ahead of her and insisted they end their night before it got too late. As she walked him to the door, she could feel his breath on the back of her neck. Rayne didn't get a chance to open the door, when she felt Troy grab her by her waist and press her up against the wall. His assertive behavior caught her off guard. She could feel his erection bulge through his pants as he grinded her ass in slow motion.

"I want you so badly," Troy whispered into her ear. Her mind was telling her no, but her sexual urge intensified as he moved his hand up and down her side, then to her breast, kissing her neck and earlobes. Troy turned Rayne around so that they would be face to face. His intense stare was keen and penetrative, her body cocooned with nervous excitement, she flutters. He parted her lips open with his tongue, slowly eased her legs apart and inserted his finger into her aching pussy. She was warm and wet as his fingers delved into her fleshy pink inside. Once he finished exploring her mouth, he unbuttoned her shirt, and began to suck and lick her erect nipples as if they were milk duds. "Umm, you taste just like candy," he implied. Unconsciously aware of her actions, reality started to sink in.

Rayne's guilt brought an abrupt halt to her behavior and her reaction to Troy's seduction. She pushed him away. "I'm sorry, we shouldn't... we can't...oh my God, what we are doing is so wrong." Rayne promptly buttoned up her shirt, covering up her disclosed breasts.

Troy apologized and begged her to reconsider how she felt, but Rayne was adamant. They should not give into temptation and cross the line. With his head down, Troy sulked out of her condo.

Troy reached out for Rayne's hand.

She quickly recoiled.

"Don't."

Troy ached for this woman. She put up a wall. He had to tear it down.

"You know how I feel about you. You've known for years. I can't just turn that off like a light bulb."

"Look Troy, you and I will never work. It's not such a good idea."

The brown-skinned waitress with short hair interrupted their conversation. It was just what Rayne needed to ease the tension between them two. The waitress took their orders then turned and walked away.

Troy took a sip of his drink. "I didn't mean to upset you. I only want you to see things from my perspective. You wouldn't be in this mess if you would have listened to me and not married Rashard. I told you he was no good for—."

Rayne quickly cut him off. "Whatever your personal feelings were, it doesn't matter anymore. I married Rashard, now we are divorced, and I've moved on."

"Don't give up on wanting to be happy because one jerk fucked up."

Rayne chuckled at his cynicism. "Why mess things up between us by getting into a relationship? If it isn't broke, why fix it? You know I really care about you. I appreciate you being that shoulder to lean on and helping me through my difficult time, but I think we should keep things between us strictly platonic."

Rayne found herself over the course of six months constantly battling temptation because she was truly falling for him. That's one ghost she had to keep in the closet. She couldn't let anyone know she secretly desired the six feet, handsome, dark chocolate brother. Not even Troy. They've become closer since her divorce with Rashard. She kept telling herself she was developing feelings because she was lonely and missing Rashard. Her head could tell her anything and she would believe it, but the heart doesn't lie.

Troy spent countless nights sitting up listening to her cry over the phone, running to her every beck and call. He was sensitive with words which had an arousing effect on her. He profusely complimented her beauty; he would walk up behind her wrap his arms around her waist and tell her how sexy she was. He showered her with gifts, took her to plays, to the movies, fancy restaurants, and brought her flowers for no reason at all. They sat up many nights listening to oldies but goodies, and sang along to the lyrics. He was kind. He was charming. He was compassionate. His sexy voice, his sexy laugh, and the way he looked at her was comforting. His tender touches had aroused her curiosity, wanted to know what his penis would feel like thrusting against her aching sugary walls. More importantly, he was her friend, her confidante; he seemed to make her life safer. Rayne knew he was very taken with her and made no secret of it, but it was her gut feeling that kept telling her not to tread those deep waters.

"You have this pensive look on your face," Troy replied. His voice started to sound defeated, "Damn. I really hope you didn't feel this way."

With reluctance Rayne looked up at Troy. She could hear the irritation and disappointment in his voice. She wasn't telling him what he wanted to hear. "I'm still in love with him."

"He didn't deserve you Rayne. You are a good woman."

"Sometimes I think I was too abrasive, and I should not have let my marriage end so quickly. I feel like I should have tried to work things out."

"Really? Do you think he deserves a second chance? I don't mean to pour salt on an open wound, but he betrayed you with a woman you despise. Don't be so naive about this."

"I know. As much as it hurts, I can't help the way I feel." Rayne cupped her glass with her hands and started twirling the straw around in her soda.

Troy became agitated and downed the rest of his drink.

Rayne said with concern, "I don't understand the animosity towards Rashard. He's your cousin and you act like you don't even care about him. What's the deal, Troy? I mean for years you two have been at each other's throat. Neither one of you have a good reason not to like each other." Rayne raised an eyebrow. Has he hurt you?"

With a cold stare in his eyes, Troy replied, "Look, I don't want to talk about Rashard anymore. I don't give a fuck about him. Never have. Never will."

The manner in which he said it sent goose bumps up Rayne's spine. His tone and his words made her nervous.

"Let's change the subject." Rayne said defensively.

Troy was getting angry.

"I don't get you Rayne. Why would you still be in love with a man that had an affair and fathered a child in the process?"

"Excuse me, what the hell did you just say?" Rayne tried to keep her voice down so that she would not make a scene and draw any attention to them.

Her dumbfoundness did not surprise him at all. As a

matter of fact, it worked out just like he had planned— he would be the one telling her about the baby.

Troy put on a shame-faced apology to cover up his deceit. "I'm sorry. I thought Rashard would have told you by now. I wish I wasn't the one to tell you."

Rayne eyed him suspiciously. "I don't believe you. You would tell me anything to draw a wedge further between Rashard and me. Why would you be so cruel?"

"Baby, I wish I was lying, but I'm not. Rachel told me Rashard was the father of her son and that they had a DNA test done.

"This has to be some kind of sick, twisted joke. I can't believe Rashard had a child with that bitch!"

"Rayne..." Troy reached out to touch her hand.

"Don't touch me!" Rayne snatched her hand away from his. Her eyes began to well up with tears. She couldn't process the information she just received. "You loving this aren't you?"

"Rayne, I wouldn't intentionally hurt you. I'm not some kind of monster."

Rayne didn't know what to believe. The only thing she knew was that she needed answers. "I can't do this." Rayne grabbed her purse and got up to leave.

"Wait, where are you going?"

Rayne stormed out of the restaurant.

Troy was not fazed by Rayne's emotional outburst. He was foolishly in love, although Rayne's feelings were not mutual. You see, when the time is appropriate, all evil reveals itself. No one knew the depth of Troy's infatuation over Rayne. There's a thin line between good and evil, and evil lies in Troy's determination to win Rayne's heart. He was determined to get what he wanted, and he wasn't going to stop until Rayne was his.

Rayne sped down Hull Street trying her best to avoid an accident. She dodged through cars like a mad woman. At this moment, she didn't care if Chesterfield County Police pulled her over. Maybe it would be for the best. She wasn't sure what she would do when she came face to face with Rashard. The thought of him having a child with Rachel made her sick to her stomach.

Thirty minutes later she was pulling up in front of

Rashard's office. Rayne stormed passed Tracie, the receptionist, as she headed towards Rashard's office.

Tracie jumped up from out her chair, "Mrs. Armstrong, you can't—."

"Go to hell!" Rayne hollered.

Tracie grabbed the phone to alert Rashard, but by then it was too late.

"You son of a bitch!" Rayne shouted. She was so mad she didn't care about the three gentlemen who were present.

Taken aback by her sudden outburst, Rashard began to stammer, "Ra...Ra...Rayne, I'm in a private meeting."

"Fuck your meeting; I need to speak with you, now!" She ordered.

The three gentlemen looked on in shock. Rayne's deranged behavior was not helping his business any. Rashard had to quickly defuse the situation before it got even uglier.

He looked at his clients in embarrassment. "Can you all please excuse me for a minute? I need to handle this situation. I'll be right back."

Rashard could tell by the look on their faces that they were displeased he had to interrupt the meeting. He knew this little episode would be the talk of many business gatherings. As much as he loved Rayne, he wanted to smack the shit out of her.

"Let's go!" Rashard ordered.

When they got inside the conference room Rashard laid into her. "What the hell is wrong with you storming into my office while I'm in the middle of a meeting acting like a fool?" He demanded to know.

"You better take some of that bass out your voice when talking to me, because right now I'm so pissed I want to kill you."

"Rayne, what the hell is this all about?"

"Is it true?"

"Is what true?"

"Did you have a child by that bitch, Rachel?!"

His secret was exposed. His eyes widened, not knowing how he should respond. It was a simple question. Either yes or no.

He hesitated for a while.

"Well did you?" Rayne demanded an answer.

Rashard lowered his head. He wasn't man enough to look her in the eyes when he responded, "Yes it's true."

"You bastard!" Rayne couldn't restrain the urge to slap him. Her hand sent a sharp blow across his face.

"How could you? It is bad enough you slept with her, but to get her pregnant. If I didn't find out, you probably weren't going to even tell me."

Rashard nursed his stinging face. "What do you mean when I was going to tell you? I don't owe you a damn thing. We're divorced. I'm just finding out my damn self and trying to process this information. So don't be coming into my office with this bullshit. I love you, but I'm not going to deal with your dramatics. How did you find out anyway?"

Rayne stood their stunned. He never talked forcefully to her before.

Rashard questioned her again. "How did you find out?"

"It doesn't matter. You're right we're divorced." Rayne brushed passed him in a hurry.

"Rayne wait!"

It instantly hit him that it was only one person behind Rayne finding out—Troy. His resentment towards Troy was growing minute by minute. Rashard knew it was a matter of time before his true colors would be revealed. And when it did, he would surely pay for turning his life into a living hell.

# Comforting the Soul

## 7

Zoey received a call from Rayne saying she needed her, and by the sound of her voice she was really upset. She sped to Rayne's house turning a twenty minute drive into ten. Zoey let herself into Rayne's condo with the spare key she had given her in case of an emergency. There were no lights on so she couldn't see; and as she carefully stepped inside she could hear pieces of glass crunching under her feet. Zoey carefully maneuvered her way through the dark living room searching for the lamp, trying not to knock anything over. When she found the lamp, she turned on the switch only to be startled by Rayne. She was wrapped in a chenille throw in the fetal position on the sofa. The living room was in total disarray. From the way things appeared, Zoey thought Rayne had been in a fight. The floor in the foyer was covered with broken glass, paper and magazines were ripped and thrown across the living room floor.

Rayne looked a hot mess. Her tears had vanished, but they left traces of smeared makeup on her face. Her hair was all over her head. Zoey started to believe she was in a bar fight and got her ass beat. She sat on the edge of the sofa and started rubbing Rayne's back. She softly said, "Whatever it is bothering you, let it all out. I'm here for you now."

Rayne's speech was muffled from her crying and Zoey couldn't make out what she was saying. Before she could ask her to repeat herself the doorbell rang. Zoey eased off the sofa to answer the door.

"Who is it?"

"Tyreke, let me in." He brushed pass Zoey. "Where is my sister?"

Zoey pointed towards the living room. "In there lying on the sofa depressed. She is really a mess right now."

Tyreke rushed to his sister's side. "Baby girl, it's me," he said, easing down onto the sofa. "You sounded really upset over the phone. Why don't you tell your big brother what's wrong?" Tyreke asked, eager to comfort his sister.

Rayne's voice began to tremble as tears started to pour down her distressed face. "Why...why...why did he betray me? All I wanted to do was spend the rest of my life with him. Have his babies—." Rayne's voice trailed off.

Zoey sat down on the floor beside Rayne and began to stroke her hair. She looked at Tyreke searching for ways they could help her friend.

"It's going to be alright. We're here to help you now. You better off without him. The hell with that two timing dog. Let Rachel have his ass."

Tyreke shot her a look. He asked in a subtle voice, "Do you think your last statement helped?"

Zoey quietly responded, "Shut up, I don't see you saying anything to snap her out this rotten mood."

Rayne removed her throw with feverish haste and slightly sat up. She said in an annoyed tone, "Don't you two start that damn arguing back and forth. Ya'll always manage to take the focus off me and center it on yourselves. I'm so over ya'll childish behavior."

Tyreke directed his eyes at Zoey and smirked, as if to say, see what you done did. "I'm sorry, sis. You know I didn't mean to upset you anymore than you already are."

"Would you like me to fix you some tea?" Zoey asked.

Rayne sniffled, "Tea would be nice." She looked back and forth between Tyreke and Zoey. Her eyes were puffy and red from all the crying.

"For what it's worth, Rayne, you'll find true happiness again. You're smart, beautiful, sexy, and intelligent. Trust me; some man would be lucky to have you." Zoey said. She headed to the kitchen to fix a pot of peppermint tea.

"She's right. You can have anybody you want. But you

won't be able to do that if you keep dwelling over Rashard. Baby girl, you have to let go and move on. I know you don't want to hear that, but he fucked up—not you." Tyreke said in agreement.

Rayne continued to whimper. Tyreke quietly consoled his sister until Zoey returned twenty minutes later with three cups of hot tea. They sat in silence. Quietness filled the room as they sipped their tea.

Zoey decided to break the silence, careful with her choice of words she said, "You never really said what it is that have you so upset. It's clear it has something to do with Rashard. You care to share with us what's the matter?"

Rayne sat her mug down on the end table. She pulled the comforter completely over her body. She clasped her hands tightly, her lips formed a frown, her wrinkled forehead tightened, and she stared back and forth at their inquisitive faces. Suddenly she released a screeching scream and a piercing cry. Rayne forced her words through her screams, "Rashard is the father of Rachel's child!"

As painstaking it was for her to say it, Rayne's monstrous outburst put Zoey on edge. Tyreke held his sister tightly in his arms, stroking her hair like she was a child.

Zoey got up from the floor and looked away. Her perplexed face unnoticed. The nerves in the pit of her stomach flew around like butterflies. She knew it would have been a matter of time before Rayne learned the truth. Her guilt of knowing jeered at her; secretly shamed by her disloyalty. She started to think about Anthony and felt more horrible. Rayne would learn of her betrayal, the consequences of her actions would be unforgiving. Watching an emotional Rayne weep in Tyreke's arms, Zoey knew if she did not conceal her emotions, they'd only ridicule her even more. As she stood over Rayne and Tyreke, knowing she took part in her friend's despair, she knew she had to free herself from her own shame.

# Been there done that

## 8

What's done in the dark will come to the light. In this life, we think we are safe from recourse, for what we do in private, what we do in secret....no one else will discover. However, what we say...whatever we have done...can be seen by others, sooner-or-later.

*Ru Paul's Drag Race* filled the screen, as the ceiling fan blew and the sounds of Brian McKnight played in the background. Tyreke clutched the phone to his ear. He was in desperate need of pleasure. Not even his absent lover could create an ejaculation to take him out of his misery. He lay across his bed naked massaging his balls and stroking his penis, relentlessly trying to force an orgasm. But he couldn't come. Becoming pissed off, Tyreke just stopped trying. He never had a hard time coming and was frustrated he couldn't let his orgasm take control. Maybe it was all the stress he was under dealing with Craig, and juggling his affair with King.

Lost in his thoughts, tuning out the voice on the other end of his call, thinking about Craig and how he was going to break their relationship off was weighing heavy on his mind.

"Tyreke, are you listening to me? You're awfully quiet." King asked.

"Yeah, yeah. I'm listening." It was a lie. In fact, Tyreke wasn't listening to anything his lover had to say. Thoughts of Craig were all in his head and he wanted to bust a nut.

"It don't seem like you were listening. As I was saying, no one can ever find out about us."

"I told you and I'm not going to tell you again, you have nothing to worry about. Our secret is safe."

"I sure hope you right."

For three months, Tyreke had been having an affair with a married man. His three year relationship with Craig had hit a snag which led him into the arms of the lover he named, King. Tyreke loved Craig, but he knew he had a lot of shit with him. Rayne couldn't stand him, and thought he could do better. Craig was controlling and sneaky, but Tyreke overlooked his flaws. Even the time he caught Craig being unfaithful, he forgave him, and stayed in the relationship. Then one night temptation presented itself, and Tyreke was happy to oblige. It was a mere payback for Craig's unfaithfulness. Fools usually do not understand when a situation is risky, so they are not afraid to do things that scare sensible people. The problem was that Tyreke was not sensible. His behavior was irrational, the consequences did not scare him the least. Although two wrongs don't make a right, the way Tyreke looked at it, what's good for the goose is good for the gander.

"Relax. You stressing for nothing. Everything is under control. I miss you," Tyreke said seductively through the phone.

"I miss you too. So what did you get into last night? You never called me like you promised."

"I stopped by my sister's house, then later on that night Craig came over and we chilled out."

There was a brief silence.

"Did you sleep with him?"

Tyreke sensed jealousy in his voice. "What kind of question is that?"

"Just answer the question. Did you?"

Tyreke was getting annoyed. He flicked off the TV, lifted off of the bed, removed his boxer briefs from the floor, and concealed his naked body. He fluffed his pillow, propped up his head, and stared up at the spinning ceiling fan. He wanted to curse King, but decided not to waste his energy on his jealous tirade.

"What I do with Craig is none of your business. Do I

51

question if you having sex with your wife? You need to quit while you're ahead?"

"It's just the sound of Craig's name makes me furious. He's no good for you. You need to cut your losses and fast."

"You telling me something I already know. I'm working on that. I just haven't figured out how I'm going to break things off."

"I sure will be glad when that day comes."

"You know he's leaving to go out of town this weekend."

"Good. I can break free from the wife and kids."

"Well then, I plan on fucking and sucking you real good. So good you won't be able to stand up."

"Damn, Ty, talking like that is making my python nice and hard."

Tyreke couldn't contain his smile. King's comment sent chill bumps up and down his spine. He started to rub his throbbing dick through his boxer briefs once again. Now they were getting somewhere. Maybe he could produce an orgasm.

Tyreke hated to ruin the moment, but he needed to get what he had to say off his chest. "You know, we been walking on dangerous ground with this affair we been having. It has become much more obvious that there are feelings involved. I thought we both agreed we were in this to have fun...no strings attached." King said he could handle a friend with benefits type of relationship with no problem. Tyreke was confused and needed to know where they stood.

"Tyreke, I can't help the way I feel about you. I didn't intend for me to catch feelings, but you make me feel so good inside. No one has ever made me feel the way you make me feel."

"But we both agreed since you're married and I'm in a relationship, we would not take each other seriously. Sex complicates things. I told you getting too connected will ruin everything."

"But you are not happy. Besides, you the one that said you were breaking things off with him."

"And..." Tyreke said nonchalantly.

"Don't I make you happy?"

Tyreke tried to evade the question. "What about your

wife?"

"What about her? This is not about her and me. This is about us."

"I thought you were concerned if your wife was to find out about us. Don't you care about your precious little secret being exposed?"

King huffed in agitation. "It's too late to be thinking about all this now. We done already crossed those lines."

Tyreke sat up on the edge of the bed. "Look, your non-caring attitude is starting to piss me off."

Tyreke's hostile tone did not bother King none. "Stop acting like you don't have any feelings for me, because you know you do."

"I told you from day one I was not in this to fall in love. You know we will never work. You are hiding your sexuality from the world, your family, and yourself. You got married to hide the existence of who you really are. Me on the other hand, I'm true to myself. I don't have to hide or pretend to be something I'm not. Everybody knows Tyreke is gay. I'm proud of who I am. I can't be in love with someone who is not true to themselves and lies to those around them. Been there done that. I learned how to stand up to the judgmental, negative attitudes, stereotypes, and ignorance. I suggest you do the same. If you want to finally step out of the closet you hiding in, then embrace who you truly are my brother. So if you really want to know how I truly feel, no I'm not in love and I don't have feelings for you. I'm only treating you the way that you're treating me."

"Why are you being so heartless, Tyreke? Are you trying to imply that I'm using you?"

"I'm just calling it how I see it. It's all good though. We are using each other. I'm just the one keeping it real."

"Shit! I just heard my wife come in with the kids I have to go. Are we still on for the weekend?"

"Umm. Whatever, I'll think about it," Tyreke said, sounding pissed off and hung the phone up, slinging it across the bedroom.

Tyreke continued to watch the ceiling fan in silence. His head felt like the spinning blades, bombarded by negative emotions and flooded with disorderly thoughts and limited clarity. Mad at Craig for the hurt and pain he constantly puts him through, and disappointed by his lover's homophobia. His nonchalant attitude made Tyreke realize he had no regard for his marriage. This unnerved Tyreke because he did not want him getting too connected. He knew that as long as his lover could keep his gay life clandestine, his tacitly same-sex relationship would remain underground. Tyreke was starting to realize his perception of his lover's attitude about same-sex attraction was all about the sex, making quickie dates and rendezvous. How could he fall in love and have an openly gay relationship? Tyreke was pissed knowing that King had more than enough internalized homophobia still stored inside his confused mind; and yet he had a thing—a very strong thing—for him.

# Eye Candy

## 9

It was Wednesday; the day of the Realtor's Expo. If it wasn't for the expo, Rayne would have stayed home in bed. She was in a miserable mood and did not need to be around anyone. She had trouble sleeping. Her thoughts raced all night after learning Rashard had fathered a child. Despite Zoey's and Tyreke's efforts to cheer her up, nothing could quickly cure her pain. She was leaving her apartment complex in route to the Richmond Convention Center. She took a familiar route, southwest on Coppermill Trace toward Mayland drive, right onto North Parham road, merged onto I-64 East towards Richmond. Memories of Rashard kept playing over and over in her head.

A smile crossed her face as she reminisced about her wedding. The church was decorated in beautiful lavender and ivory flower arrangements, which matched her four bridesmaids and maids of honor's lavender dresses. Her best friend, Zoey, was her maid of honor. She wore the most elegant satin side-draped A-line gown with beaded inset dress.

Each pew was dressed for the occasion, accented with gold and champagne ribbons hanging, a bouquet of ivory and crème roses with a touch of lavender and a variety of purple lily of the valley, sweet pea, and hydrangea flowers. It was a beautiful spring wedding that was held at her home church, Second Baptist, complete with a host of friends and family. The only thing missing was her best friend, Kenya, who she loved like a sister and had not seen or talked to since she moved away in the middle of their Junior year of high school. Ten minutes into her memory, she arrived at exit 75 and merged onto North 3rd street toward Coliseum/Downtown. Surrounding her was the Jackson Ward area. On her right was the 533 Club where her Aunt Jean had her retirement party. It was a moment she will never forget. Her mother caught her and Rashard making out in the back seat of his car. Gloria yelled at her all the way home and grounded her for a month. Rashard's parents only grounded him for two weeks. A faint smile crossed her face. Just past E. Clay Street, she had finally reached her destination. Rayne circled the block several times until she found a parking spot a block away from the Convention Center.

She gathered her composure before she got out of her car; looking herself over in the mirror to assure her hair and makeup were on point. She didn't want Terrence to see her looking like a hot mess. If he did, he would surely ask a lot of questions. She didn't want to sulk over Rashard while at the conference. Terrence Jackson was her Associate Broker, and they had a great working relationship. It was nothing she couldn't talk to him about. She briskly walked to the front entrance to meet him like they had planned.

"You look absolutely ravishing." Terrence admired how she looked in her dark grey pant suit that accentuated her curves.

"Thank you." Rayne smiled a sweet blushing smile. "I'm glad you are back from your vacation. You must tell me all about it."

"I can't wait because I have so much to tell. After you madam." Terrence held open the door, and extended his hand so that Rayne could enter into the building.

Rayne always admired Terrence. She always thought he was a gentleman, and she loved the way he took care of and treated his wife, Debra. Although she felt he possessed the same loving and nurturing qualities as Rashard, she sometimes couldn't help being envious over what he and Debra shared. She couldn't see him ever betraying their union, and now she couldn't help but wonder if he would ever step out on his wife like Rashard had done to her. She realized she couldn't put anything past any man. Even if they are married; they will always be on the prowl.

The Convention Center was a packed whirlwind. The Expo was a big event with numerous real estate classes, hundreds of people, speakers, networking, and cocktails. Registration started an hour before the first sessions and the lines were long—elbow to elbow, with agents and others looking for industry insight. The attendants hustled and bustled, passing out name badges and seminar packages in an orderly fashion. Rayne scanned the room recognizing several faces. She waved and smiled as they acknowledged each other's presence. There were two adjacent rooms filled with over fifty exhibits. Vendors were setting up their spaces before the convention started. As soon as Rayne and Terrence finished registering, they began to mingle and talk with other colleagues. Rayne was delighted when she noticed Kenneth Poindexter walking towards her; accompanied by a good-looking man.

Kenneth greeted her in his baritone voice. "Ms. Rayne Armstrong. You're just the young lady I was hoping to run into."

"It's so nice to see you again, Kenneth." Her voice was light and friendly as they embraced. Real estate had always been Rayne's passion. She started as a real estate sales agent right after college, and within two years became a multi-million dollar producer at Sale 4 U Realty, Inc. where Kenneth was the broker. After her third year being a sales agent, she decided to get her broker's license and became the company's Associate Broker. She stayed with the company one more year before she decided to start her own real estate company, Armstrong Realty.

"How are you doing?" Rayne asked.

"I'm doing well. I've been meaning to call you because I have some news I want to share."

"Is that so?" Rayne teasingly asked with a raised eyebrow.

"Yes, ma'am," Kenneth nodded. "I've decided to retire from real estate."

"Oh no, you can't. The Richmond market will not be the same without you. You taught me everything I know. What made you come to that decision, and what are you going to do?"

"I've paid my dues and I'm tired, so I decided it's time that the Mrs. and I start traveling around the world. Now that the kids are all grown up and out of the house, I'm looking forward to spending a lot of time with my wife. But I'm not sure if she's looking forward to spending a lot of time with me."

Everyone laughed, amused at his sentiment.

Kenneth turned his attention towards Terrence and lightly nudged him in his right arm. "Terrence, I see you still hanging in there. Rayne is keeping you on your toes." He chuckled.

Terrence extended his hand to shake his. "Kenneth, I see you still quite the jokester. It's nice seeing you again."

Kenneth cleared his throat. "Excuse me, but where are my manners?" This is a good buddy of mine, Bryce Underwood. He's a real estate developer and owns his own firm. He's in town on business. Bryce, this is Rayne Armstrong and Terrence Jackson."

Bryce extended his hand. "It's nice to meet you both." Bryce said.

"It's nice to meet you too." Terrence replied.

"Same here," Rayne said, not able to hide her attraction in her smile. She was immediately mesmerized by his honey brown eyes. He looked divine in his Prada charcoal grey pinstripe suit and his coal black Prada loafers. She sized up his features: a good six feet two inches tall, physically fit, and a mocha complexion. His beautiful smile displayed pearly white teeth, and the round up from his hair cut was neat and sharp as if it was done with a razor blade. His sexy deep voice made the area between her legs purr. She glanced down at his left hand, there was a wedding ring. Another woman existed in his life. *Damn*, she thought to herself.

Kenneth spoke, "Rayne, I'll be keeping in touch. Terrence, take good care of yourself and don't work too hard." He chuckled and patted Terrence on his arm.

Bryce nodded and smiled, "Again, it was nice meeting you both."

As the gentlemen walked away, Terrence leaned closer to Rayne and whispered in her ear, "Kenneth is still an asshole."

Rayne grinned. "Oh, he's not that bad."

Rayne couldn't keep her eyes off the delectable fine brother that graced her with his presence. She couldn't help but imagine his tongue between her thighs, licking and tasting her juices while she moaned a sweet symphony. Her indecent thoughts over a married man took her by surprise.

Terrence interrupted her thoughts. "Don't be so obvious."

Rayne let out a slight giggle. "Whatever do you mean?"

"Don't play dumb. I see you eyeing him down. I know that look."

"Indeed you do. So tell me what am I thinking?"

"You thinking about how many licks will it take him to get to the center of your tootsie roll pop."

Rayne looked at Terrence and with a devious grin she said, "You know me very well."

After the seminar, Rayne was elated about another chance encounter with Mr. Fine Ass. He was walking towards her; the stride in his walk reminded her of Denzel Washington.

"I'm really starting to enjoy our encounters." Bryce smiled.

His smile was gorgeous. She was getting hot and horny. The sight of him was sending chills up and down her spine.

"I couldn't have said it better myself," Rayne replied.

Bryce reached inside his blazer jacket, pulled out his business card, and handed it to her. "As Kenneth told you earlier, I'm in town on business. I just closed a deal to start construction on some new gated community homes in Powhatan, Virginia. Kenneth had nothing but positive things to say about you. He also told me if I needed any assistance on my project that I should contact you. You are highly recommended. I hope you don't mind he gave me your business card?"

"No, I don't mind at all. So what made you come out to the conference?"

"Kenneth thought it would be a good idea if I accompanied him here, that way I could network and expand my contacts. He was right; I've had the pleasure of meeting a lot of new people, *especially* one person in particular."

Rayne had a hard time trying to contain her smile. Bryce's flirtatious demeanor made her week in the knees. Her smile was wider than the ocean. Bryce stared at her long and hard as if he was staring straight through her soul.

"Maybe I can utilize your real estate expertise. I was hoping we would get the opportunity to meet again before I head back home to Atlanta. That's if your husband doesn't mind."

Rayne figured that was his way of inquiring if she was married instead of coming right out and asking. She quickly flashed her hand to assure she was single and available. "I'm divorced."

"Oh. Sorry to hear that. I believe his loss is someone else's gain." His eyes went up and down her body.

*If I could fuck him right now, I would,* Rayne thought to herself. "I'm sure one day I will find Mr. Right." What Rayne really wanted to say was, "I wish that someone could be you," but managed to keep her forwardness to herself.

"Did your wife travel here with you?"

He looked down at his wedding ring which was a symbolic expression of his love and devotion to his wife. Rayne couldn't help but wonder now that he was in her presence, was he questioning his commitment.

"No, my wife did not come with me on this trip."

Rayne's eyes lit up. "That's too bad for her. I'm sure she would have loved her visit here." Rayne replied, in an uninterested manner. She was really glad she didn't show up. She wouldn't have gotten the opportunity to meet Mr. Fine Ass, at least not in the manner she was hoping their next meeting would entail. "Unfortunately, I must be going, but I look forward to hearing all about your project."

"I look forward to telling you." Bryce assured. "I'm leaving Virginia tonight, but will be back in two weeks to meet my contractors. I'll call you when I get in town, and if you're not busy, maybe we can make plans to meet?"

"That sounds great. I'm going to hold you to it."

Bryce took Rayne's hand and softly kissed the back of it. She blushed to let him know she approved. "I'll be waiting for that call," she said seductively.

Rayne stood frozen in a trance. She didn't even notice

Terrence standing in front of her.

"Earth to Rayne," he said, waving his hand up and down her face. "Snap out of it hon. That man got your nose so wide open, you don't know what's going on around you. Get it together because it hasn't been that long since you been around a man. You around my sexy ass every day, and I don't get the attention that you giving that brother." He giggled.

Rayne pulled him by his collared shirt. "Whatever. Don't flatter yourself. Let's go."

Terrence walked with Rayne to her car. Along the way they were chatting about work for the next business day. Intriguingly, her focus shifted on Bryce. Her body became aroused. Her thoughts were inappropriate. She tuned out every word Terrence was saying.

"Alright, Ms. Armstrong, we arrived at your car safe and sound."

Rayne blinked, her embarrassment revealed in her face. "Huh...I mean...thanks Terrence for walking me to my car."

"If I'd known any better, I would say your body is here with me but your mind is on another side of town. Are you alright?"

"Yeah, I'm ok. My mind was a little distracted."

Terrence stared at her oddly. "I bet. I don't even want to know what you were thinking. I'm sure it wasn't good."

She wondered if Terrence could read her mind. Did he pick up on her dirty clandestine thoughts about a married man? She laughed it off and gave him a hug. "I'll see you tomorrow at the office. Make sure you're there on time. We have a 9'oclock sales meeting."

"I'll be there on time, just make sure you not late." Terrence held the door open for Rayne and closed it once she became situated in her seat."

Rayne started up her car and rolled her window down. "You need a ride to your car?" Rayne asked.

"Naw, I'm good. I'm not parked far, just two blocks over. The walk will do me some good, plus I have to make a phone call."

"That call sounds suspicious to me."

"What?"

"You heard me. Is there someone else besides Debra?"

Rayne jokingly implied.

"There you go assuming. I am a faithful man."

"Yeah right, Terrence. That's what they all say. See ya." Rayne pulled off and headed down 3rd Street, not even catching the look of guilt on Terrence's face.

Rayne was glad to be heading home. She had another long and exhausting day and had her taste buds set on the baked Tilapia, steamed asparagus, baked potato, and mouthwatering cornbread she was going to prepare for dinner. She felt her day turned out to be productive because she left the convention brimming with new ideas and ways to expand her network. She was especially elated she had the opportunity to meet Bryce. The thought of him made her coochie tingle with pleasure. She was eagerly anticipating the moment to get to know him not only professionally, but on a personal level as well.

She envisioned them in her office, staring at each other in silence, speculatively. She could feel his spellbound eyes slowly undress her. Rayne was consumed with longing, feverish with desire, which created an electrifying urgency for his touch. He leaned in to kiss her lips and she reciprocated, welcoming his tongue into her mouth. She began to run her hand up and down his chiseled chest, and ended at his full erect penis bulging through his pants. He grabbed her hands, put two fingers in his mouth and began licking, sucking them, greedily. Rayne was flushed; her cheeks turned red from lust. Once he finished pleasuring her fingers with his tongue, he laid her across the desk and spread her legs until her sex was fully exposed. He glides his hand languidly up and down her thigh, coming closer to her wet fold with every upstroke. Finally, he takes Rayne out of her misery, and inserts two fingers, repeatedly rotating and moving them in and out her wetness while sucking and flicking her swollen clit with his tongue. Her body began to jerk, and an orgasm rippled through her as she moaned from the pleasure her clitoris received.

"Oh shit!" Rayne yelled out. Her mind was so busy in the gutter; she almost ran the red light. As she slowly regained her composure, Rayne popped in her Maxwell CD, licked her lips and a seductive smile covered her face. She had finally found her distraction.

# Ulterior Motive

# 10

Troy could hear the conversations of dancers in the hallway as they walked passed his closed office door. Noon was approaching and Troy was up to his ears with business: dealing with his accountant for almost most two hours, invoices, dancers, and going over the floor plans for his newest addition to the Back Door— Seduction. Seduction was a VIP room exclusively for male clients who wanted to have one on one time with the dancers. To complicate matters more, he'd been wrestling with his feelings for Rayne.

He had noticed Rayne was being resistant and started to wonder if she had someone new in her life. But he would have known that as much as he sat outside her apartment complex night after night. It was a good thing he had not noticed any male visitors to her home. He didn't want to have to hurt anybody. He would look up at her apartment which was located on the second floor facing the parking lot, contemplating whether or not he should knock on her door. He would imagine that she would let him in, they would talk and laugh over a glass of Merlot, things would get steamy and he would take her to newfound heights she had never imagined. He would fuck her so intensely, with so much passion, that every thought of Rashard would be erased. He would leave his trademark inside her wet walls, his thrusts more profound than his words. He would punish her for years of rejection, but in a magnificent way.

He became bewildered about the past six months. He was persistent. His every move was calculated. He did everything he needed to do as planned to win her heart. Why was it taking so long to rescue this damsel in distress? Eleven years of being in love with Rayne was getting to him. Troy remembered the day he laid eyes on her; his dick hardened and his heart beat a thousand beats per minute. One night while lying in bed, he couldn't get her out of his mind which made him stroke his little man until he ejaculated. He masturbated for the first time at the age of 14.

He wondered if being in love with her was one of the reasons why he couldn't stay in a committed relationship. Not that he was looking to settle down with anyone anyway. Besides, too many women were on his dick and monogamy was not in his vocabulary.

During a brief moment during college, Troy and Rayne became closer than they had ever been. Needless to say, that didn't last long before Rashard got mad seeing them together and decided to work his way back into her good graces. The next thing he knew, Rayne and Rashard were talking about getting married right after college. The day Rayne married Rashard sent a sharp wrenching pain through Troy's chest. It was a marriage he felt should have never taken place. When the preacher said, "Speak now or forever hold your peace," Troy hated himself for not seizing the moment. It was his last and final chance to tell the woman he longed for how he truly felt, and expose Rashard for the two timing liar that he was. Bitterness was deep rooted in his heart after losing Rayne to Rashard.

Troy sat at his desk flipping through a Black Enterprise magazine, not really reading any of the articles. He couldn't because his mind was too preoccupied with Rayne. *How could one woman have such a spell over a man?* He thought.

He hadn't talked to Rayne since their lunch date, so he decided to give her a quick call and see if she had gotten the bouquet of roses he sent to her.

"Hello." Rayne's soft voice echoed through the phone.

The soothing sound of her voice sent a slight sensation through his jeans straight to his heart.

"Good evening, love. Did I catch you at a bad time?"

"No."

"I just called to see how you were doing. Did you get the roses I sent you?"

"I'm doing ok, and yes I got the roses you sent. Thank you. They were lovely."

"I'm glad you liked them. Look here Rayne, for what it's worth, I really do care about you. Just know I am here for you when you need me. I hope you know I never meant to hurt you."

"It's all forgiven, Troy. Thank you for your concern, but I'm a big girl and I can handle myself."

"You shouldn't be dealing with this alone."

"I'm not."

"Have you spoken to Rashard?"

"Yes, but let's not talk about him. I have had enough of this Rashard situation."

Troy sensed he hit a nerve and decided he better leave well enough alone. "Ok. I understand. Not another word about Rashard."

"I have to go. Call me later."

"Take care of yourself, Rayne."

"I will. Talk to you later, Troy."

Troy decided he needed to get out of the office, and he knew just the person to go see to get him out of his foul mood. He grabbed his blazer from the back of his chair. As he headed to his car, he ran into his bouncer, Boss Hogg. "Yo, Boss, I'm headed out for a couple of hours. Hold down the fort while I'm gone."

"I got you covered," Boss Hogg replied.

Troy pulled out his cell phone and quickly dialed the seven digits.

"Hello," a seductive voice came blaring through the phone.

"From the way you sound, you already know what I want."

"Are you coming over?"

"I'm leaving the club now. I'll be there in fifteen minutes."

"I'll be right here waiting for you, daddy."

Troy couldn't wait, his manhood sprang to action. He had a lot of built up tension, and a serious nut that needed to be released.

He merged onto I- 95 South and floored the accelerator, picking up speed. He was doing fifteen miles over the speed limit. The weather like Troy's mood was gloomy. He noticed how cloudy it was and suspected rain was coming soon. The weather man had predicted a 70 percent chance of rain and thunderstorms. As he changed gears on his 5-speed Volvo S80, his mind toyed with images of Rayne. He explored every inch of her body with his tongue, and she shuddered with pleasure as his manhood penetrated and pillaged her insides. He thought about how beautiful Rayne is when she is making her love faces. He wished he was heading to her house, and that it was Rayne that would send him into a sexual bliss. Rashard was the impediment standing in his way of what he could not have. What he could not feel: true love.

Troy made a left on Lauderdale Street, finally arriving at his destination. The small two bedroom brick rancher with green shutters was in a cul de sac, surrounded by six other houses. A swing hung from the tree in the front yard. The house belonged to an older couple before the wife died, and her husband decided to rent it out instead of selling it. He hopped out of the car and hurried up the walk way noticing the grass was about four inches tall and was in a desperate need of cutting. "This is definitely what the doctor ordered." Troy said out aloud.

He didn't get to the door good, before it swung open, and Rachel stood naked wearing only a pair of teal stilettos. Her hands were positioned on her hips, her hair was pulled back in a ponytail, and a devilish grin broadened her face. She had no shame in her game displaying her one hundred sixty five pound figure. She definitely didn't care if she was giving a free show for all her neighbors to see. That was the freaky side of her that Troy loved. When it came to sex, she cut to the chase. Troy had been with many freaky women, but Rachel was the freakiest of them all. The only reason why he dealt with her was because her head game was off the chain. Superhead had nothing on Rachel. But she was definitely not the kind of chick you would want to bring home to your momma.

Rachel pulled him inside and shut the door. Troy grabbed her by the waist and shoved his tongue in her mouth. He guided her to the bedroom and threw her on top of the king size bed. Rachel smiled and licked her lips. He climbed on top of her and kissed her with aggressiveness. He stopped for a brief moment to remove his clothes. Rachel watched attentively while he unbuttoned his collared shirt, exposing his toned arms and six-pack. Troy definitely gave meaning to the word, fine. She licked her lips when her eyes stopped at his erect penis that stood at attention like a soldier. She became even more excited from the heat that made her clitoris pulsate. She stuck two fingers inside her wet pussy, and began to slide them in and out with a slow rhythmic motion.

"You like watching me play with myself?" she asked.

Troy replied while standing completely naked. "You know I do."

She removed her fingers and slid them slowly in her mouth. She licked her juices from her fingers as if she was licking melting ice cream. With the same two fingers, she gestured for Troy to come get what he was anticipating.

Rachel wrapped her perfectly manicured hand around his penis. He wasn't working with an average size. Troy had a nine inch pretty dick, and nothing pleased Rachel more than taking his manhood into her mouth. He loved how she wrapped her mouth around the head of his penis and sucked it as if she was sucking from a straw. Rachel pleasured his penis which sent him into a frenzy. The more he moaned the faster and harder she would move her mouth up and down his shaft. Troy reached down and grabbed a fistful of her hair, pushing deeper into her warm, moist mouth. He was relishing the feeling of her constricting her throat muscles around him. Before he would climax, he decided he wanted to feel the inside of her sugary walls. He lifted her up and laid her across the bed, taking her 34 C breasts into his mouth. He nursed her breasts like a new born baby being fed.

"I want to feel you inside me," Rachel said.

"I definitely want to feel this good pussy," Troy said.

Without any further hesitation, Troy thrust himself inside her. His girth stretched her like a rubber band. His forcefulness caused her to dig her nails into his back. But this didn't matter to him; this just made him move inside her even harder.

"You like it rough?" Troy asked.

"Oh, yes," Rachel cried out and gripped onto him even tighter, her pussy clamping around him like a vice grip.

"You love the way I give it you? You love my dick, don't you?" Troy boasted.

"Yes, I love every bit of it. This is the best dick I ever had," she moaned.

So full of himself, Troy pumped in and out of her, pushing deeper with each thrust. After sexing one another crazy, they both fell into a deep sleep.

Troy slowly opened his eyes and he could tell through the slightly opened blinds, the sun had set. He looked over at the clock which read 7:00 pm. He had no intention of staying late, but funny how time flies when you're having fun. He jumped out of bed so he could take a quick shower and head back to the club.

Before he got in the bathroom good, Rachel came through the bedroom door.

"You were sleeping so peacefully and I didn't want to wake you."

"I wish you had because I'm late getting get back to the club."

"I thought you could stay and hang out with me and Moses for a little while. My grandmother dropped him off an hour ago."

"I can't. I got some business I have to take care of."

"Can it wait?"

"No. Enjoy your night off because I need you at the club tomorrow."

Rachel patiently waited for Troy to get out of the shower, twirling a strand of her hair with her finger, and flipping through an Ebony magazine.

Troy exited the bathroom with a thick brown towel wrapped around his body.

"Troy what are we doing?"

He looked over at Rachel confused by her question. "What do you mean what are we doing? What kind of question is that?"

"I mean us. What is going on with us?"

Troy tried to choose his words carefully as he spoke. He

didn't want to hurt her feelings, but he couldn't believe she was so stupid she did not know the answer to her own question. "We are having fun." Troy said looking away.

"What the hell you mean we having fun? That doesn't make sense."

He threw the towel on the bed and started getting dressed. "What do you want me to say, Rachel? I'm trying to be nice. You can't expect me to believe you don't know what is going on between us."

"Look, I know you will never picture me as your girlfriend, but considering the circumstances, I figured you would treat me a little differently."

Troy smirked. *This chick is really delusional*, he thought. "I think you not in touch with reality. So I'm going to break it down for you. We are just fucking. Nothing more will come out of this. We will never be a big happy family."

Troy could tell his response did not sit well with her. The frown that formed on her face yelled that fact.

"You bastard! Get out of my damn house!" Rachel rose from the bed. It seemed like a cloud of anger rose with her.

Troy couldn't believe how Rachel was reacting. He didn't even care. He never wanted to confuse his fucking her with love making. With her, he could never make love. He desired no connection with her. He did not want the sex to complicate their situation, stirring up a bond that he did not want to create.

Troy turned the knob to the bedroom door, turned to face Rachel and said, "It is what it is. Just make sure you have your ass at the club tomorrow."

***

It was no surprise to Rachel that Troy treated her like a two dollar whore. Rachel took the tissue and wiped her tear drenched eyes. Besides her thick thighs, thick waste, and voluptuous ass, she had nothing else to offer. It was her dick sucking skills that impressed all the guys. Her reputation from high school preceded her. Rachel was not a bad looking girl, but behind her mask, she was broken. She would have been a fool to think there could have been more between her and Troy; what they had was an arrangement.

They shared a special bond and that was the farthest it would ever go. Rachel knew she was just his booty call, but she was addicted to that snake that filled her pussy with its venom. His nine inches was powerful, and she loved to deep throat it every chance she got.

Rachel grabbed her phone from the nightstand and dialed the only person she knew she could talk too, her best friend since high school, Charlene.

"Hello," Charlene said sleepily.

"Hey. You sound sleep. I didn't mean to wake you." Rachel replied.

"It's ok girl. I was just lying on the sofa taking a nap. Those damn hardheaded kids of mine drove me crazy. I had to beat Junior's ass and ground him for a month. That boy got suspended from school for five days for calling his English teacher an asshole. I had to get some rest, plus I worked a double last night."

Rachel's laugh barely escaped her lips. "I hope Moses don't get out of control as he gets older. I can see me now jacking his little behind up against a wall."

"Well, if you don't nip it in the bud early that is exactly what's gon' happen." Charlene said in between yawns. "So what's going on with you, girl?"

Rachel sighed. "Girl, I'm so frustrated with Troy's asinine behavior; I don't know what to do. He doesn't care that I am a struggling single mother. As long as I continue to suck his thang, he's content with our situation. I asked him today what we were doing and his response was 'we just fucking'. Then he had the nerve to tell me we would never be one big happy family."

"Baby girl, I am going to have to stop you right there. You know I'm your best friend and I love you dearly, but why do you expect Troy to act any differently? He's an arrogant S.O.B., and as long as you keep opening up your legs inviting him in, he's going to keep treating you like a whore. Rachel you been selling yourself short since I've known you. I know a lot of your behavior has to do with Sabrina and Greg. You should have reported them to the authorities. I still don't know why I let you talk me into not telling my mother. Don't you realize you have a lot more to offer a man than just what's between your legs?"

70

Hearing her mother's name sent her mind twirling around memories she wish she could forget.

Sabrina walked into Rachel's room catching Greg zipping up his jeans. A month prior to that, Greg forced himself onto Rachel and raped her when her mother wasn't home. He told her he would kill her if she ever told anyone. Every chance he got, he would force himself inside her room and make her have sex with him. He was the first grown man she ever gave a blow job to. Rachel broke down crying hysterically and tried to explain to her mother that Greg raped her and was forcing her to have sex with him. Of course Greg denied it calling Rachel a liar, saying she was the one that wanted to have sex with him. Sabrina cursed Greg and ordered him out of Rachel's room, but Rachel never expected her mother to turn on her. Not her own flesh and blood.

Rachel sat on her bed with her arms wrapped around her legs that were drawn to her chest. She was crying uncontrollably. Her mother stood over her taking a long drag from her Salem cigarette. She exhaled the smoke and blew it in Rachel's face. "What the fuck you crying fo' you little bitch?" With her free hand, she smacked Rachel hard across her face making her whimper in pain. She pointed a finger, slightly dirty with chipped nail polish in her face and said, "You think you grown because you done fucked my man. That doesn't make you a woman. That makes you a common whore. When I told you to use what you got to get what you want, that didn't give you permission to go after what is mine. You want to be like me don't ya. You will never be me. You will never be classy like yo momma. Look at me girl! Your momma is a bad bitch!"

Sabrina turned around and struck a pose as if she was on Rip the Runway. Her black dress hung loosely on her one hundred ten pound frail body. Her stockings, which had a tear from the toes up to her thigh, sagged. Her hair was disheveled. Her eyeliner smeared into dark bruise-like circles under her eyes, and her burgundy lipstick was on her crooked teeth more than her lips. Rachel stared at her mother, comatosed by fear. Her mother was right; at one time she was a bad bitch. She was fly and she was beautiful, but the ten years she spent working at Daddy

Rabbits had taken a toll on her physically, mentally, and emotionally. Sabrina was a wretched mess, and she treated Rachel like trash. She figured her mother was taking her resentment and frustration out on her because she got pregnant at 18 by a customer she met while working at the strip club. When her mom told her dad she was pregnant, he laughed in her face and told her it was no way he would get a stripper pregnant. He told her to get lost. He was happily married with three kids. The only thing she knew about her sperm donor is his name— Jerome. That's if he's even her father. Sabrina leaned in closer to Rachel's face, her breath smelling like cigarettes and dick.

"Don't you ever disrespect me again as long as you living in my damn house, because if you do I will snap your fat ass neck in two." She spit in Rachel's face followed by another sharp blow to the right side of her cheek.

Rachel finally got tired of her mother's abuse and Greg molesting her; so she packed her things one night and went to live with her grandmother. Every time her grandmother asked her what went on that house, she would just say she and her mother just couldn't get along. To this very day, her mother is still with that low down dirty bastard. Rachel pushed her terrifying memory back into the strongbox stored in her brain.

"I'm just keeping it real. I'm worried about you and Moses. Just promise me you will be careful and take good care of you both."

"I'm going to be alright and don't worry about me and Moses because we're going to survive this." Rachel assured.

"You say one thing but your actions are showing me you are spiraling out of control. Slow down baby girl and stop letting Troy use you. You have a son now and you need to stop thinking about yourself and think about his well-being. I love you so much and I don't want you to get hurt."

"I need you to do me a favor?"

"What's that? Charlene asked.

"I want you to hold on to my diary in case anything happens to me."

"Girl, what is going to happen to you?"

"I don't know. Just in case. I'm thinking about leaving town."

"Excuse me."

"You heard me. Richmond is not for me anymore. I'm tired of the people here, I'm sick of the club and those filthy men touching all over me. I detest my mother and she still lives here. I'm sick of how Troy is treating me…basically, I hate my life. I just want a fresh start in another city with me and my son."

"Are you sure about this? I mean this is all of a sudden."

"No it's not. I've been planning this for two years now. I've been saving and I'm almost where I need to be so I can pack up and leave this wretched place."

"I don't know about this. You're scaring me. Have you gone and gotten yourself in some trouble?"

"I can't tell you about it now."

"What the hell you mean you can't tell me now!" Charlene scoffed.

"Moses is crying so I have to go. I promise I will tell you everything later."

"Girl don't you hang up this—."

Before Charlene could finish her sentence, Rachel disconnected the call. Moses wasn't crying. She just needed a quick excuse to get her off the phone. As much as she wanted to tell her what was going on with her, she couldn't. She didn't need a lecture, and she didn't want her to talk her out of leaving.

The phone started ringing and Rachel looked down at the caller ID. It was Charlene. She ignored her call.

Rachel walked over to her closet, pushed a pile of jeans to the side revealing a safe. She opened it and removed something from the top shelf. Hiding inside the metal box was her chance to freedom. Freedom from Troy. Freedom from her mother. Freedom from Greg. Freedom from the reverberating memories that haunt her in her sleep. A sudden stream of tears rolled down Rachel's face. It wasn't because she was sad, but irrevocably happy that she was going to finally leave her past behind.

# Unthinkable

## 11

"Good morning, Jennifer," Rayne said to her secretary stopping at her desk.

"Good morning, Ms. Armstrong."

"I need you to run me 20 copies of the agenda for the ten o'clock sales meeting, pull the Turner and Williamson files, and call Russell to schedule a home inspection for the Williamson's no later than this Friday."

"Sure thing Ms. Armstrong. I'll get right on it."

"Thank you."

Rayne walked into her office, flicked on the light, sat her Frappuccino down on the desk, placed her Dooney and Bourke purse in the chair next to her desk, turned on her computer, opened up her blinds to let in the sunlight, sat down at her desk, and mulled over the course of events that transpired over the past two weeks.

Her red light was blinking on her phone, indicating she had voice messages. She pressed the button. "You have 16 messages," her phone announced. After the tenth message, his sexy deep voice chimed in her ear, dispelling her depressing mood. It had been two weeks and he called like he promised. Rayne jotted down the number he left, contemplating whether or not she should call him. She remembered how being in his presence had aroused her sexual senses. Knowing that he was married made her want him even more. She figured he wasn't going to be about any games. Rayne believed he was a safe choice, and she couldn't get hurt because he was committed to his wife. Her hypocritical thinking was scary. Her thoughts betrayed her. *I'm no better than Rashard. Infidelity is what destroyed my marriage. Think about how Bryce's wife would feel if I interfered in her marriage?*

Rayne took a sip of her Starbucks Caramel Frappuccino. She enjoyed it after standing in a long line that was practically out the front door. She stood in that line, amused by people's addiction to caffeine, while picturing in her mind a cultural nightmare if coffee was no longer sold. There would be a caffeine withdrawal epidemic, and the streets would be filled with a bunch of caffeine-addicted zombies. Her thoughts shifted back to Bryce. Fascinated at how his smile sent fireworks through her coochie like the fourth of July. Her indecent thoughts about Bryce were so surreal. She had an hour to spare before her sales meeting started. What the hell? Rayne picked up the phone and hesitantly dialed his number. Her heart was racing and her face was flushed from her nervousness. After three rings, Bryce picked up.

"Hello, this is Bryce." His deep voice was sexy and gave her chills.

"Hello, this is Rayne." A smile parted her lips.

"Well, if it isn't the lovely Ms. Rayne. I'm so glad you called."

"Did I catch you at a bad time? You did say you had some business you wanted to discuss. So why don't you tell me all about your project?"

"This isn't a bad time. In fact, I was hoping we can get together tonight to discuss business," Bryce suggested.

Resistance shows self-control. Rayne had to play it cool and not sound desperate. "Is there a reason we can't talk now?" Rayne asked candidly.

He began to stammer. "I...I...umm... apologize for my assertive behavior. Where are my manners?"

"You don't need to apologize," she smiled warmly. "I guess it won't hurt if we discuss business over dinner. Do you have somewhere in mind?"

"I was hoping we can go to the Martini Kitchen."

"You can't be talking about that club on West Main Street. This doesn't sound like a business dinner." Rayne said bemused.

"I figured since I'll be in Virginia for a few days; why not spend it with a beautiful, radiant woman while I get some work done."

"Maybe I'm wrong, but are you coming on to me?" Rayne laughed nervously.

"Am I making you uncomfortable?"

"No. I'm actually flattered, but I think we should keep this strictly business."

*Ok so I'm lying, but he doesn't need to know that,* Rayne thought. "How did you hear about the Martini Kitchen?"

"Kenneth told me. He said he takes his wife there all the time and she loves it. It's been a while since I been in Virginia, so I don't know all of the hot spots. I do see a lot has changed. I was hoping maybe you can bring me up to speed on what's been going on in the state that bears the slogan, 'Virginia is for Lovers'."

"Well, me bringing you up to speed about Virginia could take all night."

"I have all the time you need."

Rayne was speechless. His confidence was sexy. Shocked by her own sexual impulse, she unbuttoned the first two buttons of her blouse, slid her hand down her bra, squeezed her firm breasts and caressed her nipples that were hard as pebbles. Bryce had her senses on fire.

Rayne was startled by the knock at her office door and quickly withdrew her hand from her breast.

Terrence opened the door and poked his head inside. "Am I interrupting?" he whispered.

Rayne pointed to the phone and mumbled, "I'm on the phone."

Terrence got the hint and nodded. He shut the door behind him.

"Sorry for the interruption. Now where were we? Oh, I think you will love the club. I've been there several times. It is a very nice club with, great food, great ambiance, live band, and to die for cocktails."

"So what do you say...are we on for tonight?"

"Bryce..." Rayne hesitated. Her body now calm. "Why don't I call you before I leave the office and let you know my decision?"

"If you insist. If you think it's not a good idea, I'll understand. I will talk to you soon Ms. Armstrong?" He hung up the phone.

Rayne stared at the phone in silence, the beeping sound continued in her ear before she decided to hang the phone up. Rayne didn't want her impulsive response to be one she would regret, but the mere thought of being with him was so daring. Knowing he was married did not make a bit of difference, because she was not looking for a commitment. For a few moments, she just wanted to have fun.

\* \* \*

Rayne remembered her mother telling her the best way to heal is to move on. Hard as it has been to take her advice, it wasn't until Bryce came along that she had a reason to test the waters.

*Now I know that damn shirt is in this closet somewhere?* Rayne was getting impatient and upset because for the life of her she could not find her Baby Phat halter top she just bought last week. She had a huge walk in closet with nothing but the finest clothing. She loved her clothes and her clothes loved her. From BabyPhat, Michael Kors, Versace, Prada, Chanel, Armani, Calvin Klein, Gucci, Roca Wear, you name it, Rayne wore it. Her intelligence, style of dress and classiness signified the successful business woman she had become. She always carried herself in a professional lady like demeanor. She never strived to match her peers in spending or social standing. Keeping up with the Joneses was never her style.

After what seemed like an eternity of searching, she finally stumbled over the halter top. It was a quarter to seven when Rayne peeped at the clock. She was pushing for time. She thought if only she was a genie in a bottle; she'd wish time would stop for a brief moment so that she could transform into Cinderella rushing off to see her Prince. But in her story there was no evil stepmother or wicked sisters, and she damn sure was not rushing to get back home by midnight. Rayne headed to the bathroom to take a quick shower.

Just when she thought she was making good timing

getting dressed, the phone started ringing. Damn!

"Hello!" Rayne said sounding real impatient.

"Hey, chica. What are you doing?" Zoey said, dismissing the edginess in Rayne's voice.

"I am trying to get ready so I can leave."

"I see I caught you at a bad time."

"Yes you did." Rayne flatly stated.

"May I ask where you're going?"

"I'm going out on a date."

"Date?" Zoey asked, with an unusual amount of curiosity.

"That's what I said."

"Could the lucky man be Troy?"

"No."

"What!" Zoey shouted.

"Don't act surprised. You know how I feel about the Troy situation."

"You know he would be devastated to learn you going out with someone else as much as you turn down his offers."

"He's not going to find out, because you're not going to tell. So don't go running your big mouth."

"Who is he? Do I know him?"

"No you don't know him and stop with all the questions. I have to go. I'll talk to you later."

Zoey hastily asked, "I thought we were friends and share everything?"

"We are friends, but I have to go. I got a date and can't be late." Rayne giggled.

"Whoever he is, he must be worth your time. He manages to take your mind away from Rashard and that whole baby fiasco. Damn, I'm impressed!"

"I'm not going to say all that, but let's just say he's fine, sexy, and intriguing."

"Sounds like my kind of guy." Zoey confirmed.

"Got to go." Rayne quickly stated and hung up the phone before Zoey could get another chance to talk. She knew if she hadn't, she would have kept on rambling. Zoey has always been the chatter box.

It was eight o'clock on the dot when Rayne pulled into the parking lot of the Martini Kitchen. Bryce was standing outside of the club waiting for her.

"Hello, Ms. Armstrong. You look beautiful," he said, kissing the back of her hand.

Rayne smiled, "Thank you, sir. You don't look bad yourself."

As soon as they walked into the club the live band was singing Mary J. Blige's song, "No More Drama." That's exactly what Rayne didn't want, any more pain in her life. She had called earlier that day and made reservations. Bryce followed her to a cozy plush black leather sofa towards the back of the club. As soon as Bryce sat down close to Rayne she became nervous. The waitress timing was perfect. Rayne ordered an apple martini and Bryce ordered a Corona with lime. Crab balls, wings, and loaded fries with cheese and bacon crumbs followed the drinks. With the sounds of the band mixing with his intoxicating cologne, Rayne felt like she was on a natural high. She was in a zone, too spaced out to hear Bryce ask her if she wanted to dance.

"Rayne did you hear me, I asked if you wanted to dance." Bryce was close to her ear, close to her body. She wondered if he could feel the sexual excitement her body was releasing.

Rayne was startled by his closeness and started blushing. "I'm sorry, my mind got away from me." She looked down at the floor nervously.

Bryce grabbed her hand. "I know what you need. Come with me."

Bryce led her to the dance floor. They danced to a fast song, and Rayne was impressed at how quick and smooth Bryce was on his feet.

Rayne leaned close to his ear and shouted over the music, "You got skills. I love the way you move."

"Thanks. You not a bad dancer yourself," Bryce chuckled.

"I can dance better than you." Rayne said bragging, turning her back towards him, winding and rotating her hips, pressing her soft flesh up against his hard body.

Everything around them started to fade away, just the music pounding in their ears, lust cast upon them like darkness, in their own world they created fantasy. The touching of their skin, their body heat creating an aching desire, the aroma of Rayne's perfume filled Bryce's senses, he drank her in, as if he was stranded on a desert island, his thirst unquenchable.

A sinful grin crossed Rayne's face as she felt Bryce's hardness against her stomach, her fingers trailing along his neck. Like a stampede of troops he intruded her space, pulling her closer, gliding his hand up and down her back. Finally, they were mere inches apart from each other, their molten heat at bay; he led her back to the sofa.

"We danced up a storm. I'm tired as hell." Bryce said panting, trying to catch his breath.

Rayne playfully nudged him in the arm and replied, "Oh oh, let me find out you can't hang."

"Oh, I can hang. Let's see who can't hang when we go for another round."

"Not after I eat and drink," Rayne said, picking up her Apple Martini, bringing it to her parched mouth.

"That really hit the spot," said Rayne.

Bryce sipped his Corona and sat it down on the glass table in front of them. "You come here a lot."

"Occasionally, I actually was here four months ago. My brother, best friend Zoey, and I brought my mother here to celebrate her birthday."

"That was really nice. She's a Sagittarius."

"That's right. So your birthday is in December as well?"

"No. November."

"What day?"

"The 24th."

"The day before Thanksgiving."

"Yep. I have a lot to celebrate and be thankful for. When is your birthday?"

"July 17th."

"That will make you a Cancer."

Rayne smiled.

For the next thirty minutes they continued to enjoy each other's conversation. They talked about sports, politics, and education. He made jokes. Rayne laughed, her hand grazed across his leg. She was flirting. She wanted him to know she was into him. Wanted him to know he had her attention. He didn't hide the fact he was flirting as well, sitting real close touching her arm, legs, and thighs. The sexual energy between them was evident. The pulsating between her thighs was turning into a drumbeat. The desire to make love to a married man was being clouded by the effects of the three martinis. She was relishing his company, and smiling seductively in his face. There was an air of mystery about him that had her aching for more. She figured if she played her cards right, she could soon find out.

The club's party was coming to an end because the MC announced last call for alcohol. The hours they spent dancing and talking the night away had quickly come and gone. Rayne was not looking forward to saying good-bye and parting ways. Bryce walked Rayne to her car. The moment she dreaded where they would end a wonderful date but hopefully leave with the intentions of wanting to see each other again. There was a brief silence before Bryce spoke.

"I really had a great time tonight. I've felt like I've known you for years. You are so easy to talk to, outgoing, funny, beautiful and one helluva sexy lady."

His compliments began to make her blush the same way she blushed back in the day when Rashard use to give her flattering compliments. She admitted to herself that she wanted to sex him right there in the parking lot. She didn't give a damn who would be watching. Her rosy cheeks indicated she was taken by his charm.

"Thank you."

Bryce put his strong masculine arms around her waist. "I hope I get to see you again before I head back home to Atlanta."

"I think that can be arranged. How about at my place and I'll make you dinner? I'll call you tomorrow with my address."

Bryce sealed the night with a kiss that Rayne hoped would never end. His kiss was passionate and mind blowing. When they were done exploring each other's mouth with their tongues, he gently put his finger under her chin and placed a soft tender kiss on her forehead. That was the moment she knew she had to have him. This was just the beginning of the point of no return...

# Leopard doesn't change its spots

## 12

Like Goldilocks testing out chairs and porridge, the weather went from one extreme to the next— too cold, too damn hot, rain and thunderstorms, until finally it was just right. It was a bright, warm Saturday afternoon. Rashard decided to meet Rachel at Short Pump Towne Center so he could spend time with his son, Moses. He figured meeting at the mall would be safer than Rachel bringing him over to his house or him going to her place. After all, he didn't trust her as far as he could throw her. He left Foot Locker after purchasing a pair of Jordan sneakers for Moses, and headed towards Build-A-Bear to meet Rachel. Rashard became enraged watching all the mothers enjoy time with their kids laughing, holding hands, and shopping. Rachel stole his chances of having children with Rayne. It was hard for him to accept Moses, as his son. It was his mom who convinced him that despite the circumstances, Moses was innocent and should not be penalized for his mistake. Rashard had a feeling he was not the father no matter what the DNA results said. How could he forget a night that turned his life into a living hell? Still, whatever led up to him sleeping with Rachel was vague.

Rashard and Rayne were having an intense argument that led him to storm out of their home. Their marriage became emotionally strained ever since Rashard learned his mother was diagnosed with stage four lung cancer. They'd been arguing off and on for a week, and the tension was becoming unbearable. He wanted to clear his head so he

82

headed over to the Back Door. Out of all places he could have gone, he ended up at Troy's strip club where Rachel danced. If Rayne knew that's where he was headed that night, he would have been a dead man. Being near Rachel was like signing his own death certificate. Rayne despised her with a passion. She could not disguise it. Those two were rivalries ever since high school. The feud continued through college; but eventually tapered off when Rachel dropped out of Norfolk State. Since that night at the Back Door, Rashard thought he would never see or hear from her again. That is until she sent a messenger to his home with a package that contained incriminating pictures of him in bed with her. The lewd photos of him and Rachel in the throes of passion were images he wanted out of his mind.

Walking inside the Back Door was like walking into Pandora's Box. In their provocative outfits, female dancers showed off nearly every inch of their body as they danced around the stage performing tricks and sliding down the brass pole in their acrobat moves while men and women held out their tips from the edges of the stage. Rashard sat down at an empty table, watching a man at the next table take pleasure in a dancer jiggling her large breasts in his face. He waved for the waitress and ordered a shot of Patrón. Rashard unenthusiastically watched the dancers work the stage, circulate the crowd of horny customers, encouraging them to buy drinks, or offering a private lap dance.

Rashard saw Troy emerge from the back of the club. They locked stares. Rashard felt a hand touch his shoulder and looked up to see Rachel standing behind him. "You look like you need some company." Rachel offered.

"I don't need any company, and I damn sure don't need yours." Rashard hissed.

Rashard raised his shot glass to his lips, but slammed it down in agitation when Rachel decided to join him anyway. As she pulled the chair out from under the table, he couldn't help but notice how good she looked in her thong that accentuated her curvaceous big ass and thick thighs. She looked a whole lot better than she did back in college since she lost quite a bit of weight. Memories of them being together began to flood his mind. They had a tryst during their senior year of high school. When Rashard and Rayne broke up, Rachel saw a window of opportunity that would only come around once in a lifetime. Rachel was a snake and that was one of the many reasons why Rayne had so much disdain for her. He pleaded for Rachel to never tell Rayne, but there was no way she was going to give up the chance to rub Rayne's nose in the fact she slept with her man. Rashard and Rayne finally got back together after five long months.

Rachel could see something was wrong so she positioned herself again to prey on Rashard's weakness. Truth of the matter is, the way Rachel looked and flirted with Rashard made below his waist stir, but he managed to keep his cool. Back in the day, her underhanded games would have worked. How could he forget the countless blow jobs Rachel gave him in the school auditorium, which almost cost him his relationship with Rayne. It was her skilled mouth that almost cost him his quarterback position, her attention to detail had caused him to be late to football practice several times.

It was a rough senior year for Rashard, and he couldn't believe he allowed himself to get involved with Rachel. But once he got to experience her bomb ass head game, Rashard couldn't get enough. Every time he protested her advances, she would reel him in offering to suck his dick. Her lips were like a powerful suction cup, she would suck all his juices from his body leaving him lifeless. What can he say, he was weak. The flesh is weak. You would be too if you understood she was a pro and sucked dick better than a grown woman.

"Come on Rashard, stop being a wuss," she teased. "I'll make it worth your while."

"I have practice and I can't be late. I was late twice last week and Coach Jackson been riding me hard." His mind was telling him no, but the bulging knot in his jeans was telling him yes.

"I promise you won't be late. I'll be really quick. I have a new trick I want to show you."

"Trick," Rashard said curiously.

"Sure, and you won't find out if you don't let me show you."

"Is there some kind of school you attend that teaches you this stuff because you know way too much?" Rashard asked amusingly.

Rachel started laughing, "Stop kidding around Rashard, the longer you keep fighting me the later you will be to practice."

He couldn't refuse. She was a very freaky girl. All he could think about was her warm mouth around his penis. Rachel grabbed him by his hand and led him to the auditorium. They slipped behind the curtain; she pushed Rashard up against the wall, tugged at his jeans until his lil man sprang to full attention. She let her fingers graze his length, causing him to mutter not much of a response.

Rachel was teasing him and he was getting impatient. "Get this over with already." Rashard jeered.

She looked up at him and grinned. "Patience is a virtue." At last she descended on his penis, spit on its head, swirled her mouth around it, moving her mouth up and down, taking more of him in her mouth with each pass.

Rashard closed his eyes and placed his hand on the back of her head, indicating for her to go deeper. His penis engulfed her warm mouth, moving it all the way down her throat until her nose brushed up against his pelvis.

"Damn, girl you magnificent," he whispered, reveling at how her throat muscles worked around his penis. If heaven existed, Rashard found it in John Marshall High School.

Rachel waved her hand in Rashard's face. "You seem to be distracted by something."

At that moment, Rashard realized he was no longer in high school. Although he was hurting, no one including Rachel was going to come between him and Rayne. He was madly in love and committed to his wife. Every chance Rachel got she would seductively move her hand up and down his arm and nibble on his ear. He could still see Troy looking on from a distance. He wondered what was spinning through this mind. Knowing Troy, he would love to run straight to Rayne and feed her with his lies, but Rashard refused to give him the satisfaction. The more aggressive Rachel got he would push her away; hoping she would get the hint— what she wanted was not going down on his watch. Troy decided to join them at his table.

"Don't you think you had a little too much to drink, cuz?" Troy questioned.

Rashard frowned before responding. "What's it to you? Mind your damn business."

"I make it my business when I see you downing shots like a mad man. Indulge my curiosity...you and Rayne having problems at home? Is that what brought you up in here?" A smirk marked Troy's face as he waited for a reply.

"Go to hell!"

"Looks like you already there my brother."

"I'm not your brother."

"Thank God for small favors."

The angry look Rashard gave Troy told him he should back off. They've been down this road many times before. Rashard knew how Troy felt about Rayne and any indication that they were having problems at home would have him running to her side playing on her vulnerability. He started to question himself, why in the hell was he there in the first place?

"Rayne and I are just fine. Don't you have some work to do?"

Troy looked over at Rachel. "You got this fine ass women in your presence. Why don't you let her service you? I'm sure a lap dance will make whatever troubles you're having disappear."

Rashard laughed hysterically at Troy's statement. He waved for the waitress to come to his table.

"You funny. Why the hell would I let her of all people give me a lap dance?" Rashard words were slurred as he pointed to Rachel.

Troy was about to speak when Rachel put her hand up giving him the sign that she wanted to answer the question. She leaned towards Rashard and gently placed her hand on the knot that bulged through his jeans before slightly giving it a squeeze then whispered in his ear. "Because any nigga in here will tell you I could flex in 30 different positions that will have you speaking in many different languages. You would think I was Rosetta Stone."

Troy let out a slight chuckle.

The waitress came over to the table to take Rashard's drink order.

"Hold up Dee Dee, no need to take this order, this round is on me." Troy said smiling as he got up from the table.

When Troy returned to the table, in his hand were three shots of Grey Goose. He handed one to Rashard and Rachel. He nodded at them both then said, "Bottoms up."

They all downed their shots and the last thing Rashard remembered was waking up in Troy's guest room. He couldn't believe he allowed himself to get caught up into temptation. He was not consciously aware of his actions and that one night of indiscretion had cost him a lifetime of pain. And if he known any better, he would bet any amount of money Troy had something to do with it.

Rashard's thoughts escaped him when he entered Build-A-Bear, scanning the store in search of Rachel's presence. Rachel was standing in the back of the store holding Moses in her arms talking with a sales associate. She saw him heading in her direction and her face lit up like a Christmas tree. The only thoughts that ran through his mind were how could he kill the bitch and get away with it?

"Hello, Rashard," Rachel said grinning from ear to ear.

Rashard glared at her with contempt in his eyes. He wanted to put his hands around her throat and strangle her mercilessly—but. There was always that but. He didn't want Moses to witness him murdering his mother in front of a store full of witnesses. He tried to suppress his smile at the thought of actually killing her. It was tempting. But, the last thing he wanted that day was to go to jail for murder. Dealing with her was just going to have to wait.

# Fistful of Tears

## 13

Rayne and Zoey had made plans to meet at California Pizza Kitchen for lunch at the Short Pump Towne Center. Zoey was sitting in the restaurant sipping on an ice tea and looking over the menu when Rayne walked in.

"Hey, chica," Rayne said, as she approached the table.

Zoey stood up and held out her arms to give Rayne a hug.

"Girl, I can't wait to sink my teeth into this Jamaican Jerk Chicken pizza," Rayne said, taking her seat across from Zoey.

The friendly brunette hostess came over to the table, looking at Rayne, she asked, "What can I get you to drink ma'am?"

"I'll have a pink lemonade. Thanks."

"I'll be right back with your drink," the hostess said before walking away.

"How have you been?" Zoey asked. The last time she had seen Rayne, she was a wretched mess. She couldn't help but to think that most of the pain she was enduring; she had played a part in.

"I'm doing fine. How about yourself?" Rayne asked. forcing a smile. In all actuality she was feeling miserable. As much as she wanted to hate Rashard, perhaps kill him for his betrayal, she still loved him pass the moon.

"I've been doing fine." But the pensive look on Zoey's face told Rayne otherwise.

"Come on girl. It's me you talking to. I can tell something is wrong." I can look into your eyes.

Zoey let out a long exaggerated sigh. "Ok. I didn't want to bother you since you had a lot of your own problems to deal with, but I have been under a lot of stress lately. I been trying to help my mother stay sober and off the damn bottle."

"Oh my God. I thought she was getting better and going to her AA meetings?" Rayne asked, reaching for Zoey's hand across the table and squeezing it real tight.

Rayne felt bad for her friend. She saw the pain in her eyes. "Why didn't you tell me this sooner? Maybe there was something me or mom could have done to help."

"You were dealing with your own problems and I didn't want to burden you with mine."

"That doesn't matter. We always come to each other with our problems. I would have made time for my best friend. You know it's nothing that I wouldn't do for you." Rayne smiled, hoping she realize she was being genuine and that would make her relax a bit.

Rayne happened to look up and saw Tyreke heading in their direction. "What's my brother doing here?"

"Oh, I invited him. We both decided you needed to get out for a much needed therapy session."

"A therapy session," Rayne said puzzled, raising an eyebrow.

"Yes. What is the best cure for relieving stress?" Zoey quizzed.

"Eat and shop till you drop," they both said in unison and fell out laughing.

"Hey, hey bitches! What's going on? What's so damn funny?"

"Why are you prancing in here so loud and ghettofied?" Rayne asked, standing up to embrace her brother with a hug.

"Because I can bitch." Tyreke threw his Louis Vuitton purse on the back of the chair before sitting down. Tyreke looked at Zoey. "How you doing wench?"

"You know what Tyreke; I can't stand your ass. I can't be nice to you because you always have something smart to say." Zoey scoffed and rolled her eyes.

Tyreke waved her off, "Love you too boo! But enough of that, I have some good news!" Tyreke said with sheer excitement in his voice. "I have been highly recommended to be a hairstylist for an upcoming fashion show in Atlanta. My boy Kamel hooked me up. He called me today and asked me to come out to Atlanta in two weeks. It's preliminary, but I'll be going down there to show off my skills. If they like what they see, then I'm hired. Trust and believe, them mofo's will like what I'm going to do to those bitches nappy ass heads. Ya'll know I'm fierce when it comes to hairstyling." Tyreke snapped his fingers with attitude.

Rayne and Zoey started laughing.

"You are a mess. I'm so happy for you. Congratulations, I know you are going to go down there and do the damn thing." Rayne said excitedly. Awkwardly Bryce's face intruded her mind at the mention of Atlanta. Her body reacted strangely to her irrational thoughts. She felt ashamed, quickly dismissing her unorthodox thinking.

"Yeah, I'm happy for you too, jackass." Zoey said, leaning over and smacking him playfully upside his head. She started laughing then blew him a kiss. Although Zoey and Tyreke argued back and forth, she loved him like a brother. After her nine year old brother, Anthony died from a severe asthma attack; he was the closest thing to her brother.

Tyreke directed his attention to Rayne. "So what's been going on with you lately little sister? How have you been holding up?"

"I've been holding up just fine," Rayne insisted.

"Before I forget, I'm going to D.C. next weekend to see my Aunt Linda, so we will have to cancel our spa plans." Zoey announced.

Rayne took a sip of her lemonade. "Ok, no problem. Is everything ok with her? I remember you said she had to get bunion surgery."

"Girl, her surgery went fine."

Tyreke burst out laughing. "What's it with you women and ya'll damn hammer time toes? This chick came in the shop yesterday and had the nerve to be wearing open toe sandals with corns on her toes bigger than a quarter. I was like what the hell! She thought she was cute, but that shit was not cool." He frowned, his brow furrowed slightly.

90

Zoey rolled her eyes. "Shut the hell up, Tyreke!"

The line from Boomerang popped in Rayne's head and she fell out laughing. "Tyreke you are too much."

"Girl, I don't know why you entertain your stupid ass brother."

Having paid their bill, they sat for a few minutes talking, laughing and finishing up their drinks. They left the food court and headed into the open-aired mall. Turning the corner, Rayne stopped dead in her tracks. Her day immediately took a turn for the worse. Out of all the people to run into she had to run into her Rashard, the whore he cheated on her with, and his son. Seeing Rachel with Rashard made her heart sink deeper than the Titanic. Her immediate instinct was to strangle Rachel, but she didn't want to traumatize the child. Both Tyreke and Zoey saw the evil glare in Rayne's eyes, and pulled her arms in the other direction avoiding a public altercation.

Rashard called out, "Rayne wait, can we please talk?"

Rayne ignored him and continued to walk, tears running down her cheeks. Never in a million years would she think that Rashard's child would not be her own. It's funny how life changes even if it isn't how you planned it.

# If loving you is wrong

## 14

Less than twenty four hours ago, Rayne was in the company of a man that intrigued her beyond her sexual savvy. He was charming. Mysterious. Unattainable. She could hardly contain the excitement she was feeling. The thought of being in his presence had her senses on fire. She let her imagination run free as she envisioned a night of erotica with a man she didn't even know. A man she knew she should steer clear of. The anticipation of her submission to her passion caused her nipples to harden. Her desire to seize the moment was astounding. Rayne felt like she'd been bit by a lust bug. Her sexual conscious was yearning to be with Bryce, and knowing he was off limits aroused her even more.

After several exhausting hours of showing potential homes to her clients, Rayne decided to call it quits for the day. Some clients are just hard to please. After house hopping, listening to her client's repeated debate over which house served their needs best, the difficult couple of the day finally compromised and contracted an immaculate four-bedroom tri-level home. She decided to head over to Massage Envy and enjoy the needed relaxation.

The masseuse, Nicole, massaged her body and took it into a joyful state. The moment gave her the opportunity to explore what was churning inside her after seeing Rashard at the mall with Rachel and his son. The image of them looking like one big happy family pounded in her head. A mental picture she wanted to erase. Rayne knew they would never be a happy family. Rachel could never take her place. She wasn't woman enough to conquer Rashard's heart. She felt sorry for the child. He would suffer from having Rachel as a mom. As devastated as it was seeing them together, as ironic as it may seem, Rayne figured it was for the best that Rashard was no longer a part of her life. There was no way she could be a step-mother to her arch enemy's child. She couldn't stand the possibility of coming home to the man she adored everyday knowing that he had betrayed her. As much as she wanted to hate Rashard, deep down she couldn't because he still had a special place in her heart.

Rayne felt a slight sensational twitch between her thighs. It was Nicole's delicate, sensual, and gentle touch that made her tingle and yearn clandestinely for Bryce. She tried not to let a moan escape her lips. The mere thought of him had a bizarre effect on her and caused the thought of Rashard to dissipate from her brain. Thinking about a married man in a lustful way was sinful. Trying to avoid her impromptu urges was scary like running through a house full of burning flames. But...there was always that but. Rayne was tempted to embrace her newfound desires. She could put the brakes on this madness, but the feeling of sin intrigued her beyond her wildest dreams.

"Ok Ms. Armstrong, we are done here. Be careful climbing down from the table. Your equilibrium may be a little off. You can put on your clothes and wait outside the hallway for me. I'll be back with you shortly." Nicole exited the room. Rayne slowly lifted up from the table and cautiously climbed down until she felt her feet touch the ground. The sound of her cell phone stopped her from putting on her shirt. She took her cell from her purse and answered it.

"Hello."

"Good afternoon, lovely."

A faint smile appeared on her face.

"Good afternoon, Troy. How can I help you?"

"I only wanted to see how you were doing?"

"I'm doing good."

"Where are you?"

"Massage Envy."

"Umm. I could have joined you. Why didn't you tell me?"

"I didn't need the company."

"You still are resisting me."

"I have to finish getting dress. Let me call you back when I leave."

"Is that a promise?"

"Yes." Rayne hung up the phone, grabbed an envelope for the tip and headed out the room.

Rayne talked to Troy all the way home. For once they had a casual conversation and he was not being self-absorbed, expressing his endless negative attitude about Rashard. Rayne was getting tired of their constant years of bickering, afraid that somebody was bound to get hurt.

"I'm pulling up in front of my apartment. Thanks for talking to me all the way home."

"No problem. So what are you getting into tonight?"

"Nothing. I'm going to put a Healthy Choice meal in the microwave, take me a nice hot shower and watch a little TV until the sandman takes me as his prisoner."

Rayne had to make up a lie. It was no way in hell she was telling Troy she invited Bryce over for dinner. That's one ghost she would keep in the closet.

"Sounds like you have an exciting night planned. Maybe we can make plans for dinner and a movie. We can cuddle and watch your favorite movie, *Love Jones*."

"I'll think about and let you know. Goodnight, Troy."

"Goodnight." Troy did not like her response and pounded his fist on the table. It was hard getting her to let her guard down. He figured he would have to take another approach when it came to getting what he wanted.

\*\*\*

Rayne walked into her apartment feeling refreshed from her massage. She kicked off her Jimmy Choo pumps at the front door and headed towards the kitchen to prepare an exquisite meal of steak, sweet potatoes, salad, and steamed broccoli. She lit several sensual amber scented candles and placed them in the living room and bedroom areas. She set the dining table with her finest china. The lights were dimmed to set off an intimate effect.

Rayne was ready to take a nice hot bubble bath. She pulled her long locks back into a ponytail bun, and then stood in the mirror admiring her five feet-nine inch naked silhouette. The sight of her naked flesh aroused her sexual urge. Her libido was on fire. The erection of her nipples needed her mouths attention. Rayne cupped her breast and began to give them what they desired. She found her spot and began to gyrate to her own melodic rhythm. Rayne began to moan. She was in pure ecstasy. She moved two fingers rapidly over her clit. Her breathing escalated. She started to feel her body tremble, her legs gave in and she screamed out in pleasure. Losing her balance she fell back into the sink, grabbing it for balance. Her juices ran down her hand. Rayne opened her eyes. Still leaning up against the sink she was at ease. This was just the beginning of her satisfaction.

Rayne's sanctuary was her bathtub. She closed her eyes and enjoyed the aroma of dancing waters while the sweet smell penetrated her flesh. It had been a long time since she felt so serene. She stepped out of the shower and wiggled her feet on the plush carpet as she dried her body.

She had just slipped on her goddess spaghetti strap maxi dress that hit right at her ankles when she heard the doorbell ring. She hurried to the door and took a deep breath before she opened it. There Bryce stood looking handsome wearing a pair of blue jeans, white button down collared shirt, and a pair of Stacy Adams' tan bicycle toe slip-on dress shoes. His smile full of charm made her heart melt like butter. His Cool Water Cologne tickled her nostrils and made her body ache in places she wanted to be satisfied. He had a dozen of roses in his hand. Not only was he handsome, but a gentleman.

"Hello, Rayne."

She wanted to skip the formalities and head straight to the bedroom. Then again if she could have her way at that very moment, she would be all over him like bees making honey.

"Hello, Bryce. Come in."

Bryce stood in a trance admiring her before he spoke. "These are for you." He handed her the beautiful arrangement.

"Thank you." Rayne smelled the fragrance of the roses. "They are lovely. Make yourself comfortable on the sofa while I put them in some water." She pointed to the living room.

She came back to the living room and said, "Dinner is almost ready. Would you like a glass of champagne?"

"Sure."

"Would you care to do the honors opening up this bottle of Dom Pérignon?" She handed him the bottle and a corkscrew.

Rayne became sexually aroused from watching Bryce unscrew the cork from the bottle. Her eyes moved up and down his muscular arms, visualizing them wrapped around her waist tightly, while they were enthralled in a passionate kiss. She imagined the way he turned the screw inside the cork, he was moving his penis in a slow circular motion inside her sugary walls. Without him noticing, she licked her lips. The loud pop of the cork snapped her out of her lustful state of mind.

Soon after they were enjoying their meals, and engaged in candid conversation about their personal lives and business. Bryce told her he loved his wife and was married for four years and had two kids, a boy and a girl. He then went on to tell her he grew up in Boston, Massachusetts. That was a bonus point for him because that was also the home of her favorite group New Edition. When he was 13 his family moved to Atlanta, where his dad started his own construction company. He started working for his father's company at the age of 18. He always loved the construction business. His dad inspired him to start his own property development company, Underwood Construction. He told her he had just purchased some land to start construction of Sunny Pine Estates, a gated community of new homes in the Powhatan, Virginia area. He was looking for a realtor in the Virginia area to help sale the homes and was hoping Rayne would consider being that realtor. Rayne was flattered and told him she would consider his offer. She enjoyed knowing he was intelligent, business-minded, and articulate. He made her feel comfortable and she loved being in his company. She stared at his sexy lips. She wanted to kiss them, but that notion disappeared when

Bryce interrupted by saying, "Enough about me, tell me a little about yourself, Ms. Armstrong."

Rayne smiled, he had put her on the spot. She almost didn't know where to begin. She started from the beginning telling him a little bit about Rashard. She relived the night of their marriage falling apart when she learned of his affair. Felt a lump form in her throat, fought those emotions hard, and kept her tears from escaping her eyes. She saw his eyes light up as she spoke in volumes about her passion for real estate. It was the love of the business they both had in common. She then shifted gears and told him she had a brother, who was gay, he seemed very curious.

Bryce asked, "Do you and your brother have a good relationship despite him being gay?"

Rayne answered, "I love my brother no matter what his sexual preference is. We have a wonderful relationship and I wouldn't trade him in for anything."

Bryce smiled. "I can tell you are an amazing woman."

"Thank you," Rayne blushed." Oh my God, it's getting late. Why don't I clear the table and we can finish our conversation in the living room?" Rayne suggested.

"Why don't I help you?" Bryce offered standing up from his chair.

"I can manage. Why don't you take a load off and watch TV. The remote control is on the coffee table."

"Are you sure? I really don't mind helping you." His gracious smile and look in his eyes expressed his gratitude for dinner.

"I'm sure."

Rayne quickly loaded the dishwasher and cleaned the kitchen and dining room.

One of her pet peeves was leaving a sink full of dirty dishes overnight. Cleanliness was next to Godliness and she always kept her house clean. Once she was done, she joined Bryce on the living room sofa.

"I see you're watching *The Game*," Rayne said as she sat down next to Bryce who was deep into the television.

"Yeah, I never watched this show before but it seems pretty interesting."

"I love this show. It's one of my favorites. You're watching the re-runs of last season. The new episodes don't start until January."

When the show ended they started small talk. Bryce gazed at Rayne. He slowly leaned into her. She didn't object. He placed his hand on her thigh and moved closer to her. Without any hesitation, he moved his hand up and down her thigh. He looked into her pure hazel eyes and smiled. Excitement and nervousness became evident as their gaze intensified. Rayne was allowing her libido to be her guide. A price to pay for her sinful indiscretions was worth the crime she was willing to commit. She was ready to leap into that fiery furnace of passion. His gentle touch set her mind and body on fire.

He parted her lips with his tongue. He moved his tongue around her warm mouth as if it was a snake moving to a hypnotic rhythm. Rayne wanted him. She needed to feel him inside her moist walls. She pulled away and tried to catch her breath. "I haven't been with a man since my divorce."

"We don't have to do this if you don't want."

Knowing that she wanted to, Rayne pulled him up from the sofa and led him to her bedroom to finish what they started.

Bryce teased her with his fingers; running them along her arms, her legs, and her thighs. Each stroke gave her a tingly sensation causing her pussy lips to blossom like a rose. He removed her spaghetti straps from her shoulders, and gently kissed each. Each kiss trailed to her neck. He took her breast into his mouth circling his tongue around the sensitive skin surrounding her erect nipples. A sinful moan escaped her lips. Two naked bodies standing in front of one another; Rayne stared him down daring him to make the first move. She was captivated by his physique-strong biceps, solid thighs, and his abdomen was tight. Not to mention the brother was packing.

Bryce pulled Rayne down on the bed. He buried his head between her thighs, and traveled his tongue along and around her warm labia. He sucked and flicked her clitoris as if it was strings on a guitar. His fingers moved in and out her at a rapid pace while still stimulating her clitoris with his tongue. He worshipped her with his tongue and Rayne loved it. She tugged and bit at the sheets as if she was having her own personal war. As her back arched she could feel a wave come over her body. She screamed out to the heavens. Her orgasm released like a rapid wave.

Bryce put his thick, long pole deep inside her walls and instead of rapidly plunging into her depths, he deliberately moved slowly. She felt him writing his image in the depth of her soul. He moaned in her ear, telling her how good she felt and how he wanted her to take all of him. Rayne was taking his dick very well, tightening her vagina muscles around it. This excited Bryce even more and he began to pick up the pace.

"HARDER!" She screamed, followed by a series of moans.

He took the opportunity to mark his territory licking…biting…sucking at her breasts. Rayne purred into his ear. Her nails dug into his biceps, her hips moved to his every thrust as he moved in and out of her aggressively. She could tell he was ready to release and another orgasm over took them both. At the height of their lovemaking, their synchronized moans escalated to orgasmic screams. Rayne was in heaven. That night Rayne rode Bryce long and hard until she had no more strength left in her one hundred thirty five pound body. She realized that was what she needed; she needed to be fucked three ways into Sunday

# The Morning After

## 15

Irish writer, poet, Oscar Wilde quoted, "The only way to get rid of a temptation is to yield to it. Resist it, and your soul grows sick with longing for the things it has forbidden to itself." It was the morning after and Rayne was coming down from an orgasmic high, trying to recapture last night, submitting herself to sinful pleasure. Bryce left his trademark deep inside her with every thrust, followed by heavy breathing and merciful cries that rang out to the heavens. While sexing they barely did speak, but with his each and every stroke her secrets were exposed. Secrets she never told a soul. Sex had given her the desire to learn about Bryce. For the first time in a long time since her divorce from Rashard, Rayne yielded herself and did not hold back from her feelings.

Awakened from a night of erotica, Rayne could barely open her eyes. Her body was filled with aches, being maneuvered in so many different positions as if she was an acrobat. The smell of sex filled the air. She removed the comforter from her naked body and walked to her bedroom window. Slightly opening up the blinds, the room gleamed from the bright sun. She turned around to see if she had awakened her lover, but his motionless body did not budge from his position. Bryce was still under the sandman's spell. The sun warmed her naked body as she stood meditating, trying to create positive and peaceful thoughts. She couldn't believe Bryce had fulfilled her deepest fantasies. She wanted something exciting and new to keep her mind off of Rashard. He had managed to heal her open wounds when his dick entered her pussy and started stroking her. At that moment, Rayne began to erase the boundaries of her own sexual essence.

A few times throughout the night, Rayne wondered how his wife would feel if she found out her husband was sexing her. Would her eyes open wide with a look of horror? Would her jaw become unhinged as it dropped to the floor? The images shook her like a thunderstorm profusely rumbling through the sky. Her imagination ran wild as she envisioned Bryce fulfilling his wife's every sexual desire by licking, sucking, fingering, and penetrating her pussy so deep with his penis. Does he fuck her as good as he did her? Jealousy and envy toward a woman she didn't even know made Rayne angry. Feelings of insecurity made her sex and do things to Bryce that would make his wife become a figment of his imagination. Even though he was with her for a few stolen moments, it did not take away the fact that he was still married. He belonged to someone else; no matter what, when he leaves Richmond he would be heading back home to Atlanta to be with his wife and kids. She would be left all alone. The experience would only leave an empty feeling inside, guilt eating away at her conscious, causing her to wrestle with the perception of her own self-respect.

Rayne heard Bryce clear his throat and she turned to face her handsome lover.

"Look who's finally awake." She smiled feeling the heat rise between her thighs in a matter of seconds.

A desirable grin marked his face. She walked over to the king size bed, climbed on top of him and placed a soft gentle kiss on his lips. He reciprocated inserting his tongue into her mouth. Their tongues mixed with morning breath was not her idea of sensual, but was not a bad way to start off the morning. She pulled away and stared into his beautiful honey brown eyes then ran her hand up and down his torso.

Bryce's seductive look was pure magic sending chills down her spine. He licked his lips. "I really enjoyed last night."

"So did I." Rayne reached over and grabbed the glass of Dom Pérignon from the night stand, dipped her finger into the warm liquid, and then traced the outside of Bryce's lips.

"Now let's see how you taste." Rayne licked his lips, her temperature rising like a furnace. She was on fire. His moans increased her excitement. She desired his dick. She was slightly wary of her own impulsive behavior. *What has gotten into me?* Rayne thought to herself. She couldn't quite put her finger on it, but this man was making her want to do things that her mother wouldn't be proud of. Sex with him was a different experience. Nothing compared to the way she and Rashard use to make love. Rayne loved Bryce's aggressive side. He was wild like an untamed tiger. Bryce ravaged Rayne. He was in control. He turned her around, held her wrists behind her back with one hand, and then wrapped his hand around her hair, lightly pulling it. Rayne moaned with delight. This let him know she was into it. She surrendered to his aggressiveness, screaming out for more. He penetrated her doggy style. Afterwards, he turned her around, placed a hand over her neck and penetrated her frantically in the missionary position until she came. Intense orgasms induced states of euphoria. His sensual touches released emotions of transcendent happiness combined with an overwhelming sense of contentment.

Bryce ran his fingers through Rayne's long silky locks and gazed into her eyes. "I hate to do this, but I must be going. I have a flight to catch."

"Will I see you again?" Rayne asked, hoping her question would not scare him off.

"Most certainly you will be seeing me again."

"Will that be possible?"

"Anything is possible," Bryce assured her.

Rayne gave him a bold look and then smiled. "You sound pretty confident about that."

"I can show you better than I can tell you." Bryce challenged.

"Is that right—" before she could finish her sentence, Bryce slid his penis into her welcoming pussy.

Her back arched as she rotated her hips, feeling his girth stretch her insides; she rode him slow as their synchronicity began to manifest.

"Oh, yeah baby...that's how I like it...it feels so good...don't stop," Rayne begged, trying to control the inevitable.

She began to speak in such vulgar tongues about the way she was feeling. Amazed at how this man could make her act out of character, without any self-control, begging for mercy, begging for pure pleasure. He was passionate, but his every stroke was relentless and Rayne was not afraid. She was receptive. If words could paint a picture, there wouldn't be any words to say what she was experiencing. Moans filled the room creating a perfect sound. Rayne closed her eyes trying to create new memories. She wanted the memories that existed of Rashard to go away. The only thing that mattered to her at the moment was being pleasured. She didn't want to trade the feeling for nothing. Not even for a minute.

# Pot calling the kettle black
## 16

Rayne was heading to Friday's on Broad Street to meet her brother and Zoey for happy hour. She couldn't believe she spent last night doing the unthinkable. As somber as she was to see Bryce leave, she knew it wasn't the last time they'd see each other again. Rayne finally was able to let go and live in the moment. Never did she think in a million years it would be with a married man. Six months ago she discovered her husband's infidelity which dissolved her marriage. She had no room to point the finger at Rachel now, when she was now guilty of the same thing—committing adultery and not taking Bryce's wife into consideration. They yielded to temptation for their own selfish motives not realizing wrong deeds will cause you to reap what you sow.

Rayne arrived at Friday's and lucked up on a front parking spot. She pulled down her car visor to check her hair and makeup in the mirror. She applied a little more of her Viva glam Mac lip gloss to her lips, then climbed out of her Mercedes and sashayed inside of Fridays as if she owned the place.

Once inside, she headed for the bar to look for Tyreke. Tyreke saw her coming, and stood to give his sister a hug.

"Hey, sis. How are you doing?" He asked in his most flamboyant voice.

*Damn how that annoys me. Why can't he just talk normal?* Rayne thought to herself. "I'm good. And you?"

"Girl, my day is always fabulous."

"Well that's good to hear." Rayne playfully tapped him on his arm. "Look at you diva, looking all cute. I see you rocking the skinny legs and stilettos. Can't do shit with you. Daddy would turn over in his grave if he saw you dressing like this."

"I know that's right. This is me. Love it or hate it." Tyreke put his hand on his hip to strike a pose.

Rayne stared intently at Tyreke, her lips quirked up into a smile. She adored every characteristic about her brother, but his lifestyle is unfathomable. Tyreke has a quintessential handsome appearance with a tall, lean, well-defined build. One can read kindness in his face. He has a mocha complexion, wavy, black hair and mysterious hazel eyes. Besides his lively personality, he has an overall charming demeanor.

The waitress approached their table, and Rayne ordered a Long Island Iced Tea. She then turned her attention back to Tyreke. "I see somebody got started with the drinking early. I see two empty glasses on the table."

"That's right bitch and I'm on my third. Girl, I got me a good piece of dick sliding through tonight. That nigga gon' get it." Tyreke fell out laughing.

"TMI. Please spare me the details about you and Craig." Rayne said waving him off.

"Who said it was Craig?"

Rayne looked at him mysteriously. Something was telling her she shouldn't ask questions. "I don't even want to know."

"Good. Cause I wasn't going to tell."

Rayne grabbed the menu and opened it up. "So knuckle head, you treating your sister to dinner?" Rayne laughed finding her statement quite amusing.

Tyreke did not find it funny. He started snapping his fingers and snaking his neck. "Hell naw. No you didn't. I know you don't think I'm treating you to dinner when you sashaying your ass all up in here wearing an outfit that probably cost more than what I pay for my damn rent."

"Wow, do I detect jealousy?" Rayne giggled.

"No bitch, but see if you can detect my foot coming towards your ass." They both fell out laughing.

"Hey, divas. What ya'll laughing about?" Zoey asked while taking her jacket off and placing it on the back of the chair before sitting down.

"What's up girl?" responded Rayne.

Tyreke frowned and sucked his teeth. "What's with all the damn questions? If you were here on time you would have known what we were talking about. "Yo' ass always fashionably late. You ain't cute."

"Don't start with me, fool. I can't stand you. You lucky the waitress here, because you been saved from this good old fashion cursing out I was about to give you."

"Please, don't you two start this crap this evening?" Rayne protested.

Zoey ordered a Margarita on the rocks with no salt. Tyreke and Rayne ordered another round, plus three orders of wings and two orders of loaded baked potatoes.

Zoey said, "If ya'll order all that I don't need to order. I'll just eat ya'll food."

"Typical black folks always free loading. Order your own damn food." Tyreke said flatly.

Zoey shot back, "Shut the hell up, Tyreke. I know you not paying. I'm sure Rayne footing the bill. Your broke ass can't even afford happy hour."

"Don't let the stilettos fool you boo boo." Tyreke threw his hand up in the air.

Rayne just shook her head as the two argued like fools in front of the waitress. The waitress thought they were hilarious and started laughing.

Rayne was dying to tell them all about Bryce, but with all the bickering back and forth, they were killing her excitement. When the waitress walked off, she had to quickly break up their spat.

"I wish you two would shut up! I have something to say." She felt tingly all over as if she were going to explode.

Finally, the two stopped arguing and Rayne was ready to dish out her news.

"I just had the best sex of my life last night."

Confused, Tyreke raised an eyebrow. "You let Rashard back in your cookie jar?"

"Yeah, when did Rashard come back into the picture and why wasn't I informed?" Zoey asked.

Rayne made a face and rolled her eyes at them both. "Damn. Who said it was Rashard I gave the nookie too? There you two go assuming."

"Then who the hell was it?" Tyreke barked.

"Oh my God!" Zoey's voice boomed with excitement. "You finally gave up the goodies to Troy."

"Hell to the no!" Rayne shot back.

"I'm still waiting for a damn name!" Tyreke snapped.

"Well it's nobody you two know. I actually met him at the Real Estate conference I—."

Tyreke cut Rayne off mid-sentence. "You mean to tell me you fucked a man you barely knew. Have you no shame?" He asked with emphasis.

"None whatsoever," Rayne said proudly.

"What brought on this new attitude? What's his name? What he do for a living? What he look like?" Tyreke quizzed as if Rayne was on a witness stand being interrogated by a prosecutor.

"Pump your brakes. One question at a time, please." Rayne took a long deep breath. "First of all his name is Bryce. He's a real estate developer and lives in Atlanta. He's tall, handsome, articulate, charming, smooth, and his voice got bass, a body like The Rock with a Denzel face." Her words seductively flowed from her mouth.

"Aigh't. Enough with the Salt-N-Pepa rap lines. You not fooling anyone. It's more to this Bryce character then you telling us," Zoey implied.

"I agree. I know my sister and I can tell when she's leaving out information. I would bet you any amount of money that nigga is married." Tyreke and Zoey looked at Rayne wide eyed while waiting for her response.

Rayne hesitated before answering, "As a matter of fact he is married."

Tyreke's face cringed as his drink shot from his mouth.

"Now you know you need your ass whipped." Zoey stated.

Tyreke was stunned. "Rashard really messed your head all up."

Rayne became defensive. "What does Rashard have to do with this?"

"Look sis, I'm not throwing any stones. Trust and believe we all have skeletons in our closets. I just thought you would have used better judgment. That's all."

"Did you feel awkward sleeping with him knowing he was married? You mean to tell me his wife never crossed your mind?" Zoey asked.

"No. I mean…I had my reservations, but I couldn't help what I was feeling. The moment felt so right. I may not even see him again. So what I borrowed him for a few stolen moments?"

"Well damn, don't sound so nonchalant." Tyreke stated.

"Why do I feel like I'm being ridiculed?"

"No one is passing judgment, Rayne. We are just surprised you stooped to Rashard's level. Don't forget that your marriage ended over the exact same thing. Don't you remember how devastated you were and how you felt your world was turned upside down?"

"Listen, what I had was not a revenge fuck. I'm not out to hurt anybody. A girl just wanted to have fun. I felt being with another man would help me get rid of my pain. I got caught up in the moment, that's all. No harm intended, so get off my back." Rayne said, then took a sip from her Long Island Ice Tea.

"How the hell sleeping with a married man will help rid you of your pain?" Tyreke laughed, then continued. "If anything it's going to make matters worse. Look, your brother is no angel. I've done and I am still doing things I'm not proud of. I just hope this don't come back to bite you in your ass."

"Trust me, I'm a big girl. I can handle myself. If it happens again and I choose to sleep with Bryce, let that be my problem. Capiche?" Rayne knew deep down they were right. It was the same internal conversation she had with herself.

Zoey shook her head in disbelief. She never thought Rayne would have the nerve to sleep with a married man considering what happened to her own marriage. But she knew she had no place to criticize her actions. She felt bad that Rayne was even in that predicament. She could barely look her friend in the face because her conscious consistently nagged her. The only thing she could do was pretend to be happy for her and feed into the conversation.

Zoey forced a smile and decided to make fun of the

situation. "Well if you not worried we not worried, but just answer one question. Was it good?"

"Hell yeah! It was explosive. Believe me when I say that brother is working with a package, and he dicked me down real good. His sex skills were so raw and passionate that I nearly lost my mind." Rayne was so full of herself; she couldn't contain how she was feeling inside. Recapturing the whole night again in her mind made her moist in between her legs.

"I know what you mean sis, heyyyy." Tyreke raised his hand to give his sister a high five. "On the real though, the only thing I'm going to say is be careful. Don't get yourself caught up in a situation you cannot get yourself out of."

Zoey took a sip of her drink before adding in her two cents. "Sad to say, I think you should listen to your brother. You know what happened to me when I got involved with Kevin's no good ass. Being the mistress is no picnic in the park." Zoey said, taking her napkin and dabbing the corners of her mouth. "Karma is a bitch."

"Thank you both for looking out for my best interest, but like I had said before I can handle myself."

"I'm curious though. I thought you and Troy were going to hook up?" Zoey inquired.

Her question completely befuddled Rayne.

"What gave you that notion?"

Zoey shrugged her shoulders. "Well I just figured since you two been spending a lot of time together that you both were getting serious. Honestly, I was hoping you two would become an item."

"Well, you thought wrong and there is no chance Troy and I will hook up. What I don't get is why you're always advocating on his behalf?"

Rayne was becoming annoyed and Zoey could sense her tension. Bad enough Troy was constantly in her ear talking about them getting together, now she had to hear it from her friend.

"Thank God the food is here!" Tyreke said, as he pushed his drink to the side.

"Well personally..." Tyreke paused for a second to take a bite out of his chicken. "I would love to see you and Rashard get back together."

"Ok. Stop. Stop. Stop. Let's clear the air once and for all. I do not have any intentions on getting with Troy, and when people in hell start getting ice water is the day Rashard and I will get back together. Get it in your thick skulls it's not going to happen. Enough of the Troy and Rashard spill. Let's change the subject because you two are blowing my buzz with all this non-sense." Rayne said in a matter of fact tone.

"Still a bitch on wheels," Zoey laughed and shook her head.

"And you know it," Rayne confirmed.

The three ate, drank, and jammed to the music being piped through the restaurant. Tyreke yelled out, "That is my song!" Beyonce's song, "Single Ladies" blared loudly. He stood up from his chair, threw his hand in the air, arched his back and twirled his ass.

Rayne smacked him on his arm and told him to sit down and stop making a spectacle of himself.

"Girl please, you just mad you can't move your ass like me."

Rayne shook her head and Zoey just laughed. They were all enjoying each other's company, eating, drinking, laughing and trying to maintain civilized conversations. None of them were trying to step on each other's toes. They chatted about work, music, family and any other topics that didn't have anything to do with sex or relationships. Smiles and laughter were just false pretenses to cover up the fear and pain that they all were really feeling. Rayne couldn't help but think about what Zoey said about karma being a bitch, but she enjoyed the way Bryce made her feel and really don't care if he's married. Zoey nervously thought about the dark secret she was desperately trying to hide, and praying that it would never reveal itself. Tyreke pondered over his sister's situation knowing he too was indulging in guilty pleasures with a married man.

We fail to realize that we "stone" people for their mistakes all the while making mistakes of our own. No one at the table had room to point fingers at the other because doing so would be the pot calling the kettle black.

# So hard to say goodbye

# 17

Rashard was awakened by the sound of his phone ringing. He peeped at the clock. "Five o'clock in the morning are you kidding me," he muttered. He thought who could be calling him at the crack of dawn. He fumbled for the house phone on the night stand, almost knocking over the lamp. In three hours he had an important meeting to attend and couldn't believe his sleep was being interrupted.

"Hello," he said in a groggy voice.

Rashard's mind couldn't process quick enough with what was being said on the other end of the phone. He sprang up from his bed. He could feel the blood drain from his face. He didn't hear what he just thought he had heard.

"I'm on my way."

Rashard grabbed his True Religion jeans off the chair, a wife beater, and a pair of socks from his mahogany chest. He slipped his feet inside his Nike flip flops, snatched up his keys from the nightstand and made a dash to his Range Rover.

The ride to MCV Hospital was only twenty minutes away from where he lived, but it felt like an eternity getting there. He sat at the stop light at Broad Street waiting to make a left onto Marshall Street, tapping his fingers nervously on the steering wheel as he contemplated running it.

"Change fucking light!" He yelled out loud.

Rashard quickly parked and rushed inside the main entrance of the hospital. Five minutes later he was on the third floor headed towards his mother's room. Walking down the long hospital hallway felt like walking into his own demise. Rashard detested hospitals. The hospital's disinfectant stench made him nauseous and sick. Every time he came to visit his mother, the smell would bring back memories of his grandfather. Smells have a way of bringing back memories associated with them in an extremely graphic fashion. Rashard's mind became flooded with images of his grandfather being hospitalized in the same hospital. He died there due to complications of a severe stroke.

Rashard hadn't quite reached his mother's room when he heard a loud cry coming from his father's voice. He stood outside his mother's room dreading to go inside. He knew he wasn't prepared to handle seeing his mother's lifeless body lying in that hospital bed. Tears began to fill his eyes as they confirmed his worst fears. His mother was always strong and a fighter, but it was clear she had lost the battle against cancer. Rashard couldn't digest the fact his mother was dead. There was no holding back his tears as he entered into the room.

Mrs. Armstrong lay on the bed. A white sheet covered her entire body but stopped at her neck. All he could see was his mother's angelic face, lying there peacefully, finally out of her misery. His father sprawled across her body, sobbing uncontrollably. "Come back to me baby...don't leave me...you can't leave me...I need you." Mr. Armstrong said between cries. The image broke Rashard's heart into pieces.

Rashard slowly walked towards his mother's bed, his anxiety began to manifest as he dropped to his knees and wrapped his arms around his father and began to ball; letting his emotions escape his body.

Finally, a tall thin doctor along with the hospital's chaplain came into the room. It was time to take his mother to the morgue.

"Please sir; can we have a few more minutes with her?" Rashard pleaded. He wasn't ready to let his mother go.

"I'm sorry sir," the doctor said in a sensitive tone. "But it's time. We have to take her. I wish I could allow you to spend more time but its hospital procedure."

Fuck hospital procedure, Rashard wanted to say out

loud, but held his composure. They had a job to do and as much as he didn't like it, he had to grasp the fact they were about to carry his mother off to a cold icebox.

Rashard wrapped his arm around his dad shoulders. "Come on pops. Let's go."

The pain of watching his father fall by his mother's side once more crying out in agony was unbearable. He managed to pick his grieving father up from the floor and carry him out of the room. They wept in each other's arms. Rashard saw Troy heading in their direction.

"Uncle Alex, I'm so sorry." Troy said, hugging his uncle. He caught the evil glare Rashard was giving him out the corner of his eye.

"Glad you can break away from your hoes to be here with family." Rashard said, with disdain in his voice.

"Fuck you," Troy said, breaking the embrace.

"Both of you quit it right this instant!" Mr. Armstrong demanded, lifting his cane up and pointing it at both men back and forth. "I will take this cane and crack both of ya'll skulls wide open if you two stand here in my presence and argue like two fools when my wife is dead. Show some damn respect!"

Rashard placed his hand on his dad's shoulder. "I'm sorry pop."

Mr. Armstrong shoved Rashard's hand away. "You both are sorry." He walked away, his sorrow draped across his shoulders.

"Nigga you got some nerve coming at me like that." Troy said looking at Rashard square in the eyes.

Rashard got up in Troy's face. "I got nerve. Naw nigga, you got nerve. I know you had something to do with how Rayne and I broke up. I'm two seconds off your ass. But you can consider yourself lucky. This is one ass whipping put on layaway."

"You making a grave mistake threatening me," Troy said through clench teeth.

"Naw motherfucka, you made the grave mistake when you interfered with my marriage."

Rashard heard the doctors talking and turned around to see them wheeling his mother out of her room. The white sheet covered her face. Tears stung his eyes and a hard lump formed in his throat as despair washed over him, engulfing him. He stood still as he watched them wheel her body away; his feet glued to the floor not allowing him to run after her. She was gone and it was nothing he could do to bring his mother back. He brushed pass Troy to quickly exit the hospital. He felt alone. He felt his mother had abandoned him. Pain turned into anger. Anger turned into rage. He stopped and pounded his fist into the hospital wall. His knees buckled as he dropped to the floor. With his hands covering his face he let out a tortured scream.

"Why? Why did you take my mother? She didn't deserve to die! She didn't deserve a disease so evil and painful. I need my mom."

Rashard flinched as he felt a hand touch his shoulder. He looked up to see Troy standing over him with tears falling from his eyes. For once he let his ill feelings toward his cousin cease for the moment as he embraced Troy and they shared a tearful good-bye to his mother.

The loss of a loved one can bring family closer together or further apart. Rashard never thought he would witness his father do the one thing he said he would ever do—cry. He had never seen his father cry before. Rashard didn't know he could. Besides Rayne, Rashard had lost the most important person in his life. He felt like a scared little boy facing the rest of his life without his mother. It wasn't supposed to end like this. Not like this.

As he left the hospital, Rashard knew he had to notify Rayne about his mom's death. He reached into his pocket and pulled out his cell phone and nervously dialed Rayne's number. He prayed she would answer the phone. He sounded relieved when she picked up.

"Rayne, she's gone."

"What do you want Rashard?"

The tone of her voice made him realize she had a guarded attitude which made him apprehensive. Rashard dismissed her tone, choking back tears, he said, "My mother passed away about an hour ago."

The news shocked Rayne. "Oh my God! I'm so sorry, Rashard." She couldn't believe Mrs. Armstrong was taken away from them so soon. "Please forgive me for my snappy attitude. It's just—."

114

Rashard cut her off. "No need to apologize. I understand."

He knew how she felt, so there was no need to justify her attitude. It was because he saw her while with Rachel and Moses, appearing as if they were one big happy family. Looks can be deceiving and Rashard despised being in the company of Rachel. Her presence made his stomach turn. He could see Rayne struggle as she fought the melancholy in her eyes. This made him want to grab her, hold her tight, and undo the pain he had caused her.

They both shared an emotional conversation, at one point Rayne just broke down crying. They stayed on the phone for hours consoling each other, before they knew it, noon had settled in. Unfortunately, it took the death of his mother to encourage them to put aside their differences and talk with one another rationally. Rashard needed Rayne and she was there for him. He couldn't ask for anything more.

# R.I.P.

## 18

Five long intense days had passed and it was finally the day of Mrs. Armstrong's funeral. The ride to the church was very somber. Rayne sat in silence and stared out the window of the moving car. There was no sun and the sky was gloomy. The ground was covered with puddles of water courtesy of a night of rain. Tyreke, Gloria, and Zoey accompanied Rayne to the funeral. Rayne was tired and hadn't gotten much sleep because her mother-in-law's death had really shaken her. She had a close relationship with Mrs. Armstrong, and she had to come to terms that not only had she lost her husband, but she'd lost a mother she truly loved. The day Rashard called her with the news that his mother had died was heart wrenching. Listening to him cry made her want to be by his side. She felt bad that she wasn't there for him the way she truly wanted to be because of the bitterness that tainted her heart. For that moment, she did manage to set aside her ill feelings.

Her grief began to manifest as all the memories of great times she shared with her mother-in-law came to mind. Tyreke intruded her thoughts when he announced they had arrived at the church. They were forty-five minutes early, but there were a few people whom she did not recognize standing outside of the church talking amongst themselves.

Gloria put her hand on Rayne's shoulder. "Are you sure you can handle this, baby?"

"I'm fine, Ma." Rayne took a deep breath before she got

out of the car. She was glad she was not alone and her family by her side. Out of nowhere, Rayne heard a familiar voice.

"Oh my God! Looka here, looka here, looka here. Girl you still fine as ever." Tony walked towards Rayne with open arms. "It's so good to see you again." He placed a huge wet kiss on her cheek.

Rayne cringed as she forced a fake smile. Tony was Rashard's uncle who thought he was the next Eddie Murphy. His jokes were cornier than ever. He had crooked teeth, a lazy eye (which spooked her), walked with a limp, wore loud suits, and thought he was a fashion guru; and to make matters worse, his hair looked as if it was painted on. Uncle Tony annoyed her every time he was in her presence. She always complained to Rashard that he reminded her of a dirty old pervert because he was a fresh talker.

"Turn around and let me look at you." Tony grabbed Rayne's hand and twirled her around.

*I wish I could kick this nigga in his balls*, she thought to herself. Rayne hurried to get the attention off of her. "Tony you remember my mother, brother, and best friend Zoey."

"Of course I do." Tony grabbed Gloria's hand and gently kissed the back of it. "I see where Rayne gets her beauty."

He turned his attention to Zoey. "Zoey, you still a pretty little thing. Give your Uncle Tony a hug."

Zoey twisted her lips and hesitantly gave him a hug. He scooped her up in his arms and lifted her off the ground.

"Damn, girl you light as a feather. What, you don't eat? I need you to eat so you can get some meat on them bones. Girl you so skinny, I could blind-fold you with dental floss." He fell out laughing.

Rayne, Tyreke, and Gloria were flabbergasted, and felt embarrassed for Zoey. They could tell from her expression that she was displeased with Tony's insensitive remark.

Then he extended his hand to shake Tyreke's. Tyreke cringed at Tony's lazy eye that made him nervous. "It's nice seeing you again my man. So why don't ya'll follow me into the church. I'm sure everyone would be happy to see you all were able to make it."

Before they made it through the church doors, Rashard came walking out. Rayne's eyes locked with his and her heart began to beat wildly. A thousand emotions ran through her body.

"Can we talk?" Rashard apprehensively asked.

They gazed into each other's eyes for a long moment before Tyreke's voice broke the silence. "We'll be inside if you need us."

Everyone went inside the church leaving Rayne alone with her ex-husband. They walked away from the front entrance and off to the side so they could talk in private.

"You don't know how much it means to me that you are here." Rashard said nervously.

"Rashard, you know I loved your mother very much. So being here is not an issue."

Rashard stared deep into her eyes. He couldn't keep his eyes off her and Rayne was eating up every minute of the attention he was giving her. She was smiling inside. She made sure she showed up at the funeral looking stunning and fabulous, wearing the best outfit that money could buy. Her fitted black dress was straight enough to show off her curves and accentuate her small waist.

Rashard couldn't contain himself, he reached to take her hand, but Rayne pulled away.

"I'm sorry. I shouldn't have done that. But I miss you so much. You look so beautiful."

"Thank you. You look good yourself." Rayne couldn't believe she said that. She wanted to take it back but it was too late.

Rashard cleared his throat before asking, "How have you been?"

"I've been doing fine. I can't complain. I'm finally putting my life back in order." Rayne let out a deep sigh. "I'm so sorry about your mother. My heart goes out to you and your family."

Rayne could see the pain in Rashard's face. A tear fell from his soulful eyes and made it's pathway down his cheek. Rayne was overcome by intense emotions watching a grief-stricken Rashard break down in tears. She stepped closer to him and wrapped her arms around his neck, so grateful to be back into his arms. They held each other in a tight embrace, sharing the silence gracefully. The smell of his Burberry cologne tickled her nostrils. *Damn, he smells divine.* Their bitter sweet moment was interrupted when Troy and Rachel, who was holding her son, walked out of the church. Rayne released their embrace and stared Rachel up and down as if they were about to square off in a boxing match. The sight of her made Rayne's blood boil with indignation. It took everything in her not to finally beat that bitch's ass.

"Hello, Rayne." Troy walked towards Rayne and gave her a hug and gently kissed her on the cheek.

Rashard became uptight as he watched Troy kiss Rayne on the cheek. Troy smiled. He knew his affection towards her would infuriate his cousin. He could feel the condemnation from Rashard as his gaze settled on Rayne's lovely smile.

Rayne couldn't believe Rachel had the nerve to show up for the funeral. After all, who needs an invitation to show up at a funeral to pay their respect? Rayne figured the only reason why she was there was because she was the mother of Rashard's baby. Rayne was sure that Rachel loved the moment she had to flaunt her and the baby being there in her face. She knew Rachel could never take her place. Never had. Never will. But Rayne also wasn't going to give her the satisfaction of knowing her being there was bothering her. That was until Rachel came at Rayne sideways.

"Rashard doesn't need you comforting him. He has me. That's why I'm with him and you're not."

No this bitch didn't! Rayne's face was twisted in anger, and she slightly pushed Troy to the side. She walked up to Rachel and looked her square in her eyes. "Look here you trifling heifer, you keep running your mouth and I'll smack fire from your ass! Don't you ever disrespect me again?!"

Troy grabbed Rayne by the arm. "Come on, let's go inside the church. She is not worth it."

Rachel smirked and said, "Whatever. Don't come at me talking like you bout to do something. You don't scare me."

Rayne couldn't believe she was bold enough to talk to her like that. Obviously, she didn't remember their fight in high school. Rayne beat her ass. Trust and believe it would be another fight she wouldn't win again.

Rashard grabbed the baby from Rachel because he knew

she had just barked up the wrong tree. "Let's go Rachel," Rashard said, trying to defuse the situation. As much as he wanted Rayne to beat the hell out of Rachel; he didn't want her to do it at his mother's funeral. It wasn't the time or the place.

Rayne yanked her arm away from Troy. "No, Rashard. There is no need to save this trick. She got all that mouth. Maybe I should shut it up for her."

"No. Not here. Not at my mother's funeral. Troy, take Rayne inside the church." Rashard said, in an ordering tone.

Rachel kept running off at the mouth. Rashard knew the two women needed to be separated quickly. He knew how Rayne got down. She was the type that kicked ass and took names later. Rashard and Troy quickly tried to separate them but to no avail, it was too late. Rayne balled up her perfectly manicured nails into a fist and before Rachel could finish the next sentence, she punched the shit out of her, knocking her to the ground. Envisioning Rashard and Rachel in the throes of passion which caused their marriage to end pushed Rayne to become irrationally infuriated and act out of character.

Rachel touched her mouth and was in shock at the blood gushing from her bottom lip. Tears instantaneously welled up in her eyes. Rachel cried out. "You bitch! You gonna pay for this!"

Rayne didn't respond. She had a fiery look in her eyes. She felt she did what she had to do. Rachel needed to be put in her place. There were a few people standing outside the church that were astounded by what they had just witnessed. Rayne looked back and forth at Troy and Rashard. Their facial expressions were priceless. She smoothed out her dress, turned around and made her way inside the church as if nothing had happened. It was time to do what she came there to do— pay her respects to the woman who was her beloved mother-in-law, Mrs. Katherine Armstrong.

# The Thrill of the Forbidden
## 19

A blare of sunlight flooded Rayne's office through her opened blinds. She sat at her desk twirling her pen. It was two o'clock and the afternoon was winding down. Terrence left the office earlier that day to pick up his sick son from day care. Rayne pressed her intercom button.

"Yes, Ms. Armstrong," her assistant, Jennifer responded.

"Things are pretty slow so why don't you leave for the rest of the day with pay."

"Thanks, Ms. Armstrong. That's really nice of you." Jennifer said excitedly.

"You're welcome. Lock the office door behind you. Any agents wanting to get in can use their key."

Rayne got up to lock her office door. She walked back to her desk and stared at the computer monitor. She decided to browse the MLS in search of a four bedroom home, two car garage, with a family room, possibly two and a half baths, with a huge back yard in the Henrico District. Mrs. Turner was a persnickety client and refused to be shown houses that didn't meet her exact requirements.

An hour had passed and Rayne started to get restless. She picked up her bottle and sipped the lukewarm water. She decided she had enough of the computer and shut it down, leaving the work for the next day. It had been a few nights since she'd spoken with Bryce. Confusion started to consume her because talking with him on a regular basis started to feel good. She flinched at the sensation that pulsated between her legs. Rashard was the only man that could make her act so impulsively, but something about Bryce made her feel bold and rebellious. Ever since Rayne and Bryce started their affair she was not hoodwinked to believe that he would leave his wife for her. She knew up front he was married and became involved with him anyway. Many people will label her as a "home wrecker" with no conscious or morals. Rayne would beg to differ. Her intentions were not to destroy another woman's marriage; although it was done to her. Just like Adam and Eve eating from the Tree of Knowledge of Good and Evil, Rayne was tempted. Bryce was that evil serpent, and she gave into her desires. She craved the forbidden fruit. This made Bryce even more desirable. He consistently stole her thoughts like a thief in the night. Rayne wasn't looking for a commitment. A married man had to always go home to his wife. Rayne professed she would never let another man have her heart. She was not going to be broken down and become weak and loose herself in the moments simply because she was captivated by Bryce's charm and blinded from his intimacy. He was intriguing from the first moment they met. Regardless of Rayne's intentions, she knew choosing to get involved with a married man, who could turn his back on his wife even for a few hours, was setting herself up.

Soon after their first intimate encounter, their affair fell into a pattern. They would talk two to three times a day on the phone. During these phone conversations they would engage in phone sex. It made sex more fun. There was a thrill in doing something illicit and naughty. Rayne convinced herself that what she was doing wasn't wrong at all.

An overwhelming wave of desire came over her. She bit her bottom lip. Tugged at her skirt, kicked off her red bottoms, let her hair down so her long locks could fall down her back. She picked up a piece of paper and fanned the heat that pulsated from her flesh. "I need to get it together." She whispered to herself.

She tried to put him out of her mind like a burning cigarette. Then she thought about the fact that she hadn't had a good work out lately, so maybe she'd leave early as well and head to the gym. Her arms were definitely in need of toning, and it wouldn't hurt if she concentrated on her stomach as well. Two days of Krispy Kreme doughnuts was taking its effect. She should have stood to head out the door immediately, but there was Bryce in her imagination again. The Sagittarius marking his territory. She could almost feel his tongue, telling her to surrender to her desires. Surrender to intimacy. Rayne kept fanning at her heat. "Damn, it didn't work."

Temptation had won the battle, beat her into submission. She hit the extension to her private line and dialed those familiar numbers. Each number programmed in her head, like her social security number.

"Ummm. I'm so glad you called. I've been thinking about you." Bryce said, putting his TV on mute.

"What are you doing?" Rayne asked.

"I'm at home watching ESPN."

"I'm surprised you're not at work. Where's your wife?"

"I took the day off to go to my son's recital. As for my wife, she's out with the kids and her mother at the mall shopping. I don't expect them back for another few hours."

"Well, I like a naughty boy. So do you have time for me?"

"You didn't have to ask that question. I always have time for you."

"That's what I like to hear." Rayne chuckled.

"Are you at work or home?" he asked.

"I'm at work and I'm sitting at my desk hot and horny. You just what my doctor prescribed. You think you can take care of my problem."

"Well, what does your prescription say?"

"The medication is called Bryce. According to my instructions, remove one applicator and insert into the vagina once a day to help produce an orgasm, signed Dr. Make Me Cum."

Bryce laughed. "I love your corny sense of humor. Do you have any panties on?"

"Yes."

"Take them off."

Rayne stood up, slid her panties down to her ankles. She sat back down in her leather chair and propped her left leg on top of her office desk.

"Done."

"Now place your index and middle fingers in your mouth. Make them nice and wet for daddy."

Rayne did as she was told. Placed her fingers in her mouth and sucked them like a lollipop.

"Done."

"Spread your legs as far as they can go and with those two fingers massage your clit, and move them up and down nice and slow."

"How does that feel?"

"So... freakin'... good."

She moaned and licked her lips. He reciprocated with a moan. Sounds of passion collided as if they were in an orchestra.

"Move your fingers inside your wetness. Fantasize about me being inside you and let your fingers explore the depths of your walls. You're on a conquest for pleasure; let your pussy know who's in control."

Her panties hung from her right ankle, her body was leaned back into the chair, eyes closed, and her hips gravitated to the movement of her fingers pleasuring her pink fleshly insides. She held the phone tightly to her ear trying not to drop it.

He demanded like a captain ordering his men to attack, "Say my name."

"Bryce."

Rayne's pussy commanded her fingers.

Although Bryce wasn't physically with her, Rayne felt his presence. Felt his presence suck her breast, pinch her nipples, lick and suck her labia while her fingers moved in and out of her pink tunnel.

"Oh, yeah, baby, that's how I like it, it feels so good, please don't stop," Rayne said panting. "You know what I want. Give it to me. Keep talking dirty to me. Oh, shit, I'm coming, Oh damn, I'm coming!"

Rayne legs were trembling and her orgasm shook her body as if she was going into a frantic state. Her pussy opened up like a floodgate and she was having an orgasmic shower. The flow of her juices ran down her fingers. The same fingers she used to pleasure herself while Bryce spoke dirty obscenities in her ear. She removed her leg from the desk; her sticky bottom clung to the chair as she shifted her body to sit up straight. She kept her panties around her right ankle. She needed her pussy to breathe and needed her wetness to dry out without the suffocation of her panties. She slowed down her breathing, allowing the rise and fall of her chest to catch up.

There was silence.

Bryce listened as the happiness escaped her mouth. He gave her a minute to get herself together before he spoke.

"I guess my work is done." he said.

"I guess it is." Rayne said weakly.

"You didn't sound too enthused. Are you ok?"

"It's not that." She paused. "It's just it would be better if we got to do this in person. I miss you like crazy," she whined.

Rayne desired more. For the moment, it was all about the thrill of being naughty, the illicit nature of their concealed phone calls and a feeling of romance and danger about the affair. But for Rayne, the phone sex just wasn't enough. Although she loved talking to him over the phone, it was just a temporary fix to satisfy her sexual void. A day never went by when she didn't long for his sensuous touch. Rayne wanted to feel his thickness between her legs. She wanted his arms around her. She wanted and needed all of him. Her impatience was eating away at her desires. Bryce was becoming a drug and she was becoming addicted. He was the crack she so yearned for.

"Well, baby, your wish is my command," Bryce told her.

"So are you going to grant me three wishes?" Rayne asked, playfully teasing.

Bryce began to chuckle. "No I'm not a genie, but I'm about to grant you your wish. How about you accompany me to New Orleans this weekend? I'll be out that way for business, and I don't see anything wrong with mixing business with a little pleasure."

"Hum, this is such short notice, but I definitely can make it happen." Rayne said trying to contain her excitement and not trying to come off as desperate. But the truth of the matter was, she was just that, desperate. She was elated she would finally get to see her lover again. She wanted to drop the phone and start doing cart wheels.

"Good. I'm glad you will be able to join me. I will get with you tomorrow with all the details. In the meantime, as much as I don't want to, I do have to go. Lebron James is dunking on these fools, and I'm missing a really good game."

"The nerve of you to reject me over a basketball game. But since you made me a happy woman, I guess I can let you go. I will talk to you later."

Bryce blew a kiss through the phone and ended the call.

Rayne retreated to her private bathroom. She grabbed a wash cloth, lathered it up with Dove soap, lifted up her skirt and washed away her sex juices. Rayne stared long and hard at herself in the mirror and realized she was not the same person. She had no regard for another woman's marriage. She started to wonder if her affair was an element of bitterness and hurt for what was done to her. Since her divorce, Rayne had become a bitter woman. A characteristic she never possessed. Bitter is a horrible taste. Trying to convert a bitter woman can be like trying to grow a rose from concrete. Rayne did not consider herself to be malicious, but her actions proved she was harboring some hostility towards Rashard. She didn't like what she saw, but for her own selfish reasons, she needed and wanted Bryce. She was blinded by her infatuation for him. She was falling for Bryce.

Rayne stood at her window, looking down from the second floor office building that was shared with Future Financial Services and four other tenants located on the first floor. Her office faced the parking lot. There weren't that many cars parked in the lot. She could count each car on two hands. She assumed everyone had left and gone home to their families. She was so busy engaged in sinful pleasures that she had lost track of time.

She sat back down at her desk in silence. She started shuffling through the piles of papers that were now scattered across her desk. She began to rearrange every item on her desk. She paused when she came to the 24 karat gold engraved name plate Rashard had personally designed for her when she opened up Armstrong Realty. She picked up the name plate and started tracing her slender finger across each letter. She was starting to feel suffocated by the memories that lingered like the boogie man lurking in the dark. She wanted to think about Rashard less and less. Rayne never imagined her life would be thrown the curveballs from the last couple of years. The life she and Rashard had planned was destroyed by a scandalous whore, who she wanted to strangle the life out of. Tears began to pool in her eyes, and her lips began to shiver. No matter what, she knew there was no escaping Rashard. He was her first. He still existed in the most important parts of her.

# A man's gotta do...
## 20

Tyreke shuffled into his living room. He flung his Coach pocketbook from his shoulders onto the sofa; allowing his weary body to follow it. He pulled off his Coach sneakers and began massaging his toes. The twelve hours standing up doing hair had his feet aching.

It was twenty minutes to seven when Tyreke looked up at his round cherry wood clock that sat over his TV. King was coming over at 7:30 and Tyreke was starting to wonder if that was such a good idea. Lately, King had been tripping and acting possessively. The fact that King was married and on the down low was supposed to be a plus and convenient. Tyreke didn't expect he would become emotionally involved. Tyreke was contemplating telling him it was over because his behavior was starting to get on his last nerve. It wouldn't have been any love lost considering Tyreke had plenty of men wanting to share his bed.

Tyreke cut on his CD player loaded with hits from neo-soul, R & B and hip hop artists, and stepped into the steamy hot shower. He decided to listen to Chrisette Michele while the hot water beat against his skin. Tyreke loved her music because her jazzy, evocative lyrics eased his soul. Chrisette belted out the tune "Epiphany." Craig entered his mind. The last three years he had been on an emotional rollercoaster, and Tyreke was tired of the long intense ride. He met Craig at the Hippodrome while hanging out with Rayne. There was something inexplicable about him that intrigued Tyreke and made him approach the tall, dark-skinned, well-built brother. They secretly exchanged numbers that night; and within three weeks he had the straight brother opening up his eyes to a world he never thought he would be a part of. They had their share of good and bad times, but the bad outweighed the good. As Tyreke kept his eyes closed, taking in Chrisette, the water ran down his neck, made its path down his back. He moaned as if the shower was engaged in foreplay with him. He listened to four more of her songs, "Notebook", "What You Do", "Blame it on Me" and "All I Ever Think About" before he stepped out of the shower.

Tyreke rubbed lotion all over his body, sprayed Juicy Couture perfume on both sides of his neck and spritzed the fragrance on his wrists. He reached for his red silk pajamas, but was interrupted by a knock at his door.

Tyreke glanced at the clock and smiled. "Damn, that nigga prompt." He grabbed his towel from the bed, wrapped it around his waist and strode to the door. He let King inside, dropped his towel, and let him take in his nakedness with his hungry eyes.

King smiled displaying his perfect set of white teeth as Tyreke offered him his nakedness. Tyreke studied King's handsome features as if they just met for the first time. He had that same chiseled look as actor Boris Kodjoe—a smooth bald head, and neatly trimmed goatee that nicely framed his face, and complemented his entire look. His deep dark eyes were mesmerizing. Tyreke could barely form a grin as King walked towards him, pulled him closer and slid his tongue in his awaiting mouth. His kiss became more fervent, deeper, as the pressure of his lips on Tyreke's excited him. Tyreke let out a moan, hardly audible, more a whisper. He pulled away and King graciously stared into his eyes. They hold onto each other stares. King seemed to be searching Tyreke's soul as if he was looking for an answer to an unasked question.

Unspoken words. Silence was much better than words at that moment.

Tyreke grabbed King's hand and led him towards the bedroom. He quickly began to unbutton his shirt then removed it. He examined his broad shoulders and toned arms. Next, he fumbled with his pants button, but the feel of King's tongue circling around his neck excited and distracted him from his mission. They moved towards the bed and Tyreke shoved him down and anxiously found his mouth wrapped around his thick erect penis. He consumed every inch of King as if he was his last supper. Say my name, say my name, as Destiny Child would say; Tyreke's name echoed throughout the apartment. King cooed as he enjoyed the sensation of the warm confines of Tyreke's mouth.

Tyreke became pissed off while he was in the middle of giving King a bomb ass blow job. The passion of the moment aggravated by his ringing cell phone, he knew it was Craig because of his ring tone, "Only Wanna Give It To You" by Elle Varner. He was pissed he had to stop sucking King's dick to answer his call. The good thing was he didn't have to worry about him popping up because he was out of town visiting his mother. Craig was known for doing that type of shit. Tyreke walked over to his dresser where his phone was and answered it.

"Hello," Tyreke said.

"What you doing?" Craig asked.

"Nothing. I'm just watching TV." Tyreke looked over at King who was giving him a grimacing look. He ignored him and continued to talk.

"I wanted to come see you. Is that cool?"

"I thought you were in Maryland visiting your mother. I wasn't expecting you for another week. What happened?"

"Naw. I just got back in town. I decided to cut my visit short. I was missing you and felt we had some unfinished business we needed to deal with."

"Well, you usually don't ask, you just pop up. Why all of a sudden you feel the need to get my approval?"

"Look Tyreke, I'm not trying to come over there and all we gonna do is argue. I'm not in the mood for that drama tonight."

"Trust me boo, ain't gon' be no drama. I think it's time we clear the air about some things anyway. I see you when you get here." Tyreke hung up the phone.

Tyreke could tell King was mad but he didn't care.

"You kicking me out so that nigga can come over? You

130

not going to finish what you started?"

"Don't start with me right now." Tyreke grabbed King's clothes from the floor and threw them at him. "Here, put your damn clothes on so you can bounce."

"You a shiesty nigga, Tyreke. How you going to play me like this?"

"Nobody is playing you. I just don't need Craig finding out about my extracurricular activities. He's already suspicious. He's on his way over so I need you to leave. I promise I'll tighten you up tomorrow, but right now I got some shit I need to take care of."

King shook his head slightly in irritation. He knew he was in a no-win situation. He rose from the bed to get dressed; his confused mind didn't know where he stood with Tyreke. He decided to drop the issue for now. He was angry, but he wanted to avoid a confrontation.

It had been a week since Tyreke had seen Craig, but they checked in with one another everyday through phone calls. They had a heated argument the day before he left. Tyreke was livid with Craig for going through his phone to see if he had any nigga's phone numbers, checking his voice messages, and reading his texts. He was tired of his controlling and jealous ways. *How dare that nigga invade my privacy? He was out of line, and to think I wasn't going to check his ass. Then he wanted to play mind games to try and trick me into a confession. Don't that nigga know game recognize game?*

Tyreke felt Craig had a lot of nerve coming at him in a foul manner thinking he was suspect just because he's always caught doing wrong. Little did Craig know he had one foot out the door and the other on a banana peel. His days were numbered. To keep it real, Tyreke was creeping, but he managed to keep it on the down low. He wanted to keep Craig protected from the truth because he knew he wouldn't be able to handle it if he were to find out. Although Tyreke loved Craig, he knew it was time to cut his losses and move on. But before he did so, he wanted to get some of that good dick one more time before his ass was history.

He finally got King out of the apartment. He pulled his hair back into a ponytail, and slipped on his red silk robe.

He pulled the comforter back on his king size sleigh bed, lit a few candles to get the mood right, and switched the track to Ron Isley's CD. He poured himself a glass of Moscato, turned on the television and started flicking through channels to find something good to watch.

Thirty minutes later his doorbell rang. Tyreke cut off the television and CD player. He opened the door and Craig nonchalantly strolled through. His demeanor was arrogant as always. Craig sized up Tyreke to get a good sense of his vibe. Once he saw Tyreke's mood appeared to be subtle, he was all over him kissing and forcing his tongue inside his mouth and feeling on his ass. His kisses had a sweet taste. He must have had a Jolly Rancher on the way over there. Jolly Rancher candy was his favorite.

Tyreke pulled away from his grip. "You don't waste any time do you? Can a brother get a hello before you start sticking your tongue down my throat?"

"I can't help it. I miss you like crazy. I'm so glad we want to put aside our differences. Tonight my only objective is to make it up to you for being a complete jerk." Craig ran his finger up and down Tyreke's chest. "Just to think, one day this chest will be filled with a nice set of breasts that I can't wait to sink my teeth into." He started licking and sucking on Tyreke's nipples.

*Yeah nigga get all you going to get tonight, because after tonight I'm chucking up the deuces to that ass.*

A gratifying moan escaped Craig's lips as Tyreke managed to say, "I bet you do miss me since you tried to carry a brother before you left."

"Come on Tyreke, why mess up a good mood with this attitude? Don't give me a hard time when I'm here to make things all right between us."

Craig started acting aggressively. He grabbed Tyreke by his neck and started kissing him frantically. Tyreke pulled back from his kiss, grabbed his hand and they headed towards the bedroom.

Craig looked around the room and started grinning. "I see the ambiance in here is definitely seductive tonight." Craig said so full of himself. "What did a brother do to deserve all this?"

*Not a damn thing! You just don't know what is about to go*

132

*down.* "You didn't do anything special. I just want to show you how much you mean to me. I'm tired of all this unnecessary drama between us. We been together too long to keep going through all the bull shit. Now why don't you go shower and afterwards I plan on giving you a full body massage."

"Damn, Tyreke, you in a good mood tonight."

While Craig was in the bathroom washing up Tyreke pulled out his hunting knife and slid it under his bed. He wasn't' sure what type of mind frame Craig would be in once he broke it off with him, so he wanted to be prepared just in case an altercation would pop off. If Craig decided he wanted to get physical, Tyreke would be ready to whip his ass like he stole something.

Craig emerged from the bathroom completely naked. He walked towards the bed and Tyreke watched his dick swing from side to side, bouncing off his thick thighs. He began to drool at the mouth. Damn I'm going to miss that big dick. But dick come a dime a dozen, and I will have no problem getting it. Nothing is more important than my sanity.

Craig laid back on the bed and started stroking his penis up and down and licking his lips. Tyreke dropped his robe to the ground, grabbed the massage oil and climbed on top of Craig.

"I want to try something different tonight. Why don't you let me tie you up to the bed and let me have my way with you?"

"That shit sounds good. I'm game." Craig thought he had hit the lottery. "What's gotten into you?"

"Shhhh. Just relax and let me handle my business."

Without hesitation, Craig held out his hands. Tyreke placed the handcuffs around his wrists and used scarves to tie his legs to the foot board. Afterwards, he poured the massage oil all over his chest. He rubbed the oil in his hands and started massaging his biceps, triceps and abs. Next, he poured the oil on his legs and started working the oil all over.

"Damn, boo. You sure know how to please your man." Little did he know all that was about to change. Tyreke started to stroke the base of Craig's penis. He trembled and moaned softly.

Tyreke took his erect penis in his mouth and with lips sealed around it; he moved his head up and down in a slow rhythm. He looked up and saw that Craig was watching. This sent a tingly sensation down his back. This increased his excitement and he began to devour not just the penis, but everything else. Tyreke left no stone unturned. It was the last blow job Craig was to ever get from him.

Tyreke managed to sex him into a deep sleep. An hour had passed and Tyreke was ready for Craig to bounce. He slowly undid the restraints. Quietly he got dressed. He took one last look at Craig before he made his move.

Slapping Craig upside the head, he yelled, "Get up nigga! Let's go! It's time for you to gather your things and roll out of my house."

Craig didn't know what was going on. He looked up at Tyreke with confusion in his head. With grogginess in his voice he asked, "Man, what the hell is wrong with you?"

"You. That is what's wrong with me. Now get up, get your shit, and kick rocks motherfucka."

Craig lifted his body and sat up on the edge of the bed. In his own calm tone, he tried to keep cool. "Are you going to tell me what's this all about?"

"I'm tired of your shit, your games, your lies, and your controlling behavior. I'm point blank tired. I thought long and hard about this and I feel we need to end things."

"I see you tripping, so I'm going to get dress and leave. I'll give you a few days to calm yourself down. When I call, I expect you be ready to talk with some sense."

"I don't think you heard me clearly. It's over. We are finished. Done," Tyreke said with absolute certainty.

Craig stood up and came close to Tyreke's face. They stared each other down like two men ready to fight on the street.

"You are pathetic." Craig snapped. He pushed Tyreke so hard that he fell back into his TV stand before falling to the ground.

*No this nigga didn't just push me. This fool better be lucky my TV didn't fall over.* Even in the moment that was all Tyreke could think about.

Craig ran towards Tyreke and started kicking him in his side. He repeatedly stomped him in his stomach. Tyreke grabbed Craig by his right leg, causing him to stumble. Tyreke managed to get up from the floor and charged at Craig in a frantic rage. They began to throw serious punches at one another. Tyreke threw a punch to Craig's penis that made him buckle to his knees. Tyreke grabbed his knife from under the bed and pressed it hard up against Craig's neck, his face contorted in a manic expression.

"You have two choices on how you want to do this. You can voluntarily walk out that front door, or be carried out in a body bag. Take your pick." Tyreke said through clenched teeth.

Tyreke's behavior took Craig by surprise. Craig backed away from the knife, quickly got dressed and bounced out of Tyreke's crib without saying a word. As easy as it ended, no one was seriously hurt. There would be no need for any flashing red and blue lights that night, but Tyreke knew it was not the last he would see Craig again.

# Sin City

## 21

From the moment Rayne stepped off the plane at the
Louis Armstrong New Orleans International Airport, she
was welcomed by the cities unique charm. New Orleans was
known for its sexually-liberated feel and Rayne was
anticipating the next two days being spent there with Bryce.
After Rayne retrieved her luggage from the Delta Airlines
baggage claim carousel, she headed outside to catch a cab.
She was en route to the Hilton Garden Inn New Orleans
French Quarter/CBD hotel, which was nestled in the heart
of the Crescent City Central Business District. Bryce
arrived in New Orleans at six o'clock that morning because
he had an eight o'clock business meeting to attend. After
his meeting was over, he would meet Rayne in their room.

Rayne was admiring the view from the cab when it pulled
up in front of the twenty floor hotel. The driver helped her
with her luggage and she headed inside to check in. The
southern hospitality she was receiving was warm and
engaging. Bryce had already made their reservations so all
she had to do was pick up the key at the front desk and
head up to their room. She took the elevator to the 11th
floor where the uncommon lobby was located, but it offered
a spectacular view of the city. She surveyed the open lobby
which had a fire place, three plush mint green sofas and
two burgundy armchairs with a round end table in the
middle for accent. Fresh flower arrangements and
decorations were a special feature of the lobby. Rayne

looked over at the Pavilion Pantry making note of its variety of pre-packaged meals and beverages. Not that she and Bryce would need anything, it was just nice to make note of it anyway.

Fifteen minutes after checking in, Rayne walked into her one bedroom suite located on the twentieth floor and was immediately impressed with its décor. The room was inviting and relaxed with a sitting room just as you entered the guestroom. The sitting room had its own sofa sleeper, coffee table, club chair and ottoman, phone, television and work desk. As she continued to the room she passed the bathroom and entered into the immense bedroom area with high ceilings. The king size bed screamed out her name with its pearly white sheets and fluffy pillows that were stacked neatly against one another and gave an intimate feel of indulgence and sin. She would fulfill his fantasies and he would fulfill hers. A 36-inch flat screen TV sat on top of the dresser in front of the bed. Beside the bed and in front of the large windows that delivered natural light was an oversized reading chair with another ottoman, and work desk.

Rayne was feeling a little tired due to the jet lag, so she decided a nice hot shower was needed. She couldn't muster her head around the fact she was in New Orleans with a married man she knew for such a short time, anticipating another moment where her body would experience sucking and licking from every stroke of his tongue hitting her hot spots. She took off her laced red thongs, pulled her tank top over her head, and her back arched slightly as the thoughts of sensation sent pleasure through her body. She acknowledged the urgency of sex; and all of the other thoughts parading through her confused head. Two hours before she left Richmond to catch her flight, Rashard called her cell phone. She ignored the call and sent it straight to voice mail.

As the hot water pounded upon her soft flesh, Rayne pressed the instant-replay button in her mind, quickly reviewing her intimate moments with Bryce. Damn, that moment didn't last long as Rashard's face surfaced behind Bryce's, like two songs overlapping each other. As if by telepathy, Rashard knew she was thinking about another man. *Bryce...Rashard...Bryce..Rashard...*damn. Torn between temptation and true love. She couldn't fathom her emotions. But at that moment she was in a room created for ecstasy, and as wrong as it was, the only person she wanted to be with was Bryce.

While Rayne was wrestling with her emotions, Bryce was in the process of ending his business meeting on the twelfth floor of the hotel. He met with Jeff and Mike who were investors with Premier Financial Service. Bryce had known Mike for eight years and they done business together previously. Mike convinced Bryce to fly out to New Orleans to discuss a business opportunity that involved purchasing and redeveloping a 75 multi-family high rise homes. Although Bryce felt it was a little risky; he decided to go see if it would be a lucrative investment for his company. The gentlemen spent half their morning canvassing the property and the other half collaborating and negotiating. After crunching the figures and realizing the project could lead him into bankruptcy, Bryce decided not to go through with the deal. He could tell they weren't too pleased with his decision.

"Thanks man for coming out to meet with us. Too bad we couldn't make this deal happen." Mike said, extending his hand to shake Bryce's.

Jeff followed suit, "Yeah, it's too bad. It was a good meeting you."

"Thanks guys. I'm sure there will be other deals on the table."

Bryce picked up his notepad from the conference table and directed his attention towards Mike. "Hey man, when I get back to Atlanta I'll be sure to look you up so we can catch up. It's been a long time since we swung those golf sticks around. I remember it was me that kicked your butt the last time."

Mike laughed, "Ahh man, you got jokes. Don't forget I let you beat me. I'm looking forward to it. You know how to look me up. Tell the wife and kids I said hello. Maybe I and Diane can come out for the holidays."

"That sounds good and tell Diane I said hello." Bryce said, as they bumped fists.

Bryce was heading to the elevators when his cell phone

started ringing and stopped him in his tracks. He removed the phone from his side and looked down at the number before answering it. It's like she knew the perfect time to call.

"Hey, baby. I'm so glad to hear your voice."

"I'm so glad to hear your voice too. Are you still working?"

Her voice put a smile on his face.

"Actually your timing couldn't have been more perfect. My meeting just ended ten minutes ago."

"Great. How was your meeting?"

"It went great, considering the fact I decided not to invest. I felt taking on that venture would be a huge financial risk."

"Well, you're a smart business man and you know what's best for the company. FYI, I miss you like crazy. I couldn't get any work done because my mind was preoccupied with lustful thoughts all day. I can't wait to show you all the freaky things I conjured up."

"Trust and believe I've been thinking about you too and I hope those dirty thoughts were about me."

"No. Actually they were about Idris Elba," she added playfully, her voice taking on a flirtatious timber.

"Don't get Idris hurt." Bryce laughed.

"By the way, how is Mike?"

"He's doing great. He sends his hello. He's hoping he and Diane can make it to Atlanta to visit for the holidays."

"That sounds great. I can't wait to see them again. I know you two already have plans made for tonight and tomorrow."

"Just for tomorrow but not tonight."

"Well that's strange. So what are you about to do now?"

*Damn, why did she have to ask that question? A lie would have sufficed.* Bryce figured he'd been lying thus far, one more wouldn't hurt.

His eyes trailed towards the elevator.

"Umm...I'm tired so I didn't feel like doing anything tonight. I told Mike we have plenty time to catch up tomorrow. The only thing I want to do is take a hot shower, change into something comfortable, order me some food, and then watch a little television."

"And…"

"And…what?"

"You're not going to call me so we can have phone sex?"

"Well, that's something we have never done before." Bryce said, surprised by her openness.

"It doesn't hurt to try something new every now and then. We have to spice up things a bit."

"I love the way that sounds. You know I'm all for that. Let me guess, you been reading those Zane books again?"

"No silly." She giggled like a school girl with a crush.

"I should be heading upstairs so I can get settled. I'll call you within the next few hours."

"I'll be waiting. I love you."

"I love you to. Kiss the kids for me and tell them I love them."

Bryce ended the call, and a twinge of guilt hit him for lying to his wife. It's like the cliché goes, *'when the cats away, the mouse will play.'* As much as Bryce loved his wife and didn't want to hurt her, he was captivated by Rayne. Moments with her were so carefree and forbidden. That's how it is in life; we want what we can't have. Curiosity always kills the cat, but Bryce like the way this cat purred. Bryce was curious so he crossed those boundaries, drawn into unadulterated fantasy, the taste of her sweet nectar held him captured in temptation. Carelessly, not taking heed to the web of destruction that could cause him his marriage, Bryce was torn. He had selfishly broken his vows: to love, honor and cherish. He pressed the up button to the elevator, it was too late to turn back now, and his clandestine beauty was waiting. Rayne was waiting to be pleasured, and he was happy to fulfill her desires.

# Pure Pleasure

## 22

That evening Bryce had a special night planned for
Rayne. He tried to get his conversation with his wife out his
mind so that he could enjoy the evening. He had made
reservations for them to dine at the most exquisite Creole
restaurant called Arnaud's. He had heard great things
about the restaurant. He quickly scooped Rayne into his
arms when he entered the room, and immediately
persuaded her to join him at Arnaud's. He needed to
refocus and lingering around the room while his wife's offer
for phone sex would be detrimental.

He was thrilled that Rayne did not protest. They took in
the beautiful sights of the city and teased each other with
soft touches and warm kisses, as they headed to the eatery.
Arnaud's was simply elegant with its Italian mosaic tile
floors. The sparkling glass windows reflected the glow of the
crystal chandeliers. After a five minute wait, they were
seated and started engaging in an intimate and personal
conversation until they were ready to order their food.

Rayne ordered the Shrimp Creole which was simmered in
spicy tomato sauce and Creole vegetables, served with a
side of rice pilaf. Bryce ordered the Veal Tournedos Chantal
served with wild mushroom sauce, accompanied with
savory risotto. To make the night even more special was the
live music from Arnaud's Jazz Bistro. They enjoyed the rest
of the night with great food, laughter, and great music.
Rayne felt all tingly inside; like a high school girl with her

first crush.

Four hours later, after an exquisite dinner and non-stop dancing, they were back at the hotel standing inside of a closed elevator. Bryce pushed the button to the twentieth floor. Rayne had a slight buzz. He stood in front of her, his sexy smile made her heart flutter; his soft lips brushed across hers before his tongue heatedly explored her mouth.

"Yes," he moaned faintly in her ear as he cupped her hardened breasts with his firm hands through the fabric of her dress. She could feel her entire body come to life and it brought with it an aching within her very soul.

He slowly ground his stiff erection against her legs and she moaned sweetly and softly. His tongue traveled around her earlobes in circles. His passion was thuggish. She loved a man who took charge.

He eased her legs apart, slowly moved his hands up her skirt, gradually revealing her thighs, and then pulled her thong to the side. He teased her swollen clit with his thumb. It felt so good and intoxicating. He teased her until she begged for penetration.

"I want you... I want you inside me so bad. I want you now."

His finger found its way to paradise, her wetness covering him like a warm blanket.

*Ooh baby keep going and don't stop* was all her mind was saying. The cat had her tongue, but the opening of the elevator had caught her attention.

"Bryce. Bryce." Rayne quickly pushed his hand from under her skirt. "We have company," she whispered in his ear.

He was so preoccupied giving her pleasure that he did not realize the elevator had not only stopped, but opened as well. An elderly white couple stepped inside the elevator. Rayne could see the displeasing look on the gray haired woman. Rayne proceeded to smooth out her pencil skirt, her face flushed with embarrassment. Bryce flashed the couple a smile, trying to avoid eye contact. The elderly woman constantly gave them distasteful looks and snarled. Rayne didn't like her judgmental attitude. She does not know me and I don't think she wants to get to know me. They finally reached their floor and she couldn't wait to get out the old bitty's sight. As they headed off the elevator, Rayne flipped the bird to the old lady. The elevator started to close and she could hear her gasp in shock from her inappropriate behavior. Rayne knew what she did was wrong, but it was still funny as hell. Bryce and Rayne laughed all the way to their room.

"You know you were wrong for flipping the bird to that old lady."

"Well she should have minded her own damn business and kept her stank looks to herself."

Bryce put his arms around Rayne's waist. "Enough of the chit chat, let's finish what we started."

Once inside the room, Rayne was completely in shock. The room illuminated a romantic feel. There were rose petals from the door trailing to the bedroom area. Two wine glasses, a bottle of red wine, a bowl of strawberries and whipped cream sat on a folding dining table, and jazz played in the background.

Rayne looked at Bryce with a pleasing look. "How did you manage to arrange all this?"

"Oh, I made arrangements with the night housekeeper."

"So now you're friends with the housekeepers?" Rayne said jokingly, pinching Bryce in the arm.

"Ouch that hurt." Bryce said grabbing his arm. "Come here woman and let me make something else hurt." He pulled Rayne close to his body and began to unbutton her blouse exposing her breasts. Her nipples were at full attention. Before he could put her breast into his mouth, she pulled away from his embrace.

"Wait one minute. I have a little friend who wants to join us."

"A friend?" his curiosity painted his face.

Rayne retrieved a pink jack rabbit vibrator and a pair of handcuffs from her suitcase. Bryce's eyes widened.

"You plan on doing some freaky shit tonight, huh?" he laughed.

"I figured we could add a little excitement to our night."

"I don't need any help from your little friend. I think I can handle this all by myself."

Rayne walked towards Bryce, unzipped his pants, massaged his penis, and whispered seductively into his ear,

"You ready for some intense pleasure?"

"I've been ready. Bend your fine ass over." Bryce smacked Rayne's ass so hard she jumped. He removed her thong then took the vibrator from her hand and put it under skirt, rubbing the plastic head across her aching clit. "That's it baby, keep that ass bent over like that," he said, then slid down on the floor and lifted her skirt above her knees. He dug his hands into her ass and started to suck the hell out of her clit. That felt so good that Rayne pushed his head into her fiery flesh as hard as she could. The licking and sucking intensified and Rayne began to buckle at her knees. Bryce sent her body into a whirl spin, forcing her to clutch the bed comforter tightly as her orgasm released. She watched her juices explode down on his face.

Bryce helped Rayne out of her dress then laid her down on the bed. He stood over her admiring her beautiful figure. She was ready to be taken to new heights of erotica. He began to take off his shirt and dropped it to the floor. He then took off his pants and boxers, and his thick chocolate pole hung. He walked over to the table and removed the bowl of strawberries and cream. He parted her lips to her universe, placed a strawberry inside her wet fold, decorating her canvas even more with whipped cream. He ate Rayne like she was strawberry shortcake.

After Bryce savored her sex, his tongue made a pathway from her belly button, working its way up to her breasts. He lavished her breasts. He circled his tongue around her erect nipple and bit down on it, and her body jerked. He put her hands behind her back and placed the handcuffs around her wrists. This aroused her into a state of ecstasy. He turned her around on her stomach, "get on your knees," he demanded.

Rayne did as she was told and he repeatedly smacked her ass real hard. It was pain. Pain was pleasure. Rayne let out a loud long moan that left her breathless. Her ass was sore, but she wanted him to keep going. She let him have his way with every inch of her body. She heard the humming sound of her vibrator from behind. He spread her legs farther apart, and she welcomed the plastic replica of a male's penis. He pushed that vibrator deep in her pussy as far as it would go. The vibration made her shake with pleasure. She tried to grab that plastic penis with her pussy muscles. Bryce removed the vibrator and from behind he shoved his penis so deep inside her, a loud squeal escaped her lips. She screamed his name repeatedly so loud, she was certain the neighbors knew his name. His girth stretched her insides as he was fucking the hell out of her. He was abusing her insides with his deep plunges, and if that was considered a crime, then he should be arrested. Arrested for giving her pussy so much pleasure. An orgasm took over her body like a demonic being. Orgasms moved through that room like a hurricane. Orgasms took away Rayne's pain. Her mind was free. Her body was free. She allowed Bryce to dive into the depths of her soul with his every stroke. All reality was thrown out the window for that moment and she dived into a fantasy.

Finally, after hours of pure pleasure, Rayne and Bryce collapsed into each other's arms. Rayne was full off of pleasure. She closed her eyes and let go.

# The Devil is a Liar

# 23

***A month later...***
    It was a Thursday evening and Rashard was leaving American Family Fitness on Brook Road. He didn't feel like cooking when he got home so he decided to call Applebee's for carry out. He ordered his favorite, Cajun Shrimp Pasta. It would only take him ten minutes to get to the restaurant which was only five minutes away from his condo at the Villas at Virginia Center Commons. Rashard pulled up in the carryout parking space; and sat for five minutes before a blonde, petite, tall, cute in the face employee came out to his car carrying his food.
    "How are you doing sir? You ordered the Cajun Shrimp Pasta? That will be $12.74."
    "Thank you," Rashard said and handed her his platinum American Express credit card."
    "I'll be right back with your receipt." She handed Rashard his pasta and walked off.
    While he waited, he contentedly inspected his food to make sure his order was right.
    "Here you go sir." The waitress handed him his receipt Rashard signed the receipt then handed it back to her.
    "Thank you and have a good night."
    "You do the same." Rashard smiled.
    Rashard couldn't remember the last time he was in the gym as he climbed the six flights of stairs to his condo.

Legs, arms, calves, thighs, and his gluteus maximus were all incredibly sore.

He opened the front door, deactivated his alarm system and flicked on the lamp that sat on his end table. He slowly walked towards his dining room table when his cell phone went off alerting him he had a text message. He sat his food on the table and pulled his cell phone from his shorts pocket. Rashard gazed at the strange text, mystified by the verbiage that came across as suspicious.

*I need to see you. You need to know it was a set up.*
*If you want to know the truth; meet me tomorrow at the Starbucks inside Barnes and Noble on Broad Street.*

Rashard responded to the text which led to a brief but strange conversation.

*Who is this?*
*Don't worry about who I am. You'll find out soon enough.*
*What type of game are you playing?*
*No game. If you want to know the truth either you will meet me or not.*
*How will I know who are you are?*
*Trust me you will know.*
*And if I don't come.*
*Then you will never know the truth. The decision is yours.*

Rashard was curious to know who was behind the mysterious text, and what truth he needed to know. Morning couldn't come fast enough. It was after midnight and Rashard kept tossing and turning thinking about the bizarre text message he received. He grabbed his remote control from the night stand and cut on his television. He didn't want to hear the sound so he hit the mute button. He couldn't sleep. He wasn't watching the TV, it was watching him. He just stared at the ceiling, thinking about what could be about to happen in his life now. His mind was racing and he started to fume over how his life changed dramatically over the past year. It wasn't fair that he had to lose the two most important women in his life. Unfortunately, when it came to his mother he couldn't question God. Everyone had a number and when it's their time to go, they must be prepared and have their life in order. Although the loss of his mother hurt so much, at least he knew she was no longer suffering and that her soul

147

was finally resting in peace. She was in a better place and knowing she was in the hands of a loving and merciful God made his heart smile.

He reflected on the funeral, the last time he had seen or spoken to Rayne. He felt so lonely and empty without her by his side. He knew he had hurt her in the worse way, and her seeing Rachel and Moses at the funeral just pushed the stake deeper in her already wounded heart. The look in Rayne's eyes after her physical confrontation with Rachel at the funeral solidified what he had feared: there was no way in hell he was getting her back. Even though his mother's funeral was not the appropriate place for Rayne and Rachel to be fighting, he was glad Rachel got what she deserved. However, killing Rachel would have been a splendid idea. Causing him to lose Rayne would substantiate for his irrational sense of judgment. Besides, knowing he still had to deal with Rachel and Moses was not serving his life any justice. Rashard tried several times after the funeral to reach out to Rayne, but she snubbed his vain attempts.

Rashard was still restless from his lack of sleep. He turned his tired body towards his nightstand. The alarm clock! Are you freaking kidding me! He focused his half opened eyes to the large red numbers that read 7:30a.m. He reached his arm out and slapped the button on the alarm that was making an unwelcomed racket. He sank his head back into the pillow; closing both eyes tightly for fifteen more minutes before getting up. He stepped into the steamy shower, lathered his washcloth with his Irish Spring soap, and then leisurely washed his tired body from head to toe. He scrubbed every inch of his body three times. The water beating against his skin was starting to wake him up.

Rashard generously applied Aveeno lotion over his body, massaging it into his skin. His skin felt as smooth as a baby's bottom. Rashard eased into his Sean John jeans, and a white polo with his company's logo, and pulled on his Red Oak Mesa Leather steel toe boots. He took another thirty minutes drinking a cup of coffee and reading the sports section of the Richmond Times Dispatch. Once he was done, he grabbed his keys and headed to the office.

At eleven o'clock Rashard left his office so that he could stop by the Virginia Credit Union on Glenside Drive to deposit several of the company's receipts. With haste, he drove to Barnes and Noble on Broad Street and arrived ten minutes early to meet the person behind the puzzling text. He looked around the bookstore until he spotted the Starbucks on the right hand side of the store. He headed straight towards the café, looking around to see if he recognized a familiar face. He found an empty seat nestled in the corner and sat down, continued to stare at the faces of strangers sipping on coffee while reading a book or magazine. There was a Black Enterprise magazine sitting on the table, so he decided to read it while he waited. He was so deep in thought, that he was startled when he looked up to see a familiar face in disguise. Her face was almost completely hidden by a wide brimmed hat and sunglasses. Rashard was unbearably bewildered. He was still able to recognize her. *Why is she hiding behind a disguise?* Rashard thought to himself.

"What's with the shades and hat?" he asked.

She spoke softly. "My appearance is irrelevant. What I need to say to you is important." She appeared to be nervous as she took a seat across from Rashard.

He watched her with wide eyes. Her nervous energy was boundless. She sat down, fidgeted with her hands and kept looking over her shoulders. She was on edge and he could sense her tension. She finally removed her hat and sunshades, and laid them on the table. Her hair was pulled back in a ponytail and by the looks of her face, Rashard could tell she'd been crying; her large eyes were all red and puffy.

He looked into her dismal eyes and spoke in a curious tone. "You seem to be nervous about something. What's wrong with you, and who are you hiding from?"

She didn't answer him. She noticed how he was studying her face. She quickly looked down at the table. Her bottom lip began to tremble and tears began to roll down her cheeks.

Rashard asked wryly, "What is this all about?"

"I had to see you in person. I have been agonizing over this for a long time, and I don't think I can keep the truth from you any longer. Please don't hate me for what I'm about to tell you."

Rashard couldn't take the suspense anymore. "Please, just spit out what you have to say."

Everything around him started to fade away as he sat listening to the horrid details of her betrayal. He was shocked and speechless. He wanted to snap, but his body felt paralyzed. He couldn't believe what he was hearing. The more she revealed, the more anger began to manifest and he began to sweat profusely. He felt he had just been hit by a train with her words. At that moment, it felt like he had died and was attending his own funeral. She had set him up, and came to him to reveal her ugly secret. Their ugly secret. When she was done she started to cry profusely. Rashard grimaced but didn't say a word. He felt no sympathy towards her. Fuck her feelings! She had deceived him in the worst way.

"I don't fucking believe you."

"It's all true. I wish I was lying, but I'm not."

"Now...all of a sudden, after all these years, you want to have a guilty conscious. Do you realize the damage you have caused? My life has been a total hell because of you!"

Rashard reached out and grabbed her sunglasses, disintegrated them in his hands.

She looked down at the mangled sunglasses. His anger made her nervous, the deranged look in his eyes as if he wanted to devour her, had her on the edge of her seat in panic.

Rashard pounded his fist on the table. People began to stare; he had interrupted their reading. Words couldn't express how he was feeling at that very moment.

Rashard kicked the chair from up under him and left Barnes and Noble temporarily disoriented. The nauseating feeling he felt made him shudder uncontrollably. He cursed. His anger turned into a new feeling; murderous rage. All he could think about was Rayne. His marriage was maliciously destroyed and he desperately wanted revenge. Even with the truth, would it be enough to win Rayne back? So much damage had been done. Now he too had a secret.

Secrets have a way of eating at the soul. No matter what the motivation is for secrecy or how hard we try to hide secrets, there are always repercussions. Someone has to face the consequences. Although we lie in order to protect

150

the feelings of those we don't want to hurt, at some point we will eventually have to release those skeletons from their closets. As Rashard sped to his destination, he remembered reading a quote by Guatama Siddhartha, the Buddha, that said, "Three things cannot long stay hidden: the sun, the moon and the **truth.**"

# Consequences & Repercussions

## 24

Rashard felt an adrenaline rush as he pulled up at the Back Door. He had known deep down in his heart that Troy had something to do with his marriage falling apart. He stormed inside the club and was greeted by an overwhelming smell of marijuana. Two strippers walked passed him wearing revealing outfits that accentuated their curvaceous bodies, but left nothing to the imagination.

As Rashard raced down the hall in a huff he could hear loud music coming from behind one of the closed doors. He was headed towards Troy's office when he felt a hand touch his shoulder, and heard a deep husky voice from behind.

"Yo, my man, you seem a little lost. Can I help you with something?"

Rashard turned around and came face to face with a heavy set, tall bouncer looking type dude. He sized him up before responding. "I'm not lost. I'm going to see Troy."

The heavy set dude eyed Rashard up and down, and then exhaled a puff of smoke in the air from his cigar. "Do you have an appointment?"

Rashard was getting irritated. "No. I'm his cousin."

"Right this way," dude waved his right arm into his direction for Rashard to follow him.

The bouncer knocked on the door before entering.

"Who is it?" Troy asked from the other side of the closed door.

"It's Boss Hogg. You got company."

He wasn't lying when he said hog. Don't know about the

boss, but he damn sure was a hog.

"Come in."

Troy looked away from his computer. From the look on Rashard's face, he knew his visit was not a social call.

"You need anything chief before I go?"

"Naw, I'm good. Just shut the door behind you. I'll call you if I need you." Troy said, with his eyes hooked on Rashard.

Boss Hogg gave Rashard another look up and down before he left the office.

Troy leaned back in his chair and crossed his arms. He propped the sole of one shoe against the edge of his desk. "What brings you to this neck of the woods?"

"You still the same conniving, manipulative bastard. You didn't think I wasn't going to find out, huh?" The contempt in Rashard's voice sounded like roaring thunder. The anger inside of him started to come alive. He was ready to pounce on Troy like a wildcat.

Troy's lips quirked up into a smirk. He started clapping his hands together as if Rashard just made a grand speech, amused by his insult. He had a smug look on his face. "Cuz, you got balls talking to me like that. For what it's worth, I'm going to let it slide since I don't know what the fuck you talking about."

"You know damn well what I'm talking about. I know you and Rachel set me up that night. You managed to slip something into my drink that caused me to lose consciousness. Then you took me to your apartment and made it look like Rachel and I slept together by taking pictures of me and her in bed. I knew something wasn't right when I woke up at your apartment. I never wanted to believe that bull shit story you said about me being too drunk to drive home. You never gave a fuck about me. You have always been jealous of me. All these years you detested me and Rayne being together. You took advantage of me that night because your intentions were to break us up so you could have Rayne. You were always in love with her. You created an opportunity to take her. You and Rachel knew sending those pictures to Rayne would be enough to send her over the edge. I can believe Rachel having something to do with your ridiculous scheme because she's a scandalous bitch. To add insult to injury, Moses is not even my son. You're his father."

Rashard moved closer towards Troy, lips pursed, and his fists tightly clenched in anger. He locked eyes with Troy as they contemplated each other's next move.

With a sudden rage of hostility, Troy jumped up from his chair. "I find it ironic you come into my place of business and confront me with some bullshit story you made up. You got one helluva nerve to think you can talk to me like that. I suggest you turn around and walk out of my office before you get hurt."

"You know I'm telling the truth. You pissed off because I found out. Stay the fuck away from Rayne!" Rashard said through clenched teeth.

"Don't hate the fact Rayne and I have become very close. I give her what she wants and what she needs. Just ask her about that night at her apartment. Ask her how I had my tongue so deep into her pussy that I sucked the fuck out of her until she squirted cum. I guarantee you never made her squirt the way I did. Watching her body jerk back and forth was amazing."

Troy's taunting words detonated in Rashard's ear. Rashard couldn't listen to stories about Rayne having sex with Troy; knowing they were cousins. He wanted to kill Troy. Would he get twenty years or life? It circled around his brain like a marathon, his intent to get rid of the man who destroyed his marriage. Troy's snarkiness was like a constant jab to his ego. His cynicism forced Rashard to become volatile.

"You son of bitch!" Rashard snarled.

Like a speed of lightening, he leaped towards Troy knocking him to the floor. The two men scuffled, but Rashard got the best of Troy and punched him in his face. It was like watching a Heathcliff episode in Troy's office. Legs, arms, feet were in the air, as they threw blows at one another. A gush of blood splattered from Troy's lips. Rashard exploded like a ticking bomb. He continuously beat the shit out of him. Troy was struggling to handle him.

Boss Hogg must have heard the commotion inside the office because he bolted through the door and charged towards Rashard. He snatched him off of Troy, who lay on the floor defensively. His face was so bloody, and two teeth fell from his mouth. Boss Hogg had Rashard in a tight grip.

Rashard watched as Troy struggled to get off the floor. "I can assure you low down motherfucka, you and Rachel will not get away with this. You both will pay for the pain you caused me." Rashard spat.

Rashard's threat had halted Troy. Even though he was in so much pain, he managed to say with a sly grin on his face, "All is fair in love and war."

Rashard yanked himself away from Boss Hogg and quickly exited Troy's office. He knew if he had stayed any longer he definitely would have committed murder.

# If I can't have you no one can

# 25

It was midnight when Troy arrived home from the club holding a bag of ice on his face, His head was spinning like a windmill, and his mouth was in excruciating pain. Troy threw his keys on top of the table that sat in his foyer adjacent to the dining room and slowly walked towards his mini bar. His bar was filled with all kinds of alcoholic beverages from Patrón, Grey Goose, Paul Mason, Hennessey, Absolut Vodka, Ciroc, Bacardi, to José Cuervo and more. He needed something strong to help dissipate his crushed pride, battered ego, and relieve the pain that danced through his face. He poured himself a shot of Patrón, grabbed the bottle and collapsed on the sofa. He raised the glass to his aching lip. Troy hated Rashard and vowed that he would make him pay. The next time Rashard would be carried away in a body bag.

Troy sat the bottle and shot glass down on the coffee table. He pulled off his Air Jordan sneakers and gulped down another shot of Patrón. The excessive shots of alcohol led him into a wonderfully deep sleep, where his thoughts and his desires were pleasured. A knock at the door aroused his jaded state of mind as he wondered who was knocking at his door. He wasn't expecting any company. In a drunken stupor, Troy struggled from the sofa and dragged his body to the door.

"Who is it?" Troy slurred with question.

No one answered, without looking through the peephole,

Troy opened the door and his eyes widened with shock at the sight of Rayne standing at his front door. He had to play it cool, because he didn't know what her intentions were. He wasn't sure if Rashard had gotten to her with the truth. She didn't appear to be angry, so this eased his mind a little.

"Rayne, what brings you here so late at night?"

Instead of saying a word, Rayne gracefully strutted towards the living room. The smell of her perfume aroused Troy's senses even more. She stood in front of the sofa and held up a bottle of Moscato in her hand. He shut the door and when he turned around he got the surprise of his life. His heart began to palpitate, and he could feel the blood rush to his dick.

Rayne was standing with her trench coat open. Her sexy smile was seductive, and her hour shaped figure was fully exposed. She was naked and wearing a pair of red stiletto pumps. Troy's imagination ran wild as erotica began to overtake him.

He couldn't help but wonder if she was setting him up. *Is she fucking with my mind?* He needed to know what kind of game she was playing. Before he could ask her what her intentions were, Rayne placed her finger in her mouth and began to sway her hips from side to side. She had Troy hypnotized with her seductive rhythm. He wanted to know if she tasted as good as she smelled so he pounced on her like a True Blood vampire. He couldn't control his urges any longer. Rayne teased him in the worst way. He repeatedly kissed her neck with soft kisses, and then he began to lick her as if she was a Tootsie Roll lollipop. Indeed, she tasted sweet like candy.

He removed her trench coat and began to fondle and suck her breasts until sweet moans escaped from her lips. Rayne's moans reverberated throughout the room mixing well with Troy's heavy breathing. Even though he was a little suspicious, he knew the moment was once in a lifetime. He didn't want to mess it up, so he had to see how far he could go. Troy slowly eased her down on the sofa and spread her legs a part revealing a welcoming pussy. He buried his head between her thighs and began to feast on her like his aunt's southern fried chicken. His hands

fondled her breasts and he pinched her nipples as he
moved his tongue in and out of her wetness. His lips gently
sucked her labia as he placed two fingers inside of her to
increase the pleasure. Rayne rotated her hips to the rhythm
of his tongue, so he placed in a third finger to up the
tempo. He slurped up her juices enjoying her sweet taste
like a 7-Eleven cherry slurpee. Rayne let out soft whimpers
and moans as she grabbed the back of Troy's head pressing
his face harder between her thighs. She wanted his tongue
to go deeper. The deeper his tongue got, the harder her
body began to shiver. After about twenty minutes of
pleasuring her with his fingers and tongue, he asked her to
turn over. Rayne did as she was told and was on her hands
and knees in the doggie style position. Troy took the
Moscato from off the coffee table, opened it up and took a
sip from the bottle. Rayne gasped when he poured a trail
down the crease of her back. The wine traveled down to her
ass cheeks. Troy's tongue trailed from her back to the folds
of her anus, his tongue like a vibrating penis, her body
quivered with delight. Rayne clutched the pillows in her
fists.

In between her panting Rayne said, "I want you inside
me. I want you now."

Troy thought he had just won the mega million lottery.
He was grinning from ear to ear. He rubbed his penis up
and down the folds of her anus before piercing her wetness;
he desperately wanted to feel her insides. He wanted to take
his time with every stroke. As he stirred his penis inside her
like he was stirring a cup of coffee, Troy's fingers dug into
her ass, pushing hard against her resisting muscles that
hugged him in welcome. He kept moving his fingers, going
in and out, teasing her muscles into submission. Rayne
cried out in pleasure; the double stimulation was too much
for her to bear. The amazing feeling of being sexed by Troy
felt too good to be stopped. Rayne decided to shift gears
which excited Troy, moving with ferocity, cuing him to pick
up the pace. She demanded more and he gave her more.
Rayne bucked wildly and her eyes rolled to the back of her
head from her pussy and anus being beat into exquisite
pleasure. He desired this woman. He loved every minute
they were sharing—that was until he heard a sound and

knew they were not alone.

Troy was alarmed beyond words. He looked up and saw Rashard standing over them. Rashard's presence made Troy's penis go limp. He pulled out of Rayne and slightly shoved her away from him.

"You were so anxious to stick your dick inside of my wife that you forgot to lock your front door." Rashard snarled with a terrible look of disdain on his face.

"Oh my God, Rashard!" Rayne jumped up from the sofa and grabbed her trench coat to cover up. She hated that Rashard caught her in an indecent position. She could see the hurt in his soulful eyes.

A single tear ran down Rashard's face. He despised Troy even more. He pulled out a .25 and pointed it back and forth between Rayne and Troy. Rashard felt a rage flaring inside of him; a rage so powerful that he couldn't believe he was ready and willing to shoot Rayne.

Rayne let out a loud scream. Troy did not fluster at the sight of the gun. In-fact, he was quite amused by Rashard's behavior. He let out a chuckle then asked, "What are you going to do? Shoot us both because you caught me fucking your ex-wife?"

"You're one cocky bastard. You think this is funny? Nigga, we not on *Who's Got Jokes*. I'm going to take real pleasure in shooting you." Rashard snarled.

"Rashard, please don't do this." Rayne pleaded.

"SHUT UP, you trifling whore!" Rashard snapped, pointing the gun in Rayne's direction.

Rayne was lost for words. Her whole life began to flash before her eyes. The sight of the gun and the cold look in Rashard's eyes terrified her. She began to cry.

"Come on man, put the gun down. Can't you see she's scared to death? What you have to prove by killing—."

Rashard cut Troy off midsentence. "Let me think." Rashard paused for a brief moment. "I'll kill you for being a backstabbing, crab nigga, and I'll get the pleasure out of killing her for betraying me with you. Does that answer your question?"

Troy could see the fire blazing in Rashard's eyes. He knew death was impending.

Rashard waved the gun back and forth, contemplating

159

which one of them he would shoot first.

"Rashard. Baby please. You don't have to do this. Put the gun down and let's talk about this. I'm so sorry," Rayne whined.

"Fuck this! Don't plead with this—."

Before Troy could finish his remark, Rashard cut loose two shots that went straight to Troy's skull.

Troy jerked awake. He was covered with sweat and he could feel his heart beating at a rapid pace. He pulled himself together, only to realize he was having a dreadful nightmare. He snapped back to reality, feeling a little disappointed. He was mad as hell that Rashard invaded his dream. Damn, what he would give to have that moment with Rayne. It was that same moment that almost happened before Rayne's sudden case of morality.

The ceiling fan was spinning and the room was cool. The aching pain from his swollen face, and the fact that Rashard was the cause of it, aroused his fury again. The first thing that came to his mind was that there was hell to pay and certain people had to be dealt with.

Troy eased off the sofa onto his feet and wiggled his toes into the posh nude area rug in front of his antique brown leather sofa. The softness felt good against his feet. He wished his face felt as good at that moment. He scuffled across the room towards his bedroom to retrieve a bottle of Tylenol from his dresser. A gold heart shape locket caught his eye. He opened it and ran his finger across the picture of him and his mother inside. Tears filled his eyes. He was shaken by the memory of the last time he had seen his mother.

The sound of his mother's merciless screams and cries had awakened him. He followed her screams and cries all the way to her bedroom, where the door was cracked. He stood just outside the door and witnessed the most inhumane display of human torture.

His father hovered over his mother with a lighter in his hand, repeatedly flicking it, taunting her; as he listened to her beg for her life. His mother's feet and hands were duct taped to the bed posts. She tried to wiggle herself loose, but to no avail. His father would dance around the bed, laughing, taunting, flicking the lighter, as if he was playing musical chairs; because when he stopped he would put the burning flames up against her feet, then start all over again. The next time it was another part of her exposed body getting burned.

Troy watched in horror. He couldn't believe his daddy would take his cruelty so far. He was scared. Troy knew when he flew into a rage, it was like a beast being let lose. He was an abusive man, but that night his behavior was psychotic. Troy felt helpless as he stood paralyzed. As he continued to watch and listen, it was his father's words that scared him to the very core of his soul.

"Please, Joe...don't do this...it hurts so bad...please...please think about what this is going to do to Troy if he loses his mother," she said, pleading in between her desperate cries.

"Fuck that little nigga! Why should he care about losing a junkie for a mother? He ain't my son anyway! When I'm finish with you, I'm going to burn his little ass too!"

With those last words, Joe sat his mother's feet on fire. Her screams sounded like tortured souls gone to hell. When she turned her head towards Troy's direction, their eyes locked. Even through her distress, she still looked beautiful. The screams stopped, a slight smile spread across her face, and her loving caramel eyes stopped shedding tears. Without any sound coming from her voice, Troy could clearly read the words that silently escaped from her lips, "Baby, I'm so sorry. I love you."

When Troy looked away, he saw Joe staring at him with a grimace. With all the strength he could muster, Troy bolted from the house and ran to the neighbors to get help. When he came back with help, his home was engulfed with flames with his mother still tied up inside.

Since his mother's death, he harbored utter disdain for the man he thought was his father. He was eight years old that night he found out Joe was not his biological father. Joe ripped his mother out of his life. He was never given the chance to ask his mother about his real father. He still doesn't even know his name. Although he was adopted by his aunt and uncle, he still felt his life was not complete without his mother in it.

The sound of Troy's cell phone intruded his stroll down memory lane. It was for the best. Reliving his mother's demise felt like someone was taking a knife and cutting out his heart. He was all choked up, but had to pull it together before he answered his call.

"Hello," Troy barked through the phone.

"It's me. I got your message. You said it was urgent you needed to meet with me."

"Indeed. I need a favor."

"What kind of favor?"

"Not over the phone. Meet me at the club tomorrow and I'll give you all the details then."

"For sho'. I'll be there. Later."

Troy hung up the phone. He gave himself a long hard stare in the mirror. His tears were a silent language of his grief. Troy always hid behind his emotions like a mask. Hiding behind that mask only shielded his life of despair. He knew once Rayne found out about his betrayal, winning her heart would be hopeless. He was a walking tortured soul. Love, resentment, hate, flowed through his blood like a river. He resented the man who killed his mother and took her away from him. He had mad love for Rayne and what he felt for her was enormous. He hated the one person standing in his way. He was destined to get rid of him. Two tears in a bucket, Troy had an agenda, and if he couldn't have Rayne then no one could.

# Distant Replay

## 26

    The soft, gentle flames of the fireplace created an ambience of romance, intimacy and togetherness. You could barely hear the soft jams that were playing from the CD because the rain was beating ferociously up against the window pane. Bryce's tongue was trailing along Rayne's arm, neck, shoulders. While the sounds of moans echoed throughout the room, there was a sound of the strong winds blowing through the trees and the rumble of thunder. Bryce cupped Rayne's breasts with his firm hands, his tongue danced in circles around her nipples, licked...pinched...fed on her hardness like chocolate covered raisins. Lightning struck. Bryce gripped the bottom of Rayne's ass, lifted her slightly off the floor, he bent down and licked her slit from top to bottom tasting her sex. He felt a little tremble run up her legs. His tongue teased her in the worse way, avoiding penetration. He stroked her throbbing clit with his finger before he licked around it and sucked it softly. He lapped at it greedily sensing her enjoyment as he pulled away intermittently. He made a pathway of kisses from her inner thigh bringing her feet to his mouth. Kissed, licked, and sucked her toes, while he rubbed his dick up and down her moist opening. Rayne whined for stimulation as she grinded her pelvis against his shaft. He decided to put her out of her misery and began to tongue her wetness slowly and thoroughly, no area was left undisclosed. As he massaged her inner thighs and continued with his oral pleasure, Rayne massaged her

163

breasts. She pinched at her nipples and traced circles around her tender soft areola. Bryce penetrated Rayne's pussy.

Rayne moaned and screamed. She cried out to the heavens as Bryce kept penetrating her in an aggressive manner.

"Ahh, yes," Rayne cooed. "Gimme this dick!" she screamed.

Bryce pumped in an out harder and faster. "Damn, this is some good pussy." Bryce stated with such conviction.

They were so busy exchanging pleasure on her living room floor that they hardly heard the thunderstorm that screamed and swept through the sky. They were making noises of their own. Couldn't tell who was the loudest. Bryce was fucking her so intense. It was aggressive. It was magnificent. She told him not to stop. She begged him to fuck her until she was breathless. And so he did. He sexed her like a wild animal.

Rayne's pussy was on fire and her orgasm was building fast. Bryce was giving her all he had to offer. He loved how Rayne was keeping up with his pace. This excited him even more. He reached down and grabbed a lock of Rayne's hair as her pussy muscles tightened with so much force, the friction so powerful that it caused them both to erupt like a volcano. They both collapsed in each other's arms and drifted off to sleep. Rayne was beat into submission by pleasure. Bryce was just what the doctor ordered.

A month had passed since their trip to New Orleans. Rayne went into complete closure. She buried herself into her work and rarely spoke to Tyreke, Zoey or her mom. Things had become very overwhelming; from her mother-in-law's funeral, to seeing Rashard and Rachel together again. All of it was making her even more depressed. Luckily for her, Bryce managed to get away from his wife and kids so that they could spend the weekend together. They hid out in her apartment enjoying one another with great sex, conversation and great meals that Bryce cooked for her. She hadn't felt the way she did at that moment since her divorce from Rashard; being with Bryce made her feel like a new woman.

An hour later, Rayne was awakened by sweet, tender

kisses to her neck. While Bryce gently held her, kissing her and stroking her back, she quietly wept. Never in a million years did Rayne think she would be having an affair with another woman's husband. She never imagined she and Rashard would get a divorce. She was foolish to believe they were going to always be the picture perfect couple. Truth is no one can predict what is going to happen in their life, because life is a crazy ride and nothing is guaranteed.

"What's the matter? Why are you crying?" Bryce asked, turning Rayne around to face him.

"I feel so silly. I didn't think you could hear me."

"No need to feel silly. Obviously something is bothering you. Did I do anything to upset you?" Bryce kissed her lips. Whatever was bothering her, he wanted to take the pain away. He could see she was drowning in her sorrow.

Rayne sighed. "I never thought my life with Rashard would end this way. We would be divorced and I would be sleeping with a married man."

"Don't be so hard on yourself. He was the fool for messing up. Don't beat yourself up because you did nothing wrong. When you love with all your heart and soul, it's so hard to let it go. But in time, your heart will eventually heal. You're a good woman, Rayne, and you deserve to be happy. I want to be the one to make you happy."

A broad smile formed on her face. She looked into Bryce's eyes and said, "You always know what to say to make me feel better. You do make me happy, but—."

Rayne became silent. The rain drops against her window suddenly caught her attention. The sound gave her reason to stall. She didn't know if she should tell him what else was bothering her. How would he react? She divorced a man who was unfaithful. She didn't want Bryce to think she was passing judgment. Rayne didn't want to go down that road with Bryce, but she needed to know. She wanted to know.

"What else did you want to say? Obviously there is more." He asked, waiting patiently for her to speak.

"Is this your first time having an affair?"

Bryce became tense. Rayne could tell she hit a nerve. "Yes."

Although Rayne wanted to find it quite hard to believe,

she could tell by the look in his eyes he was telling the truth.

"Why me?"

"What do you mean, why you?"

"Why did you choose me to be unfaithful with?"

"Why is that so important, now?"

"Because it is. I want to know. I need to know."

"Would you think I was lying if I said you intrigue me?"

"Is that all?" Rayne took a deep breath and exhaled. "Do you feel guilty that you're cheating on your wife?"

"Where is all this coming from? I feel like I'm being interrogated. Maybe I should ask if you feel guilty." Bryce said becoming defensive.

"It's not about me feeling guilty. You're the one with a lot to lose." Rayne felt she needed to come back and defend herself. His tone was condescending. She sensed he was all in his feelings. She wasn't trying to pass judgment. She only wanted to know his intentions. There were always reasons, whether good or bad, why someone would want to cheat on their wife or spouse. Rayne knew nothing about his wife. She only knew his wife's name. She shared the same name as her best friend, Kenya. She didn't even know what she looked like. Maybe it was for the best. She wanted to keep it that way. Although they talked, they limited what they shared with each other when it came to their lives. He was not privy to any of her secrets or other relationships, and she was not privy to his. The less they knew about each other the better.

"Why all of a sudden do you care about me cheating on my wife? Does this have anything to do with your husband cheating on you?" Bryce jumped up and paced the living room floor back and forth. His muscular legs moved with such force. Stopped at the window, gazed out at the parking lot that looked like a river; the rain was finally slowing down.

Fuck you was what Rayne wanted to say. He spoke with no regard to her feelings. But she contained her emotions since she was the one who crossed the line.

Rayne sat up and folded her legs in the Indian style position.

"I don't care. Your wife means nothing to me." Rayne

sounded insensitive.

Emotions got the best of her. She tried not to be that mistress who fell in love. Sex leads to love. Love leads to disappointment and disillusionment. She could already tell their relationship was moving in a different direction. Early that evening, over a candle light dinner Bryce prepared, he gave her a beautiful Lavender Amethyst Cable Bracelet by David Yurman. His gift was completely unexpected. Rayne knew sleeping with a married man was opening Pandora's Box, and accepting the gift would just feed more into her carnal pleasures. Her reluctance in opening the box proved what she had feared— that their relationship was about more than just sex. Feelings were becoming involved. She wanted to keep hers protected. Bryce was making that hard for her. She had already crossed the threshold that could lead to possible disappointment, and there was no way she could turn back now. What the hell? Why not open the box?

The entire moment was new to Rayne. She had never been the other woman. She knew that when she and Bryce are together, she only sees the good side of him. On the other hand, his wife sees the good, the bad, and the ugly. He strays away from his marriage, and Rayne knows she'll reap the fruits of his labor.

"Oh my God Bryce, it's so lovely, I love it! Thank you so much. It's so beautiful, but you didn't have to get me a gift. The only gift I need is being with you." Rayne said, smiling seductively.

"It was my pleasure. I know you weren't expecting this, but this is my way of showing you how fond I am of you. This bracelet is a token of appreciation of our friendship, and a little thank you gift for accepting my job offer." Bryce smiled.

Yes, it was totally unexpected. Rayne reached over placing her hand on the back of his neck, expressing her gratitude with a passionate kiss.

Bryce walked away from the window and sat down next to Rayne. His eyes settled pointedly on her long hair that looked wild and fell softly across her shoulders. He put his hand underneath her chin and turned her face towards his. His eyes were searching for understanding. She had Bryce confused in some kind of way.

"I don't get it. Why are we having this conversation? It's a little too late to be asking these questions. We both have already crossed the lines."

"You right. I'm sorry, Bryce."

He was upset.

"No need to be. This is hard for the both of us. I will admit I have fallen for you Rayne. I have feelings for you. I'm not trying to hurt you. It is not my intentions."

"I know." Rayne said with a trusting look in her eyes.

Deep down Rayne knew they were both using one another for their own personal gratification. He was missing something from home. Whether he wanted to admit it or not, he and his wife were no longer connected. He was feeling empty inside. It was that emptiness that made him stray from home. Bryce was that married brother who strayed every now and then and has no intentions on leaving his wife.

And let's keep it real, Rayne needed a distraction to keep her mind off of Rashard. Neither one of them was looking for commitment. He fulfilled that void in her life. But it was Bryce who had the best of both worlds. They threw caution to the wind and continued their affair regardless of the repercussions they both would eventually have to face. Over the past five months, she got to know him and he got to know her. Physically. Emotionally. Rayne loved the stolen moments they spent together.

Silence fell upon them. Bryce pulled Rayne closer to his naked body. He pulled her mane behind her ears. He kissed her lips, slid his tongue inside her mouth, their kiss turned to passion. He climbed on top of her and Rayne allowed his dick to penetrate her pussy, releasing trapped emotions.

They lived miles apart, lived two separate lives, but were being joined together by lust and satisfaction. Every time he gave her an orgasm, the closer she would become to his world. They both created an indissoluble bond. Unfortunately for them, it was one that was forbidden.

"Promise me you won't let my wife become an issue."

"If she's not an issue for you, then she won't be for me."

As easy as it rolled off Rayne's tongue, deep down inside she was starting to have mixed feelings. First her affair with Rashard and not being able to let go and move on, second,

Troy's undying persistence to become her man, and third, her secret affair with Bryce. Her life was suddenly rather interesting and filled with too much drama.

The guilt of engaging in something so sinful and something she had been a victim of was starting to weigh heavy on her conscious. Rayne knew Bryce's wife would become an issue. Why wouldn't she? Her inconsiderate disregard towards his wife was totally out of character. The more Bryce sent waves of pleasure through her body, she thought about how awkward it was to be feeling some type of way about a married man. But, she felt so safe with him. It was those nagging doubts that started to become clear; she was certain now. She was falling in love with this man.

Bryce continued to bury his penis deep inside Rayne's sugary walls until they both fell into a zone. Nothing could break them away from their moment. Not even Rashard who was calling Rayne on her phone.

# Revenge is a dish best served...
## 27

Ice Cube couldn't have said it any better, today was a good day. Troy no longer felt insecure as he left his dentist office after getting his two teeth fixed. It was a temporary fix, and the major work couldn't be done for another two weeks. He was en route to the Back Door so he could take care of business. So far he hadn't heard from Rayne, so he assumed Rashard hadn't gotten to her yet. He knew damage control had to be done, but he already figured out how he was going to clean up his mess. It was okay though, he had a plan for Rashard's ass.

Troy walked into the club to meet his acquaintance to discuss business. He spotted him sitting at the bar curved over his drink, and smoking from a pack of Newports. His tee was crisp white and complimented his dark skin very well. Essence, who was a light skin chick with red hair, thick thighs, petite waist, curvaceous hips, huge breast and one of Troy's finest dancers, was trying to get his attention, but he wasn't paying her any mind. Troy shook his head. He couldn't understand how any man would ignore a banging ass broad like Essence. When Troy walked up, he could tell this man had been through hell and back from the deep dark bags under his eyes and the somber look on his face.

Troy looked at Essence with a grin on face. "Don't waste your time on this one."

Essence who was totally shocked quickly walked off in

embarrassment.

Troy said as he sat down on the bar stool next to his acquaintance, "Man, you look a hot mess."

"So you think you a comedian?" he said exhaling the smoke from his cigarette then placing it down in the ashtray.

"You know I didn't mean any harm. Lighten up. When did you start being so sensitive?" Troy waved the waitress over and ordered vodka with Red Bull. He stared at his acquaintance; a little empathy came over him as he watched him take down shots like they were nothing. He was three sheets to the wind.

"Don't you think you need to slow it down?" Troy asked.

Clearly the gentleman didn't feel the need for Troy's advice. "You do you and let me do me."

"Whateva man. I'm only looking out for your best interest. So since you don't need my help, let's get down to business. I need your undivided attention because I don't need you fucking this up."

His acquaintance looked at him sideways. "What is this all about, Troy?"

Before Troy could respond, the waitress returned with his drink and sat it on the bar in front of him. He gave her the cue to keep the drinks coming. She smiled and seductively walked back to the other side of the bar. Troy watched with lust in his eyes as her ass cheeks bounced up and down. He especially loved the way her ass bounced while she rode his dick. Troy sipped his drink before speaking. "On some real shit, I need a favor. I hope I can count on you."

With a raised eyebrow, his curiosity peeked at the fiery glare coming from Troy's eyes. "You have my attention. What is it you need me to do?"

Troy slid a manila envelope across the bar. "Hopefully this will speak louder than words."

Without hesitation, his acquaintance picked up the envelope and opened it up to scan the contents inside. He put the envelope down and gave Troy a suspicious stare. "You are kidding me right? Is this some kind of joke?"

Troy gulped down the last of his drink before responding. "Do I look like I'm joking?"

"When?"

"As of yesterday."

His acquaintance lit up another cigarette while his eyes wandered around the club looking to see if anyone was listening With a huge smirk on his face he looked at Troy and asked, "Why?"

"That's for me to know. You don't need any details." Troy stated firmly.

"You expect me to do you a favor, and don't expect me to ask you any questions."

With a huge devilish smile, Troy replied, "Yes."

His acquaintance mushed the remaining of his cigarette into the ashtray. He stood up from his bar stool, picked up the manila envelope, and stuffed it in his back pocket.

"I'll be in touch."

The man stood to walk away, as Troy rose from the stool, the sound of Rachel's voice behind him startled them both.

"Girl, you scared the hell out of me." Troy stated.

"What are you two up too? Look like its top secret." Rachel inquired, hoping she would get an answer to her question.

"It's nothing you need to worry about. I need to speak with you anyway. Why don't you meet me in my office? I'll be there in a few." Troy demanded.

Without another word and a skeptical smile on her face, Rachel walked away and did as she was told. When Troy called and said it was urgent that he needed to see her right away, she knew something was wrong. She wondered why it couldn't wait until she got to work that night, but Troy wasn't having it. He demanded to see her immediately. She knew whatever he wanted must was big.

Rachel walked away, her curiosity sending warnings through her body. Troy turned his attention back to the tall brother at the bar and pointed his finger in his direction and spoke sternly, "Look here, don't screw me on this. Don't tell me you would keep in touch. You take my envelope, you carry out my wishes. Betraying me will be unforgiveable."

"Your wish is my command, friend," he said then saluted.

With that said, he left the club. Troy was certain his

wishes would be carried out to the fullest. He had nothing to worry about. Now he had to go deal with that scandalous ass Rachel.

"I can't believe Rashard knows the truth." Rachel said shaking her head. "You don't think I told him do you?"

"I don't know, did you?" Troy asked with a cold look in his eyes.

"Hell no! I had nothing to do with it. There is only one other person that knows, so you need to ask her!" Rachel exclaimed.

"If I find out it was you that betrayed me, I swear you will regret you ever crossed me."

"Like I said, I have no reason to betray you. I can't stand Rayne, so I got the pleasure out of ruining her marriage. So don't come at me sideways," Rachel said with serious attitude.

Troy stroked his goatee. He was a little skeptical, but for now he had to take her word. "For now I'm convinced." Troy's face took on a serious expression. "I heard you sleeping with Malik now. That's why I can't get the pussy because some other nigga getting it."

"First of all, I don't know who you getting your information from, but you need to let them know Rachel belongs to no one. Besides, when did you start caring about who I deal with?"

"I don't care." Troy said flatly.

"Then what you bring it up for. You're such an asshole Troy." Rachel said becoming defensive.

Troy parted his lips with a smile. "I love your feisty attitude. That shit turns me on. Why don't you come over here and take out all your frustration on my dick."

"You're such a pervert," Rachel said giggling.

"You like this pervert."

Rachel stood up and took off her shirt, tossing it to the floor. She reached behind her back, unsnapping her bra, exposing her breasts. She could see the hunger in Troy's eyes. Rachel couldn't stand Troy's aloof behavior at times, but she reaped the benefits of dealing with his arrogant ass. Being that he was the boss, sleeping with him had its advantages. Rachel seductively walked towards Troy ready to give him the ride of his life. He had already pulled out his big black penis through his pants. She slid down on his lap, and began to ride him hard, bouncing up and down on his penis fast like a jack hammer. Troy closed his eyes and began to fantasize about Rayne. Then she slowed it down moving her hips slowly in a circular grinding way. Just the way Troy liked it. She knew how to send him on the edge of unbearable ecstasy.

When he opened his eyes, he was astonished to see Rayne on his lap, taking his joystick into high gear. His mind had to be playing tricks on him because he looked over his shoulder and saw Rashard in the corner watching. He closed his eyes again; maybe this time when he reopened them he won't feel as if he lost his mind. His state of mind was that of a deranged man. Rayne's face was so vivid; he reached out to touch her soft flesh, gently stroking her beautiful face. She smiled, her lips moved in an inaudible whisper. He turned his head to see Rashard rushing towards them in a fit of rage. Troy couldn't believe what was happening was real. He became enraged in this scene and wrapped his hands around Rashard's neck, strangling him merciless. He could hear muffled crying, flailing hands hitting him across his face. He opened his eyes and realized it wasn't Rashard he was strangling. It was Rachel. He loosened his grip and shoved her off him onto the floor. Rachel gagged trying to catch her breath; trying to force words from her mouth. Troy was astounded by his outburst. He scowled at Rachel, wishing she was truly Rashard that he was strangling. Realizing he almost killed her was bittersweet, because in the back of his mind nothing was more pleasurable then knowing revenge is a dish best served cold.

# Bittersweet

## 28

Rashard dialed Rayne's cell phone again but didn't get an answer. He didn't want to show up at her house unannounced, but it was imperative that he speak to her. He had to tell her about Troy's manipulative plan that ended their marriage. In the back of his heart, he was hoping Rayne would run into his arms as if nothing happened and they would become husband and wife again. Just like they both always planned. He loved Rayne with the very fiber of his being, and it was no doubt in his mind she loved him the same. She was his world. She was his everything. Falling in love with Rayne was a wonderful thing. The one thing in his life he will never regret. They dived in head first not heeding the objections of others that felt they were moving too fast and that they should slow it down. They're love was a sure thing. Rashard's life was a total chaos and he was determined to repair the damage that Troy had caused. He was ready to get his girl back no matter what he had to do to convince her they belonged together. Before heading to see Rayne, there was still one more loose end he had to deal with. Rashard called his assistant to let her know he wasn't coming into the office. He foresaw his day was going to be tied up. Rashard smacked his lips when his cell phone started ringing and he looked down to see that it was Rachel calling. She had been blowing up his cell phone calling him all last night and this morning. It was nothing she could say to undo the damage she caused.

"What the hell do you want, Rachel?" Rashard asked curtly.

"You don't have to sound so rude," she snapped back.

"Seriously, are you kidding me? You lucky I'm not face to face with you. Do you realize the damage you caused?"

"Look, it was all Troy's idea. I don't want to get into that right now. I have something really important to talk to you about."

"Don't put this all on Troy. This is as much your fault as it is his. You would have done anything to destroy Rayne. Now that I know Moses is not my son, we don't have shit to talk about."

"Look, I'm sorry you got hurt. Far as Rayne...well she's a different story. But like I said I need to warn you about Troy," she said with a sense of urgency in her voice; but one Rashard did not catch.

Rashard couldn't believe she felt no remorse for her actions. "I don't want your damn apology. You are just like Troy. Don't try to become a decent human being all of a sudden. It doesn't become you. You're a lying, manipulative, conniving, scandalous whore. What makes you think I want to hear anything you have to say about my cousin?" Rashard shot back.

"Your cousin tried to kill me!" Rachel yelled out.

Rashard couldn't believe it. He was speechless as he mused over what he had just heard, wondering how Troy tried to kill her. Sadly, he didn't complete the task.

"Rashard did you hear what I just said? Did you hear me?"

Her news diverted confusion into loud, grateful laughter.

"I have no pity for you. That's what happens when you make deals with the devil."

"You really think this shit is funny, Rashard?" she belted out, almost in tears. "How dare you be so insensitive and laugh. This is not a joking matter. You should be thanking me I'm even warning you about your crazy cousin."

"Seriously, why should I care about you almost dying? Did you care about my marriage when you were scheming with Troy?"

Rachel didn't respond. Although Rashard hurt her

feelings by laughing, she knew what he was saying was right. She really cared for Rashard, but it was Rayne she wanted to hurt.

"I'm curious though, why would Troy try to kill you?"

"I don't know. Your guess is just as good as mine. But it wasn't me he really wanted to kill. One minute we were talking, and the next thing I knew he had his hands around my neck choking me to death."

"Again, why do you feel the need to warn me? That's your problem not mine."

"Because while he was choking me, he thought I was you. In a maniac tone, he kept saying 'I hate you Rashard....die you son of a bitch...die...die...I hate you.' The more he kept saying die, the tighter his hands got around my neck."

Rashard knew Troy had some deep rooted issues since his mother died, but he wasn't sure how far he would go in hurting anyone. Now he was unnerved and he knew he had to get to Rayne before Troy did. "Look Rachel I have to go." he quickly stated.

"Wait. You don't have anything else to say?"

"What do you want me to say, Rachel? You want me to come to your rescue and console you. It's not going to happen. You want me to say I'm sorry Troy tried to hurt you. I'm not. In fact, what I will say is, I'm glad he almost killed your trifling ass. Too bad he didn't succeed. Too bad he got to your ass before I did. The only difference is you would be dead." Rashard hung up in her face before she could say a word. He was glad Troy tried to cancel that bitch like Nino Brown in that movie *New Jack City*. Rashard knew he had to be stopped before someone else got hurt.

***

On the other side of Richmond, in Henrico, Rayne was just waking up from another beautiful night of ecstasy. She was starting to like the idea of waking up in the morning next to Bryce. The sun was brightly shining and Rayne was in bliss. Bryce never ceased to amaze her. She looked over to find him still under the sandman's spell. Rayne no longer had mixed feelings about last night's events; she was now certain about one thing. She was falling in love with Bryce. There was still one problem that remained. He was married and it was not a damn thing she could do about it.

Rayne arched her back and stretched. Her erect nipples pushed hard against her sheer top. She slowly climbed out of bed and tiptoed to the bathroom. After washing her face and brushing her teeth, she returned to her bedroom to retrieve her cell phone. Rayne decided to silence her phone after the constant ringing. When she checked her phone, she saw that she had fifteen missed calls. What the hell! She viewed her missed call log and saw eight of those calls were from Rashard and the other calls were amongst Troy, Zoey, and her mom.

"What the hell was so urgent that Rashard had to call me eight times?" Rayne mumbled to herself. She then saw that she had voice messages and decided to listen to them. She could tell by the messages left by Rashard that something was wrong. She could hear the desperation in his voice. In every message he pleaded that it was urgent and he needed to see or speak with her right away. Then the message from Troy sounded quite strange. She looked over at Bryce who was still sleeping and decided that Rashard was not going to rain on her parade. Whatever it is he wanted will have to wait. In fact, she decided not to return any calls until Bryce left. If it was an extreme emergency, then the cops would have to come knocking.

Rayne was on cloud nine. She just finished making breakfast and the smell of her cooking drew Bryce to the kitchen.

"Good morning," Rayne said, softly greeting him with a smile.

He reciprocated with a warm kiss. "Good morning. Something smells good in here," Bryce said, smiling from ear to ear.

"Why don't you sit down while I pour us some orange juice?"

Bryce sat at the kitchen table and relished over the delightful breakfast spread in front of him. Rayne managed to outdo herself. She cooked pancakes, bacon, sausage, eggs, grits, and fried apples. Rayne returned to the table with the glasses of orange juice. She couldn't help but notice the goofy smile on Bryce's face as he eyed down the selection of foods like a hungry vulture.

"What's with the goofy smile?" Rayne asked laughing.

"I'm impressed. I can't believe you cooked all this. It looks like you cooked for an entire army."

"What better way than to reward the man who made the best love to me last night? Dig in before the food gets cold."

"Bon appetite," said Bryce while putting a mouthful of eggs into his mouth.

It was a bitter sweet moment for Rayne. After eating breakfast and cleaning up the kitchen it wouldn't be long before Bryce had to leave. Noon was fast approaching and Bryce had a two o'clock flight he had to catch. As upset as she was at the fact he had to go, she had to accept and deal with it. After all, he was married. He had to go home to his wife and kids.

Rayne looked on in sadness as she watched Bryce pack his bags. Deep down she wished he was unpacking his bags to permanently stay. Although they have been having an affair for a short period of time, she felt like she had known him for an eternity. Rayne still couldn't wrap around her head that she had fell head over heels for Bryce. She hated the fact she couldn't flaunt him to her friends and family. Only Tyreke and Zoey knew his name. His identity had to remain hidden. He was her best kept secret. She was his mistress.

"I wish you didn't have to leave," Rayne said sadly.

Bryce stopped in the middle of his packing and walked over to Rayne. "As much as I don't want to leave, I have to. If I don't, my wife will send out a search party looking for me. I promise this is not the last you will see of me."

Rayne began to pout and Bryce playfully tried to curve her lips into a smile with his finger. "Don't be sad," he said, running his fingers across her lips.

"I have every reason to be sad."

"Will this make you feel better?" Bryce leaned in and gave Rayne the most intense passionate kiss. Her knees started to get weak. They kissed for what seemed like hours. They both were panting as they finally came up for air.

"Whew. Now that was a kiss," Rayne said blushing.

"I knew that would make you feel better."

"Just a little," Rayne said batting her eyelashes.

Emotions were running rampant as they gazed at one another with pure lust and passion in their eyes. It was making everything inside of them stir. There was no doubt; they were feeling one another. Whoever said falling in love with a married man wasn't easy? The sad irony of it all was that Rayne fell for the right person at the wrong time.

"You think we have time for a quickie?" Rayne asked.

Bryce glanced at the clock on the night stand. He had another hour and half to spare before he had to get to the airport. "I don't see why not."

Rayne's shirt came off and hit the floor. Her panties were about to follow until they were unexpectedly interrupted by a loud bang at her door.

"Are you kidding me?!" Rayne hissed with clear aggravation in her voice. "Who the hell could that be banging on my damn door like the police?"

But then Rayne thought about all the urgent calls Rashard left insisting she call him. What if something bad really did happen and it was the cops at the door? She really didn't want to answer the door. Maybe whoever it was would realize she was not at home and leave, but the knock just got increasingly louder and repetitive.

"Whoever it is, they sure are persistent to get through that door." Rayne stated.

"Maybe you should go see who it is. It could be an emergency."

"It damn well better be or somebody's head going to roll." Rayne said, in an agitated tone.

Rayne hesitantly put back on her shirt, slipped on some shorts and stomped towards the front door. "Who is it?!" she shouted at the top of her lungs.

"It's me."

Was it who she thought it was? It couldn't be. It better not be. Not unannounced. Rayne swung open the door, and froze right where she was standing. She couldn't believe Rashard had the audacity to show up unexpected. Before her mouth could move to utter a single word, Rashard ran up to her and embraced her with the tightest hug. Rayne managed to break their embrace and shoved him off her.

"What the hell is the matter with you?" Rayne questioned.

"Before you get upset just hear me out. I have something very important to tell you. Can we talk?"

Rayne was hesitant in her response, but before she could even answer, Rashard had an unpleasant look on his face. When she turned around to see what caught Rashard's attention; Bryce was standing in the living room behind them.

# What goes around comes around
## 29

### *Rayne/Rashard...*

A few months had passed since Rayne learned the truth about Troy and Rachel's betrayal. Their betrayal had pierced her heart like a knife. Rayne cradled the phone under her neck while she zipped up her suitcase. Rayne thought that it was too early in the morning as she listened to Rashard on the other end of the phone bear his soul. His words reminded her all over again why she fell in love with him. It was too much to take in all at once considering how things progressed between her and Bryce. Her thoughts were obscured and darkened. She didn't know what to say. She didn't know what to feel. She guarded her heart; shielded that large organ in the middle of her chest that beat wildly with excitement and love whenever she was around Rashard. Now that the truth had been revealed, that large organ can't seem to pump blood through her ever constricting veins. Rayne was numb to the fact that Rashard was selfishly removed from her life, and now it's only one person standing in their way of true happiness again: Bryce. Rashard's eagerness to get things back to normal was overwhelming because not a day went by he don't profess his love.

"I love you, Rayne." Rashard said in an assuring voice.

There was a brief silence.

Rayne sat her suitcase by her bedroom door, and sat on

the edge of her bed. Tears began to silently roll down her face.

"Rashard it's not that I stopped loving you, but so much has happened between us and with me in the past year. Don't you think it's a little too soon to be saying those words to each other?" Rayne solemnly replied.

"No. I don't know about you, but I never stopped loving you. I'm not committed to anyone and I haven't been able to really date anyone seriously since our divorce. Deep down in my heart baby, I knew we belonged with each other. I was biding my time until that day came. I just wish it wasn't under these circumstances."

Rayne knew his comment about not being seriously involved with other women was for her benefit. She knew Rashard was devastated seeing her involved with another man. It was written all over his face, he didn't have to say a word. Rayne was quite surprised that Rashard wasn't serious with anyone. Unfortunately, she couldn't say the same. Although she and Bryce were just supposed to be friends (with benefits), she allowed him to climb that wall she had built around her heart; and in fact, allowed him to tear that wall down so she could feel pleasure. She no longer mourned over the pain that Rashard had caused. Now, by a twist of fate, she has the chance to be with Rashard again. Sadly, Rayne didn't know what to do.

"Rashard, this is so much for me to handle right now. I really don't know what to say at this moment and I do have a flight to catch."

With an aspirated sigh escaping him, Rashard said, "I understand, sweetheart. I'm not trying to upset you. I just wish we could pick up where we left off the day we held each other, made love for hours, professed how much we loved each other before that whole treacherous nightmare began."

Rayne peeped at the clock. "Rashard, I'm going to be late. Why don't we finish this conversation when I get back to Richmond? I don't want to be late picking up momma and getting to the airport."

"Ok. Enjoy your trip. I'll be thinking about you." Rashard said not wanting to hang up the phone, too afraid he may lose Rayne all over again.

"Talk to you later," Rayne said.

"I'll be waiting for your call." Rashard replied and hung up.

### Rayne/Troy/Rachel...

Rayne's first reaction to the truth was hatred. Troy and Rachel destroyed her life, causing her to lose the man she deeply loved. Rayne and Tyreke decided to go to the Back Door to confront Troy. When they barged into Troy's office unannounced they found Rachel on her knees giving Troy a blow job. It was no surprise since that's what Rachel was known to do best. They both had dumb-founded looks on their face. The next time they would learn to lock the door. Troy showed no remorse for what he had done. In fact, he felt his purpose was well justified. He said he did it all for love.

Rayne took great pleasure in expressing the hatred she felt towards him. He just stood there looking stupid in the face, as if he was about to cry. Tyreke wanted nothing more than to whip his ass. Rayne did more containing Tyreke from beating Troy then she did giving him a piece of her mind. Rachel stood and looked on quiet as a mouse. Rayne knew her ass was scared. She should be. Troy had the nerve to plea for her forgiveness, but Rayne spit in his face and told him to fuck off. She wanted to drive a knife in his heart like warm butter, then rip it out and stomp on it like a roach. Troy wouldn't back off and Rayne got tired of listening to his excuses as to why he did what he did, so she let Tyreke pounce on him like a hungry lion. With one quick blow to the face, she watched Troy go down like Victor Ortiz. When they were done with Troy, Rayne walked up on Rachel ready to attack. Rachel swung and hit Rayne in the eye and she almost lost her balance. Rayne pushed her to the floor, gripped her by the ears and repeatedly slammed her head on the floor. Tyreke had to pull her off before she killed the girl; but Rayne managed to get one last good punch to her face before he did. Before Rayne left Troy's office, she made it perfectly clear they were to stay away from her. Tyreke cosigned with a threat. Rayne felt good knowing they both got what they deserved. Needless to say, Troy respected Rayne's wishes and hadn't contacted her. However, she knew it would be a matter of time before he resurfaced in her life. When he did, she was going to make him wish he hadn't.

### Rayne/Bryce...

It was the weekend of the Atlanta Designers Premiere Summer Fashion Show, where Tyreke was one of the hairstylists for the models. The trip was a perfect get away for Rayne to escape all the craziness she endured in the last few months. You could feel the smoldering heat and baking earth. The temperature gauge in Rayne's Mercedes read 100 degrees. Hot and humid was an underestimate. Rayne let down the convertible top and before she could pull out of her parking lot, she received a text from Bryce.

*My darling Rayne, I hope all is going well. I know you have been going through a rough time this past month, and I'm the last person that wants to make things a lot more complicated than what they already are. I'm having a rough time as well because I haven't been in your presence. Hearing you tell me you still have feelings for me means a lot, and I can't express enough how much you mean to me. I want you to know I think about you every day and I miss the hell out of you. I definitely can't wait to see you again.*

*Forever yours,*
*Bryce U.*

Rayne didn't respond to his text message. She sat the phone down in her passenger seat, pushed the play button on her Mary J. Blige My Life CD, and headed to pick up her mother so they could meet Tyreke and Zoey at the Richmond International Airport. After explaining to Bryce how her marriage ended, he expressed his empathy but assured her his feelings would never change. As a matter of fact, he still wanted to continue seeing her. This delighted Rayne, but her feelings were now in limbo over Rashard. Rayne realized she had a problem. She was torn between two men she deeply cared about. The hard part of going to Atlanta was knowing that Bryce lived there. She hadn't seen him since the day he and Rashard came face to face at her apartment. Talk about an awkward moment. What Rashard didn't know and could never find out was Bryce's marital status. That's one skeleton had to be kept in the closet. Rayne wouldn't have wanted them to meet period, but the way she saw it; it was Rashard who had showed up unannounced. It became hard focusing on Rashard when she had developed a strong connection with Bryce. Rayne wanted to love Rashard again, but she wasn't ready to let go of Bryce. Bryce made it perfectly clear he wasn't ready to let her go so soon either. She wanted to inform Bryce so bad that she would be in Atlanta for the weekend, but decided it was for the best that he didn't know. I mean it wasn't like she would be able to see him. She already knew Tyreke, Zoey, and her mom were going to hog up all of her time and attention. For those few days, she would just have to put her own issues aside and concentrate on being happy for her brother.

Rayne turned her music down and reached for her cell phone. It was Zoey calling.

"Hey, chica. You on your way?" Zoey asked, sounding all excited. She didn't even let Rayne say hello before she started talking.

"I sure am. I'm almost at my mom's house, and then we'll be there. Where are you?"

"I'm at Wawa's. I had to stop and get me some cash from the ATM machine. I'm fifteen minutes away from the airport."

"Ok. I'll see you when we get there."

Rayne hung up from Zoey and called Tyreke.

"Hey. Where are you?"

Tyreke let out an agitated sigh. "Girl, I'm just leaving my damn apartment."

"What's wrong with you?"

"That damn Craig. I hate his trifling ass. Since I broke it off with him, he has been blowing up my cell. I have been ignoring him, so he decides to show up at my apartment right as I was about to leave and started begging me to take him back. The nerve of that nigga. He has completely lost his damn mind! I told him I was leaving for Atlanta and he went into a frenzy. It's a shame to have such good ass. These niggas go crazy and can't control themselves."

"Oh my God, Tyreke, TMI. I didn't need to know all that." Rayne said shaking her head in disgust. "I'm pulling up at momma's house. I'll see you when you get to the airport." Rayne quickly hung up the phone before Tyreke started saying something she didn't want to hear.

Rayne made good timing getting to her mother's house. With the airport's tight security, everyone figured it would be best to arrive two hours early before their flight departured. Rayne helped her mother take her luggage to the car. They loaded the luggage into her trunk then headed to the airport.

Gloria looked over at Rayne and asked, "How have you been feeling, baby?"

"I'm doing ok, ma," she said trying to sound happier than what she felt. "How have you been?"

"I've been doing fine despite the fact my arthritis has been flaring up occasionally. Other than that, I've decided to go back to the nursing home and do some volunteer work."

"That's great ma, I'm glad you keeping yourself busy. You know I worry about you being in that house alone. I told you you can always come and live with me."

Gloria smiled at her daughter's concern. "There is no need to worry about me. I think I'm capable of being alone. I can take care of myself. Who do you think took care of you for eighteen years? Besides, two queen bees can't live under the same roof. If I want to walk around naked or have a man come over, I like to do that in the comfort of my own space."

Rayne glanced over at her mother. She frowned at the mental picture of her mother walking around naked. As if Gloria knew what she was thinking.

"Don't make that face at me." Gloria chuckled. "Don't act like you don't have the same thing I got." Gloria shifted the conversation. "You don't mind me asking baby, how is Rashard?"

Rayne sighed. She averted her eyes on the road as she headed up Laburnum Avenue. Her face brightened at the sound of his name and image of his face. She felt a sudden lump in her throat, and had to fight back any tears from overtaking her face.

"He's a complete mess, ma. He's been up in arms over what Troy and Rachel did. He wants revenge. He wants closure. Not to say I don't blame him. I tell him try to maintain a level head and don't do anything reckless. I'm a firm believer that what goes around comes around and Troy and Rachel will eventually get what they both deserve."

Gloria shook her head in bewilderment. "I just don't understand why they would be so cruel and manipulative and ruin your marriage. That boy has some dark, deep rooted issues we don't know about. So what are you going to do about you and Rashard now that you know the truth?"

Rayne made a left onto Williamsburg Road.

"Honestly, I haven't given it much thought. I've been wrestling with my feelings. Deep down I still love Rashard. He calls relentlessly or sometimes he may stop by the office unannounced with a bouquet of flowers in his hand. I have enough flowers to open up my own flower shop. This is going to sound crazy, but I never thought I would say his persistence has become overbearing. I remember I wanted nothing more but for Rashard to give me attention. Now, I'm wishing he backs off..." Rayne's voice trailed off as she slammed on her brakes trying to avoid hitting the car that jumped in front of her.

"Watch where you going stupid!" she yelled out. "Like I was saying, I've been keeping this a secret."

"Secret?" Gloria wondered what was coming next.

"I've been involved with someone."

Rayne cut her eye at her mother. The expression on Gloria's face wavered between curiosity and amazement.

"Well...that isn't a bad thing. You did what you had to do. I never expected you not to move on. I mean after all, you thought your husband had cheated on you."

Rayne's voice became unsettled as she replied, "Trust me ma, it's not what you think. It's a lot I haven't shared with you."

"Look, baby, I can't tell you what to do. I can't tell you how to feel. But what I can tell you is to follow your heart. If it's Rashard you want then fight to make things right. If it's this new man you want, then remember you have to deal with a whole new set of bullshit. Men are all the same they just have different faces, so that you can tell them apart. You'll always be faced with ups and downs in a relationship. The good thing is knowing that Rashard was truly faithful and that infidelity did not ruin your marriage. One thing you should know..." Gloria paused. "All men cheat."

Rayne was stunned by her mother's stereotypical remark, and what did it have to do with their conversation.

"Where did that come from? I mean...it's not like daddy cheated on you."

Gloria turned her head away from her daughter, keeping her view on the green signs that gave directions to airport parking.

"Did you hear me, ma? I asked you a question about daddy."

Still looking away, Gloria bit her bottom lip as she pondered over away to take back what she said.

"Listen, let's talk about this at another time. We're here at the airport and I don't want any tension. If your brother senses something is wrong, he will start asking questions and I don't feel like getting into this."

"You made the comment, so obviously you have something you want to get off your chest."

Gloria turned to Rayne, tilting her delicately featured face away from the window.

"I know what I brought up. But I said lets drop it for now. We have plenty of time to finish our conversation."

With hesitation, Rayne replied, "Whatever you say, ma."

For the rest of the short ride towards airport parking, Rayne didn't say another word to her mother. She didn't want to believe her mother's remark could have been implied towards her father. It got Rayne to thinking that there is some truth to what her mother said about men. Bryce was a perfect example. Rayne just didn't want to believe that her father was capable of cheating on her mother. In her eyes, her father was the perfect gentlemen and could do no wrong. He adored her mother. She was certain her mother was the only woman he loved and he would never betray her. Rayne reached over and grabbed her mother's hand, holding it real tight. It was her silent way of letting her know she loved her. Gloria wept in silence, wishing she kept the truth concealed.

# What's done in the dark...

## 30

It was nine in the morning when the plane landed at the Atlanta airport. Everyone had retrieved their bags from the Delta Airlines baggage claim carousel. The excitement of being in Atlanta was like an adrenaline rush. The women were headed to check into the Marriott before they decided to do a little sightseeing and shopping. Tyreke had no time to spare because he had to head straight over to the event and start fixing the models hair. He was pissed because one thing he loved to do was shop.

The day flew by so fast. Kicking off at eight, there was already a line of people gathered outside the big warehouse waiting to get inside the illustrious event. The girls couldn't wait to get inside to see what the latest offerings were in the fashion industry. Not to mention, see what a helluva good job Tyreke did to the models hair. They were sure he had them looking flawless. Hungry photographers were poised outside snapping pictures. Rayne, Gloria, and Zoey felt like stars as they walked the red carpet posing effortlessly for snapping paparazzi cameras.

Rayne looked super sexy in her jaw dropping Giorgio Armani black silk gown. The gown featured a plunging neckline that was complimented by a respectable yet still daring central split. The back was dramatically open before the gown cascaded into an elegant train. Rayne's inspiration for this dress was Rhianna who walked the 2012 Grammy Awards in LA. The gown was the original look mocked after Michelle Pfeiffer in "Scarface." Rayne's hair was long and wavy with blunt bangs. A pendant necklace, black/gold clutch and pointed toe PC ankle strap red bottom shoes completed her look.

Gloria looked elegant in her Eva Longoria inspired royal blue dress with a very deep neckline and a tight fitting bodice. The skirt was flared with a train. The waist had a band around it with a bow type pattern. A white diamond Pendant, silver clutch, and silver pumps were the finishing touches to her ensemble. Gloria's hair was pulled into a bun bringing out her youthful look. She didn't even look like she was fifty six years old.

Zoey was stunning in her beautiful fuchsia designed dress which featured an exquisite asymmetrical pattern. Adding glam, were sequins sprinkled all over the dress. A gold clutch and gold platform sequin PU red bottom stilettos accented the outfit. She wore an up do with strands of flowing curls that graced her soft mocha skin, large eyes, and high cheek bones.

Fashionistas stepped out in immense numbers displaying their daring, bold, sexy, and elegant threads all in the name of fashion. Designer trends popped up throughout, including sheer dresses, evening gowns, lively and exotic prints, and high-waist skirts.

The event was hosted by Hollywood's sexy, Tyson Beckford. The night jump started with a social hour and music by DJ Cut Creator. Once they got inside the warehouse, they met up with Kamel who took them backstage to see Tyreke. They had only a brief moment to watch him work his magic on the models hair before they had to take their seats. It was amazing because they were seated on the second row right where the models entered and exited the catwalk, giving them the perfect viewing point. When the fashion show started, they got to see the garments grace them before their wide-open eyes and drooling faces. Fifty of the hottest designers were showcased. Roberto Cavalli, Calvin Klein, Juicy Couture, Rock & Republic, Sean John, Ed Hardy, Dereon, True Religion, Akademiks, Apple Bottoms, Ecko, Baby Phat, Rocawear, and many more. The models hair were sculpted in truly amazing styles that complimented each outfit. They admired the attention to detail that was extravagant and the designer's endless nights of work was vividly apparent and appreciated. Rayne, her mom, and Zoey were in fashion heaven.

The fashion show had finally come to an end and they couldn't wait to see Tyreke and divulge to him what a wonderful time they had and compliment him on the wonderful job he did. Finally, they all were joined up with Tyreke and they continued to live it up as the evening was fun filled with super stylish socialites, alert reporters, professional photographers, and crowds of celebrities. Spotted in the audience were Editor of Vogue magazine, Anna Wintour, rapper Kanye West, and Phaedra Parks along with her fine ass hubby. Then another face caught Rayne's attention, which stunned her as if she saw a ghost. She couldn't believe her eyes and she actually thought they were playing tricks on her.

"Oh my God! It can't be who I think it is." Rayne shouted, as she grabbed Zoey by the arm.

"What the hell?" Zoey exclaimed frowning. Will you let loose of my arm? What is the matter with you?"

"Look over there at the female standing next to the bald headed black guy."

Zoey stared hard at the female. "Oh my God! Rayne, it can't be."

"It's only one way to find out. Let's go over there." Rayne said.

Rayne and Zoey proceeded to walk off. "Ma, Tyreke, come on." Rayne ordered as she waved for them to follow. They were wondering what had made her so excited. When they approached the young lady, it was Gloria who got the shock of her life. She had hoped she was rid of her for the rest of their lives. It had been a long time since they had seen or heard from her, and that was fine by Gloria. It was for the best.

"Kenya Renee Crenshaw! Girl is that really you?" Rayne shouted.

The young lady stopped in the middle of her conversation and stared at Rayne for a brief moment. Her eyes darted back and forth between Rayne and Zoey until her brain registered who was standing in front of her.

"Oh my God! Rayne. Zoey!" Kenya screamed.

She ran up to them and all three women began to hug. They pulled away from their embrace and with enormous smiles on their faces started looking each other over, observing how they all changed over the years. Kenya looked breathtaking in her teal gown that snuggled her petite frame. After all these years she had finally cut her long hair. It was cut close on one side and long on the other complimenting her light skin tone, brown eyes, and high cheek bones. Rayne glanced at her left hand and saw she was wearing a wedding ring. From the looks of it, Kenya seemed like she was doing really well for herself. Rayne and Zoey hadn't talked to Kenya since their junior year of high school. Never in a million years did they think they would run into her in Atlanta.

"Wow. I can't believe I'm seeing you guys after all these years. You two look good." Kenya said.

"So do you," Zoey and Rayne said in unison.

Gloria watched Rayne's excitement being reunited with her childhood best friend. She knew Kenya meant the world to her and Rayne was devastated when she moved away and never heard from her again. It was a wonderful reunion for Rayne, but it was a painful one for Gloria; it was a reunion she wished never happened. Seeing her only reminded Gloria of Kenya's mother betrayal.

Kenya looked over their shoulders. "Is that Tyreke?"

"Yes it is, wench. Now come give me some love," Tyreke said grinning.

Kenya let go of their embrace so she could speak to Gloria.

"Hello, Mrs. Washington."

"Hello, sweetheart. It's nice to see you again." She lied. Gloria reached her arms out to embrace Kenya.

The three women and Tyreke continued ranting and raving about how happy they were seeing each other again. Kenya looked away and spotted her husband walking in their direction.

"Excuse me ya'll I be right back. I have someone that I want ya'll to meet." Kenya said stepping away.

Everyone continued to talk when Rayne zoned out of the conversation and her eyes traveled in the direction Kenya was walking. Her jaw dropped open and heart beat slowed as Kenya walked back towards them with a good looking man on her arms. She thought her mind was playing tricks on her. She saw him and a frown quickly took over her face.

"Everyone, I would like for you to meet someone very special in my life." The beam on Kenya's face gave clear indication she adored him.

They all turned around staring with big smiles across their faces, checking out the tall handsome gentleman standing before them. With the exception of Rayne, she stood frozen solid like ice. Her face couldn't assemble a smile even if it wanted to. Their eyes met as he looked in her direction.

"This is my husband, Bryce Underwood. Bryce, these are my childhood friends," Kenya said pointing while introducing each one of them.

Tyreke and Zoey knew that name sounded vaguely familiar. From the uneasy expression on Rayne's face, they knew instantly he was the married man she was involved with.

"It's a pleasure meeting everyone," Bryce said, as he shook everyone's hand. When he reached out for Rayne's hand, she was apprehensive to feel his touch. From the looks of it, she could tell he felt the same. I'm sure when he felt her sweaty palms up against his skin; he could tell she was more nervous than a hooker in church. They let each other's hand go. The tension between Bryce and Rayne was so thick you could cut it with a knife. They both tried to remain calm; so that they would not give any suspicious indication to Kenya they knew each other.

"Rayne, Zoey, and I were best friends growing up. I would like to think we still are." Kenya said, flashing them a smile. "This is my extended family from Richmond."

As Rayne listened to Kenya ramble on and on about Bryce, she struggled to keep her emotions at bay. She looked over at Tyreke and Zoey, and the looks on their faces spoke volumes. She knew they couldn't wait to get her back to the hotel and chastise her for sleeping with her best friend's man. It wasn't like she knew. She was deeply saddened that out of all the married men she could have had an affair with; she ended up with her best friend's husband.

Now ain't life some shit.

***

Rayne was standing outside next to her Mercedes as she watched Bryce pull his Bentley into the visitor's parking space. That little voice inside her head kept telling her it was a bad idea for him coming to see her. Finding out a week ago in Atlanta that he was the husband of her best friend Kenya, who she hadn't even seen in over twelve years, felt like dying and going straight to hell.

Bryce looked some kind of good walking towards her. Rayne instantly became mesmerized staring at his sexy thick lips, recalling how they felt exploring every inch of her body. Bryce's smile was warm and inviting. A hello was replaced with a hug that spoke a thousand words. They held each other long and tight as if they didn't want to let go. Rayne inhaled his manly scent which filled her senses. She quickly pulled away and put some distance between them. See, that was the type of shit she knew she had to avoid.

"I miss you." Bryce said.

Rayne folded her arms over her chest. "It hasn't been that long since we've seen each other."

"You've been avoiding my phone calls."

"I had too. What else was I suppose to do? I just found out you are married to my best friend."

"I know it's complicated. But—."

Rayne cut him off. "You think. This is way past complicated." She snapped back.

Bryce tried to plead for Rayne's understanding. "I'm sorry. I've told you many times; it wasn't my intentions to hurt you."

"Why are you here?"

"I needed to see you. We need to talk." A solemn look took over Bryce's handsome features, sad creases in the corners of his eyes.

"We need to stay away from each other."

"I'm afraid I can't do that."

Rayne was stunned after what they just found out he was still willing to take that risk.

"Are you crazy? You're looking for trouble."

"I guess I am, because I'm here, asking…no begging you not to throw away what we have. Can you please hear me out?"

"Bryce we have nothing. What we have is not real. We can't do this. Kenya is my friend."

"I know. I know I'm being unfair. But I can't help the way I feel. I know you feel the same way to. You can't just turn your feelings off like a faucet."

"Do you know what you're saying? This thing can back fire and blow up in our faces."

Bryce walked closer to Rayne. She had a somber look in her eyes. Her eyes fell to the ground. He lifted her head and gently stroked the side of her face. "What can I say? I'm a fool in love." Slowly he bent his head covering her lips with his, his tongue forced entry into her mouth, chasing her tongue, their kiss turned into full blown passion.

Rayne didn't resist, her feelings and emotions had prevailed. The agony of knowing she fell head over heels for her best friend's husband was pure torture. Torture was the name of the game building in the mind of a stranger, who grew ill watching their passion from a distance.

"I'm going to regret this," Rayne said, taking Bryce by the hand and leading him up to her apartment.

When Rayne and Bryce were out of sight, Troy pulled into a vacant visitor's parking spot near her building. He decided to sit outside and wait for her friend to leave. If he was the new man in her life, then what better time for them to get acquainted?

# Reunited

## 31

We all fall short to temptation. So who are we to judge? Inside every man or woman are evil intentions that are ready to emerge. We all have secrets we hope remain hidden. The greatest struggle in life is wanting to be a decent human being. The essence of every person's existence is the battle between good and bad, within and without. We are taught at an early age to obey the Ten Commandments. One of those commandments states thou shall not commit adultery. It is those transgressions for which we must repent.

Out of all the men Rayne had to have an affair with, why was it with Bryce? The joyous feeling of being able to talk with her friend again was outweighed by her guilty conscious. Truth of the matter, Rayne couldn't wait to get the hell out of Atlanta, because being around Kenya, knowing she was married to Bryce, made her angry.

Every day since their reunion, Rayne, Kenya, and Zoey had been talking, and playing catch up. On the surface, Rayne and Kenya were friends, but in Rayne's mind, she meditated at great length on why Bryce married her. If you were to name Rayne's strongest emotion she felt towards her friend, it would be jealousy. During this particular night talking with Kenya, Rayne listened as she spoke in great magnitude about what a wonderful husband Bryce was.

"Let me tell ya'll what Bryce did for me last night. He surprised me by having a gourmet chef come into our home and prepare me the most scrumptious meal. We had lobster, steamed crab legs, shrimp scampi, sautéed vegetables, and rice pilaf. During dinner he gave me a beautiful David Yurman bracelet, and a gorgeous Jovani Couture dress. After we ate, he ran me a bubble bath, and afterwards...well...I'm not going to indulge in any of the intimate details, but ya'll get the picture." She giggled, like a teenager having her first crush.

Rayne's heart cringed. She remembered a few months ago Bryce gave her the same type of bracelet. She rolled her eyes to the back of her head. She grabbed her Lays potato chip bag from the nightstand and started nervously munching on them. She hoped the crunching sound would drown out Kenya's nagging voice. Her smoldering guilt intensified, hidden behind her heated tears, knowing she was just with her husband a week after she left Atlanta. Rayne didn't know how long she could keep up with this charade.

"He sounds like a great husband." Zoey stated.

"He is, Zoey. He is a wonderful husband and father. I'm so grateful he is in my life. I don't know what I would do without him."

"You awfully quiet Rayne." Zoey noticed.

"Come to think of it, she has been awfully quiet." Kenya added.

Rayne cleared her throat and put down her bag of chips.

"I'm still here. I was listening. I just have a lot on mind.

"Anything you want to talk about? I'm sure you tired of me talking about Bryce?"

*You right about that. I've been damn tired of your mouth. Shut the hell up!*

"Naw. You good." She lied. "I couldn't help but notice how you and Bryce remind me so much of me and Rashard and how we use to be when we fell in love."

"Oh my God, Rayne. I'm so sorry. I've been so insensitive rambling on about me and Bryce, and not taking in consideration how hurt you must be over losing Rashard."

"You don't have to apologize. I'm a genuine believer that things happen for a reason, and this too shall pass. Rashard and I have been slowly working through things. So we good, no need to worry your pretty little ahead about us." Rayne said in an indignant manner, hoping Kenya did not catch the tone in her voice.

"I truly hope you guys find a way to make it work. All that trouble you went through to get that man. From pretending you were failing math, fighting back and forth with Rachel, sneaking out of the house, wearing those short skirts and tight fitted shirts, you really put in a lot of work to win him over."

Zoey started laughing. "Yeah, don't forget to add stalking to that list."

Kenya clutched her hands to her chest as she laughed so hard.

"You know we have nothing but love for you Rayne. We just joking around." Zoey said, trying to soothe her friend. Zoey wasn't clueless, she knew Rayne was hurting knowing she slept with her best friend's husband, and listening to Kenya boast about their happiness just poured more salt into her wounds. When Rayne confirmed that was the Bryce she was having an affair with, she confided to Zoey that she had developed feelings for him. Her biggest fear was Kenya finding out and she wasn't positive she could stop seeing Bryce. Sadly, Zoey was dubious that Rayne would put an end to her affair before Kenya found out and someone got hurt.

"Ha, ha, you two think it's funny."

Despite the fact of discovering the truth, Rayne still continued to talk to Bryce. They both admitted their feelings for one another were still strong and they couldn't see letting each other go. He had come into her life and changed her whole perspective. Because of Troy and Rachel, she involved herself into an affair that she now couldn't get out of. The sad thing was; she didn't want to. Bryce was that forbidden fruit she craved and did not want to leave alone.

"Well ladies, it's getting late and I need to get off this phone. I have some things I need to do around the house."

"You right, I should be going too, Rashard will be here in an hour."

Kenya sighed. "This sure does bring back a lot of great memories from high school. I'm so happy you guys are back in my life. I'll call ya'll tomorrow. Goodnight." Kenya said gleefully.

"Goodnight," Rayne and Zoey said simultaneously. Rayne was glad that call was over. She laid her head against her pillow that felt like absorbent cotton. She didn't want to move from the spot, and she wouldn't if Rashard wasn't coming over. She reluctantly got up and dragged her feet towards her walk in closet. She opened the closet door and stood stiff as a board as her eyes scanned for something to wear. She decided to put on a pair of Levi capris and a purple tank top. Two minutes later Rashard knocked on the door. He looked better than he had in quite some time and in a blink Rayne saw the young boy that she had allowed to help her become a woman.

Rayne handed Rashard a glass of red wine. She sat on the couch next to him, keeping some distance between them. The moment felt awkward because at one time she yearned to be that close to him.

"Thanks for inviting me over." Rashard said, after taking a sip of his wine. He leaned back into the sofa and stared at Rayne momentarily before looking away.

"You welcome. So how was your day?"

"Good. I can't complain."

"That's nice to hear. How is your dad doing?"

"He's doing well. He's gradually getting back to his old self. He decided to come back to the office part-time. It's been great having him around. I feel being at the office will do him so good."

Rayne smiled.

"That's great." She sat her glass of wine down on the coaster on top of the coffee table."

With his eyes locked to the floor, Rashard's voice trembled like a violin string, "I've been thin...thinking about us. I know the last thing you want to hear is about you and I getting back together, but do you think it's an inkling of a chance it could happen?"

Rashard turned his head towards her as he waited for an answer.

Rayne hesitated, knowing deep down she still had mad love for him, but she kept those feelings repressed because of her feelings for Bryce. She didn't want to lead Rashard into thinking they would get back together as if nothing ever happened. She had to tread her words carefully.

She bounced her left leg up and down frantically.

"You know I'm hurting just as much as you are. I never stopped loving you. I'm not saying we may never get back, but I don't want to rush things. Let's take things slow and see where it takes us. Besides, we just can't pick up where we left off and pretend nothing ever happened. We have a lot to consider, trust for starters."

Rashard was trying not to get upset, but he felt Rayne was being unfair. "I feel like you are penalizing me for something I really didn't do. You're giving me all these excuses as to why you think we should not get back together, and quite frankly, not one of them makes sense. You know I didn't do anything wrong, so why are you coming down hard on me? I've asked for your forgiveness and that's not enough. I feel like you treating me like somebody that you use to know. I don't know what else I could do to make you reconsider."

"I spent so many days trying to find ways to get you out of my system. I lost the only man that I love! I tried to hate you, but I couldn't. With every fiber of my being, I wanted nothing to do with you. I thought you hurt me, so I moved on. Now to know it was all a lie...I feel cheated!" Rayne emotions got the best of her and she broke down crying.

Rashard wrapped his arms around her. She wept heavily as he caressed her back trying to calm her down. He noticed she was not wearing a bra and that excited him, his libido kicked into high gear.

Without letting her go he said, "I love you. I will always love you. I can't see the rest of my life without you in it. I want you so badly." Rashard raised her head from his shoulders, he put his finger underneath her chin, and her eyes indicated she wanted him just as much as he wanted her.

Rashard kissed her forehead, tip of her nose, cheeks, and then engulfed the lips that he missed terribly for the past year. Rayne took him greedily giving him full access to her warm mouth. Rashard slid his hand underneath her tank top; her warm flesh felt like a furnace, he was ready to ignite her into a passionate state. Soft, tiny moans escaped Rayne as he pulled her closer to him, her nipples tightened into hard peaks that ached for freedom from her shirt.

Rayne missed Rashard like hell. She wanted to stop but she felt the intensity and pleasure in her body build up. She wrapped her arms around his neck, pulling Rashard on top of her, stimulating a part of him down below. The sensation grew rapidly. Rayne was stuck in pure ecstasy and only wanted it to keep going, so she grabbed Rashard by his hand and led him to her bedroom.

Rayne's tank top was no match for Rashard as he vigorously pulled it over her head. She returned the gesture and pulled off his shirt. Rayne touched his chest and lust pierced her body, sending a tingly sensation through her moist walls. Rashard took a moment to gaze at her round, perky breasts. He touched her breasts which felt firm; his craving became more abundant at the notion of taking her immediately on the bed. His mouth devoured her breasts and the moment was gratifying as he sucked, licked, and nurtured them effortlessly. Rayne dug her nails deep into his back as she held on to him tightly.

Rashard worked Rayne out of her capris, then her panties until she was fully naked.

"You are so beautiful."

"So are you. Now come here and show me how much you miss me." Rayne motioned with her finger, giving him permission to have his way with her.

Rashard was eager to oblige as he slid out of his jeans and they hit the floor. He climbed on top of her and eased his dick inside her wetness. Rayne mounted her legs around his waist and palmed her hands around his ass. Rashard thrusts were deep but slow as he elicited gasps of delight. His groans bounced off the walls, creating a melodic rhythm that synchronized with the sway of Rayne's hips. Before she could get comfortable in her position, Rashard flipped over so she could ride him. Rayne moved back and forth in fast motion and Rashard moved well with her not missing a beat. Her thrusts were profound as she rubbed her clit in front of him and he watched her pleasure herself. Their bodies were in tune as if nothing ever changed between them.

It sounded like a mantra as Rashard sang out, "Mmmmm, this pussy feels so great." He couldn't hold back any longer. "Baby I'm coming...shit I'm coming."

Rayne reached her peak also as her orgasm exploded and she fell on top of Rashard's breathless body. Heavy breathing flowed through the room.

Finally after catching his breath, Rashard smiled and wrapped his arms around her and they both fell asleep together until morning.

Rashard slowly opened his crusted eyes and looked about him contentedly. He stretched and yawned. He leaned over and touched Rayne's beautiful skin. She felt so soft. She looked so lovely lying in the fetal position. He wrapped his arms around her waist, and then placed a soft kiss on her neck. She slightly moved from his touch. Her back was turned against him so he pulled her closer into him. Feeling her warm body against his made his manhood rise.

Against Rayne's better judgment, she slept with Rashard. As much as he tried to resist it she just couldn't fight temptation. It was too strong. It was relentless. She woke up out of her sleep and when she looked at the clock it read 3:30 a.m. She was still wrapped in Rashard's arms. A regretful feeling hit her as her mind drifted to Bryce. She felt like she had cheated on him by sleeping with Rashard. Rayne slid away from Rashard and curled up under the covers.

Rashard cleared his throat before speaking softly into her ear. "I hope one day very soon, you'll decide to give us another chance. I don't know what it is that is holding you back from wanting me, but I have a clue. I love you with all my heart and soul."

Rayne felt a lump in her throat and the tears began to sting her eyes before they made a pathway down her cheek. She turned around to face him. His eyes had a gloomy look; one of a man whose heart had been broken into a thousand pieces. Rayne sensed he was trying to hint around to Bryce, and wanted to know if he was the reason why she was being resistant.

All choked up, she managed to tell Rashard how she felt. "I do love you. But right now, things are complicated in my life. I just need more time to sort through my feelings."

As much as Rashard didn't want to know, he couldn't take the nagging feeling anymore so he asked, "Does this have anything to do with that guy? Is it more to him that you're not telling me? Do you love him Rayne?"

Her instincts were right. "No. I mean yes. Yes and yes. Try and understand when our divorce became final, and reality hit that you would no longer be a part of my life, I met this wonderful guy. I know you don't want to hear this but I do care for him."

Rashard couldn't believe his ears. "I thought our love would be everlasting," he said sadly.

"I thought it would be too, but things have changed."

"But that was no fault of our own. We were manipulated. Don't let them win. Don't give them the satisfaction of knowing you and I can't beat this. We belong together," Rashard begged.

"Please, Rashard. All I ask for is a little time and understanding."

"Whateva. I thought we had a strong bond. I see we don't. You let another man into your heart, and I have to pay for my cousin's mistakes. This shit isn't fair," Rashard exclaimed, jumping out of the bed.

Rayne's rejection was a blow to his ego. He was upset. He yanked his pants up from the floor and quickly got dressed. He kept his back turned to Rayne because he didn't want her to see him cry. At that moment, his tears were a sign of anger. He felt like he was being betrayed by Rayne.

As Rashard walked towards the door to leave, he had taken only a few steps before he heard Rayne say, "For what it's worth, I love you and I never stopped."

Without turning around to face her, Rashard replied, "If you loved me, nobody else would be in the picture. My heart wouldn't be feeling this much pain. The way I see it, we are over. There is nothing else to discuss."

With that said, an emotional Rashard left. Rayne couldn't believe her ears. Rashard had given up on them. She wanted to run after him but she couldn't. Hurt, pain, hatred, all began to rise and those feelings made her infuriated at those who caused it. She buried her head into her pillow, balled up in the fetal position and began to cry uncontrollably.

# Malevolence

## 32

Rashard sped down 64-East pushing 75 in a 55mph speed zone. He didn't care if he got caught and got a ticket for wreckless driving. His driving was a result of how he felt. He was angry with Rayne and pissed off at how she was treating him. He wondered if she even cared. He couldn't help but wonder if she loved him the way she claimed, because if she did, she wouldn't be so reluctant about giving them another try. It felt like Rayne crushed his heart with a mallet, and knowing she had feelings for another man made him nauseous. This latest blow, coupled with his mother's death added to the mix of his woes, he felt he had nothing left. He had nobody to blame but Troy and Rachel for his marriage ending, and wanted so badly then to make them pay. Rashard's madness teetered as he thirst for revenge.

Rashard merged onto Powhite Parkway. He turned on his CD player and let the sounds of Earth Wind and Fire whisk him into a more serene state of mind. His father loved Earth, Wind and Fire and that's how Rashard came to love their music as well. He enjoyed when his father played all their records around the house; singing all their love songs to his mother. When Rashard first heard, "I Write A Song", he instantly thought of Rayne. The song expressed how he felt about her. The night on the way to their senior prom he played that song for her. He fast forwarded to track 9 and let that song play as he drove recalling making love to Rayne just a few hours earlier.

Rashard made a left into Bramblewood Estates Apartments. He had another issue he had to deal with. He pulled into an empty parking spot and gathered his composure. Rashard rang the doorbell, and his first thought was to leave, but Zoey opened the door before he could make a beeline back to his truck.

"Hey, come on in," Zoey said, stepping aside so he could enter.

He looked around her living room inspecting the disarray. There were shoes, clothes and toys sprawled across the floor. The television was playing Sesame Street, and the coffee table that sat in front of her sofa had a plate of untouched food still left on it.

"Excuse the mess. I haven't gotten the chance to clean up yet. I'm glad you decided to come. I know this must be really hard for you."

"You think." Rashard barked. "How can you do to this me? How could you keep a secret like this from me?"

"Don't come in here getting all up in my face. I did what I had to do to protect you and Rayne from the truth. I had no other choice. My back was against the wall, and that was the only way I knew how to deal with it. If it wasn't for your cousin's constant meddling and threats, you still wouldn't know the truth." Zoey said with deep emphasis.

"I still think you were wrong. How you think Rayne's going to react when she finds out? We can't keep this from her forever." Rashard snapped back.

"We both were wrong and I feel extremely bad. It wasn't like we intentionally sat out to hurt her. It was a mistake. Rayne is my best friend. She's like a sister to me. I hate the fact I'm the reason behind all her pain."

Rashard let out a long sigh. "You right. We can't undo what happened. But we don't need to tell Rayne the truth right now. It's too soon. Hell, I have to process this all myself. When she finds out, this is going to destroy her. Where is he?"

"In the back room."

"Can I see him?"

"Sure. Anthony!" Zoey called out.

"I see you named him Anthony after your brother."

Zoey smiled. "Yep. I sure did."

Anthony came running from the back room with his Halo action figure in hand.

"Yes mommy."

"Come here. I have somebody I want you to meet. Say hello."

"Hello," Anthony said, in a low soft voice.

Rashard was speechless. He couldn't believe it. He was the spitting image of him. He had a head full of curly hair, large light brown eyes, and his mother's mocha complexion. His smile brought out his big dimples. He was a handsome little fella. Rashard extended his hand out to Anthony.

"Hello, little man. Can I have a high five?"

Anthony and Rashard exchanged high fives. It was a warm feeling. For Rashard, it was a beautiful thing. He couldn't believe for the first time he was standing in front of his son. A secret Zoey kept for five years. All he could think about was Anthony never got a chance to meet his grandmother. He was certain he would have loved her as much as she would have loved him.

One drunken night in college led to an ill-fated romp between them. A night they vowed to keep from Rayne. Unfortunately for Zoey, Troy found out about that night and threatened to expose her secret. He had manipulated her for his own personal gain. When Rachel told Troy she was pregnant, they went to the clinic where Zoey worked to have DNA samples taken of them and the baby. A second DNA test was taken with Rashard. When Rashard had the test done, he had no idea Zoey was the lab technician that worked at the clinic. Rachel arranged for the test to be done when Zoey was off. It was Rachel's job to tamper with the paternity results to make it look as if Rashard was the father of Rachel's baby. The baby actually turned out to be Troy's. It was all part of Troy's manipulative ploy to break up Rayne and Rashard's marriage. It was a perfect opportunity for Troy to blackmail Zoey. Zoey agreed only to keep Troy from exposing the truth about her and Rashard to Rayne.

Zoey was ready for her son to come home and as her conscious gotten the best of her, she decided it was time that Rashard knew the truth. It was tremendously hard for her to drop that bombshell on him. She knew crossing Troy would be detrimental, but that was the chance she was willing to take. Now her biggest hurdle to cross was telling Rayne about her betrayal. Seeing the beam in Rashard's eyes as he played with his son made Zoey's nerves settle. At first she did not know how he was going to react when he saw Anthony. Rashard looked up with a warm look in his eyes. That look gave her a gleam of hope.

***

It was three in the morning when Rachel got home from the club. She retrieved her safe from the top shelf of her closet. Those men were like hungry vultures spending their last dollar to see her give them the best strip performance they ever witnessed. Rachel did her thing and it was well gratifying as she sat on her bed and counted over fifteen hundred dollars in tips. She had met her goal. All the years she had been saving had finally paid off. She had the hundred thousand dollars she needed and she was set to make her move. The twenty thousand dollars she earned from Troy for getting involved in his little scheme had put her right at her mark. The tips from tonight were just an added bonus. Even if Troy didn't pay her, she still would have gotten pleasure out of ruining Rayne's marriage.

Rayne thought she was better than everybody, so Rachel felt she had to take her down a peg or two. After all these years, it was a sweet payback for giving her a soda bottle with her urine mixed in it. A devious grin marked her face as she kissed the stack of bills before locking it inside her safe. Rachel couldn't wait until later on that afternoon to face Troy and tell him she quit that damn club. She was taking Moses and leaving Richmond for good. She knew Troy wouldn't allow her to take their son and move, but she didn't care how the hell he felt. She detested Richmond and she was more than ready to cut her ties. She wanted to escape from under her mother's shadow. When she looked in the mirror, it is her mother's face she sees. The life her mother lived, dancing at a strip club and different men sharing her bed had become hers. The only thing positive surrounding her life was her beloved grandmother, best friend Charlene, and Moses. Unfortunately, they weren't enough to make her stay in Richmond. Later on that day she was making her move.

Rachel was exhausted and ready to take a much needed shower, but first she pushed her safe back into its secret spot and called Charlene. Luckily, she was at her night shift job. She quickly dialed her work number and Charlene answered after the fifth ring.

"Hey, girl, it's me Rachel."

"Hey. Is everything ok?"

"I'm fine. I just want you to know that I love you and that later on today Moses and I will be leaving for New York."

"New York!" Charlene shouted. "Girl what has gotten into you? You go from one extreme to the next."

"Look, I will explain everything to you when I get there, but in the meantime I need you to listen to me carefully."

"Rachel you're scaring me."

"Don't be. I'm going to be just fine. Don't worry so listen up. If anything happens to me, in the top of my closet under a pair of jeans you will find a safe. In that safe are my diary and some other important items. The spare key to the safe is inside an envelope hidden on the top shelf of my linen closet underneath a stack of sheets. You think you can handle that?"

"Ok, but this sounds like some freaky shit going on. What kind of mess you've gotten yourself into? Is it anything that will land me in jail?"

Rachel chuckled. "No silly. It's nothing like that. I'm not involved in any criminal activity. I shouldn't have you all worried. I don't expect anything to happen to me, but I figure you need to know where I keep my most important information—that's all. By six o'clock in the evening, I plan to be on the road headed to New York."

It was a lot Rachel hadn't revealed to Charlene like her and Troy's scheme to break up Rayne and Rashard's marriage, nor Troy really being Moses' father. Even though she confided in Charlene a lot and she felt she could trust her, she didn't want to risk any chances of anyone finding out the truth about her and Troy. Especially not until she got all the cash she needed for her escape. Plus, Troy threatened to hurt her if she told a soul.

"I hope you telling me the truth. Well after that shit Troy

pulled almost choking you to death, maybe I don't blame you for leaving. I don't know why you didn't call the police on his black ass. I should have done it for you. Once again, I let you talk me out of doing the right thing. Maybe once you land back on your feet, you will move back."

"I don't think I will ever come back here. But you know you and the boys are welcome to come visit me and Moses anytime. I'm getting really tired and want to take a shower before I go to sleep so I will call you later on."

"Ok. Take care of yourself Rachel."

"I will."

Rachel removed her Juicy Couture sweat pants, tank top and panties, throwing them in her laundry hamper. She didn't get two feet towards her bathroom when she heard a noise from another room. It sounded as if someone was in the house with her. Moses was staying with her grandmother, so she knew it wasn't him. Before Rachel could completely turn around, a rope was around her neck. Her feet lifted from the ground as she struggled to fight her attacker off. She fell to the ground as the rope was released from her neck. She tried desperately to gasp for air. Obviously, whoever was in the house wanted her to suffer. They weren't ready for her to die. She sustained several blows from constantly being kicked in her back, legs, and side. Rachel struggled to get up as she crawled towards her bathroom. When she reached the bathroom floor, she managed to turn over on her back. She wanted to get a good look at this intruder. Unfortunately for her, a mask hid his face. But not for long; he wanted to be seen. Rachel's eyes had widened in shock. She couldn't believe it. She knew her perpetrator and knew it would have been a matter of time. Her body ached as she struggled to speak. "You...I can't believe it's—." Rachel wasn't given a chance to complete her sentence because in a blink of an eye, three shots were sent blazing through her skull.

The next day when Rachel's grandmother didn't hear from her, she called Charlene to see if she had talked to her. Charlene decided to meet her at Rachel's house. Rachel's grandmother used the spare key to get inside the house. Charlene called out her name but there was no answer. She walked towards her bedroom with Rachel's grandmother close behind. They checked the bedroom but there was no sign of Rachel. They decided to check the bathroom and as they stood in front of the bathroom entrance, they got the fright of their life. Pieces of Rachel's skull and blood splattered across the bathroom floor and walls. A grueling message written in blood was left behind. It was the killer's trophy mark. It read:

# Malevolence

Writing has always been LaShawn's passion. The vision of Forbidden Fruit came to life in her dream. Through this vision, LaShawn began to write her first chapter. As she embarked upon her journey, she realized that nothing is allowed to come into our life without a divine purpose. LaShawn had to go through the trial and errors and humbling in order to fulfill her dream as becoming an author.

LaShawn Hewlett-Wilson was born in Richmond, Virginia. She graduated from Franklin Military High School, received her A.A.S. degree in Legal Assisting from J. Sargeant Reynolds, and is currently enrolled in University of Richmond, pursing her Bachelors in Paralegal Studies. Forbidden Fruit is her first novel. She is the CEO and founder of Bittersweet Publications, LLC.

LaShawn resides in Richmond with her husband, two sons, and step-daughter.

For more information, visit her website at www.bittersweetpublications.com, email at bsweetpub@yahoo.com, and Facebook.com/LaShawn Hewlett-Wilson.